IT'S MOVING DAY
CHEZ HOLMES

Mystery writers Christopher Holmes
and J.X. Moriarity
are moving in together.

But while J.X. is off at a mystery fiction convention,
Kit, who's still not sure he's ready for this,
unpacks a crate that should contain old china.

It doesn't.

Within the mounds of Styrofoam popcorn
is a dead body.

A very dead body.

There goes the neighborhood.

*Dear Spike,
Watch out for
smiles!
Josh Lanyon*

THE
BOY WITH
THE
PAINFUL
TATTOO

HOLMES & MORIARITY 3

JOSH LANYON

The Boy With The Painful Tattoo

October 2014

Cover Art by L.C. Chase

Edited by Keren Reed

ISBN-10: 1-937-909-50-6

ISBN-13: 978-1-937909-50-5

Printed in the United States of America

JustJoshin Publishing, Inc.
3053 Rancho Vista Blvd.
Suite 116
Palmdale, CA 93551
U.S.A.

www.joshlanyon.com

This is a work of fiction. Any resemblance to persons living or dead is entirely coincidental.

TABLE OF CONTENTS

To Steve, who kept me up all night.

CHAPTER ONE

"Come with me, Kit," J.X. urged.

As promising a conversational opening as that sounds, and despite the fact that we *were* in bed, J.X. was talking about attending a mystery fiction convention. The 19th annual Murder in Midtown was being held in Las Vegas this year.

"Nah. I don't think so." I scrunched the pillow into a more comfortable ball beneath my head. "There's a hell of a lot to do here."

No lie. It was our first morning in our new home on Chestnut Lane in San Francisco. Just the words *our new home* made me feel a little lightheaded, so it was lucky we were lying down. On a mattress on the floor of our new living room, as a matter of fact. Which I thought sort of reinforced my point.

J.X. seemed unconvinced. "Nothing that can't wait."

"Are you serious? Look around you."

His warm, solemn gaze moved from my face to the stacks of boxes and crates surrounding us. The moving van delivering all my worldly goods had broken down twice on the long hot trek from Southern California. It hadn't arrived until shortly after midnight and the movers hadn't finished unpacking until the sun had cracked open a bleary, jaundiced eye.

"It'll all be waiting here when we get back."

"Exactly."

"And so what? We'll deal with it together."

"Why don't I just deal with it on my own, now, since that's what I'd prefer?"

J.X.'s eyes, the color of warm sunshine on shadowed water, narrowed. "Okay," he said mildly, at last. "But I think it would do you good to go to the conference."

Yeah. Because I always have such a fabulous time at conventions and conferences—when I'm not falling over dead bodies. I snorted—which was more polite than what I was thinking—and rolled over, folding my arms around the ball of my pillow. "Our first argument in our new home. I never thought this day would come."

At my mock-mournful tone, J.X. made a snorting sound of his own. "We're not arguing. We're discussing." His hand stroked the curve of my back.

"Ah. But only because of my sunny good nature that never takes offense." His hand made another of those slow, seductive passes down my back. I swallowed. "No matter the provocation."

"Yeah," J.X. murmured. "Let me see if I can provoke you a little more."

"We don't have time."

"Yeah we do," he whispered, pulling down my boxers.

"Hey!" I looked over my shoulder to see him grinning. Hair ruffled, he looked rather villainous. Not that that was a bad thing. He sucked with noisy deliberation on his index finger.

I gulped out, "You...have a plane to catch..."

"Shhh."

And *shhh* I did, obeying this unsettling new dynamic developing between us whereupon I let J.X. boss me around in a way I had never before allowed anyone.

His hands parted the globes of my ass, his index finger found the puckered entrance to my body and he slipped inside. That deliberate assertion of possession was electrifying. I was instantly flushed and sweating, heart pounding in desperate need that felt all too much like anxiety.

"I don't..."

"Yeah, you do." His breath was heated against my ear.

And...yeah, I did.

J.X. moved his wet, slick finger teasingly, pushed deeper...deeper.

A weird sound squeezed out of me. A helpless little cry.

I wanted that touch so badly, but even as I was pushing back into it, I was trying to writhe away from it, not feel it so keenly, so intensely.

"Say it, Kit."

Face buried in my arm, I gave a shaky laugh.

"You want me to fuck you?"

I shook my head. Yeah. Right. I didn't want *that* at all.

"No?" I could hear the smile in his voice. J.X.'s probing finger found my prostate, brushed delicately, then pushed harder. Tiny bursts of color, like miniature fireworks, went off behind my eyes, snapping and sparkling all down my nervous system.

I sucked in a breath. "Oh God. God. *God.*"

"Oh God!" J.X. said in a completely different tone and pulled his finger out of my butt so fast I could have sworn I heard a sound like a suction cup letting go. "What the hell? Who the hell is *that*?"

I heard it then too. A businesslike rapping on the picture windows a few feet from us. A female voice yoo-hooing.

"Yoo-hoo! YOO-HOO!"

Knock. Knock. Knock.

Could she see us? I wasn't sure. Luckily we were under the blankets. Still.

The knocking was now coming from one of the large bay windows along the side of the house. Through the filmy window sheers, I could see the tip top of one of those broad, straw coolie hats some elderly folks—and outright eccentrics—use for gardening.

Mid-scramble for our clothes, J.X. and I exchanged horrified glances. He looked so stricken that I started to laugh, even as I dragged my jeans on.

"Who the hell *is* that?" J.X. protested again, which struck me as still funnier.

"Welcome Wagon?"

"No way." He said doubtfully, "You think?"

"Well...no." I climbed awkwardly—it's not easy to go from pleasurable arousal to alarmed action in thirty seconds flat—over one of the many crates marked *books*. I half tripped over a rolled Persian carpet, clattered into a set of fireplace rack and accessories, and finally stumbled over to the window seat. I struggled with the catch on the window and managed to raise the sash a foot or so.

The spring morning scents of honeysuckle and freshly mown grass wafted in.

I saw a small person of indeterminate sex, dressed in baggy clothes. At first glance it appeared that one of the garden gnomes from next door had come to life. And had something to say about it.

"Good morning!" the gnome greeted me. She had one of those fluting, high voices that brought to mind Sunday school teachers and curators at the most macabre exhibits at the Tower of London. A voice like an ice pick through your left eye socket. "Welcome to the neighborhood. So sorry to disturb you on your first morning, but the movers must have broken one of the sprinkler heads along your front walk."

"Oh. Uh…okay."

As I seemed to be missing the point, she said kindly, "Water is shooting up like a geyser out there. There's a drought going on, you know."

She was probably in her sixties, but unlike my former mentor Anna Hitchcock, no effort here had been made to stave off the ravages of time. Not that she looked ravaged. Beneath the wide brim of her hat I could just make out twinkling blue eyes in a round and rosy face.

"Hell," I said. "Okay. Thanks for letting us know." Not twenty-four hours in the new place and it was already falling down around our ears. I hate to say I told you so—well, no. Actually, I kind of like to say I told you so. I couldn't wait to tell J.X. *I told you so!*

She offered a small but capable hand. "Emmaline Bloodworth. I'm on your left."

Proof of my distraction, I actually glanced to my left. "You are? Are you?"

"I live in the house to your left." She was still offering a doll-sized hand, and I leaned down to take it. She shook hands firmly.

"Christopher Holmes." I released her, started to retreat, but by then J.X. was behind me so I backed my ass firmly into his crotch, which pretty much illustrated the current state of affairs at #321 Chestnut Lane.

"Ooof," J.X. steadied us both with his hands on my hips.

The most alarming part was my body's instinctive reaction to the feel of his still-partial erection through both his jeans and my own. That level of awareness, of desire, of—oh God—of *need* was not normal, not natural. Not for me.

"Hello there," Emmaline greeted him. "We keep missing each other, but I've seen you coming and going this past week."

More going than coming. I didn't say that, obviously.

J.X. joined me in the open window and shook hands with Emmaline. "J.X. Moriarity. Kit and I are—"

"We've got a broken sprinkler," I interrupted.

"I heard. I'll take a look."

"No. You've got a plane to catch. I'll deal with it. But before I turn off the water, were you going to take a shower?"

J.X. looked over his shoulder for a clock that was not there. He felt around his jeans' pockets for his phone. Also not there.

Emmaline checked her wristwatch. "It's nine forty-five."

J.X. sucked in a breath. "I guess I'm not showering. Good thing it's a short flight."

"I can show you where to turn off the water," Emmaline told me.

"Thanks. I'll meet you out front."

J.X. caught my arm as I moved away from the open window. "What if I throw some things in a bag for you? It's just for the weekend. We can deal with this crap when we get back."

"Now you're talking crazy," I scoffed. "If anything, this should indicate why we can't both take off in the middle of moving in together." I was smiling because he had to know I was right. I now had an excellent, irrefutable reason for not going with him. I pushed him toward the doorway and the curving, walnut staircase beyond. "*Don't* miss that plane."

He didn't like it, but he didn't have a choice. The clock was ticking. Somewhere. In a box we couldn't find.

J.X. pounded up the stairs and I veered left and went out the carved walnut and glass double doors to the Corinthian porch.

The beauty of the front yard caught me by surprise. I'd been too tired to notice more than shadows and shapes when I'd arrived late the night before. Red brick walkways and short walls—not counting the twelve-foot vine-covered structure dividing our property from the house on the right—coiled their way through low hedges and sculptured ornamental trees. The weathered stone and elegant greenery created a lush and pristine setting for the Victorian-Italianate house set discreetly back from the street.

A nice neighborhood to have bad habits in, as Chandler would have said.

Emmaline came around the corner of the house. "The main water shutoff valve is on the right over here, by the little cherry tree."

"Hell. Heck. I don't have a wat—" I broke off as she held up a long, steel valve control key. "Oh. Great."

"This way. Come along, Christopher." She bustled away down the brick path. I obediently followed in her wake. A butterfly swooped languidly past my nose, as though hired by the homeowner association to add ambiance. Did we have a homeowner association? I didn't know. J.X. had pretty much been the driving force behind all this.

We found the water main, I pried up the metal lid, and Emmaline handed me the key like a good scrub nurse delivering the scalpel to the surgeon. I turned the meter valve counterclockwise. "I'll pick up a couple of replacement sprinkler heads this morning."

"It's going to be nice having young people in the neighborhood again," Emmaline said as I finished turning off the water.

At forty, I didn't exactly think of myself as "young people," but everything is relative I guess. I handed Emmaline the valve key back, and replaced the metal plate. I wiped my hands on my jeans and stood up.

Emmaline was filling me in on the other residents of Chestnut Lane. The Tunnys—"twin brothers and old codgers," according to our neighbor lady—lived to the right of us behind that formidable wall. Codgers they might be, but the wall almost certainly predated them. The Salvatierras lived across the street to the left of the walk-down parking lot. The house to their left was currently empty, but not for sale. The house to the right of the parking level was owned by Mr. Lemon. Mr. Lemon was a retired history professor.

"Ah," I said. I knew I should probably be paying closer attention to the *Who's Who*. These people were going to be my neighbors for the next however long I—we—lived here, but somehow I felt more like a house-sitter than a new homeowner.

"Now don't hesitate to call on me if you need anything," Emmaline said, walking briskly toward the ornate iron gate at the front of the yard. "I hope you'll be very happy here."

I bade her adieu and headed for the black front steps of the stately porch. Sunlight gilded the sage-green balustrade and pillars, tipped the leaves of the hedges and flowering vines in gold. Honeysuckle grew in profusion everywhere, the sweet scent perfuming the warm morning.

Emmaline called something I couldn't make out. I smiled, waved, and went through my new front doors.

Strangely, the house smelled both new and empty. Strangely because the place had been built in 1904 and was currently stacked to its skylight in boxes and two households' worth of furnishings. From upstairs, I could hear footsteps walking back and forth. I listened for a moment then crossed the dark hardwood floor of the foyer and poked my head in the living room.

This was a large room painted a satiny, cheerful yellow with creamy decorative crown molding and corner pieces. The marble fireplace, one of four, was original to the house, as were the intricate etched glass and brass chandeliers. The house had lots of these beautiful little touches, from the tall pocket doors to the hand painted tiles in the bath and kitchen. And for three million dollars, there ought to be some beautiful little touches. I studied the stacks of boxes and furniture that had yet to be assigned their place in the new world order. I stared at the mattress before the fireplace. It was a mess of blankets and sheets. The blankets and blue and white striped sheets were J.X.'s. The mattress was mine. It was destined for the guest room upstairs. We had agreed—or rather, I had agreed to J.X.'s suggestion that we start off fresh with a new bed and a new mattress. Metaphor? You decide. They were supposed to be delivered that afternoon—another reason why someone had to stay here. We couldn't both go gallivanting off to parts unknown.

Or even parts known.

I found my way to the kitchen—remodeled but still retaining vintage charm with the black-and-white parquet floors, beadboard cabinets, and hand painted ceramic tile backsplash. I saw that J.X. had found and plugged in his coffee maker. I made coffee and idly opened a few boxes, looked inside, and let the flaps fall closed again. Between the two of us there was a hell of a lot of junk here. And somehow when viewed inside a cardboard box, all my worldly possessions *did* look like junk.

More heavy footsteps overhead. What the hell was he doing up there? Pacing the floor?

I went over to the fridge—J.X.'s was newer and bigger (some things never changed) so mine had been relegated to the basement—and I wasn't sure if I was relieved or not to see he hadn't had time to do much more than pick up a carton of milk and a container of eggs.

He'd ordered Chinese takeout the night before, but I'd arrived too late and too tired for food. I was hungry now, but there wasn't time to fix something before J.X. left, and somehow it seemed rude to start cooking breakfast he couldn't eat.

How long before I stopped second-guessing my every impulse? Before I stopped feeling like a guest? Before I stopped—

No. Don't go there.

I wasn't regretting anything.

Anyway, it was too soon to know if I had anything to regret.

Preceded by a blast of John Varvatos fragrance, J.X. pounded down the staircase and breezed into the kitchen. He wore jeans, one of his ubiquitous white tailored shirts and a tweed blazer, but no amount of tweed or elbow patches could make him look like a professor or a teacher. He wore stylish boots and a gold stud glinted in one ear. Spotting the percolating coffee, he fell upon it like the wolf upon the fold. Or the wolf upon the barista. "Thank. God." He found his mug in the sink, turned on the taps to rinse it, and of course there was a choking sound from the faucet which spit out a trickle of water.

"Here." I unwrapped a mug from the half-unpacked box on the counter and handed it across.

"Thanks." He poured in coffee and glanced at me. "It doesn't feel right leaving you to deal with all this."

"It's not a problem. I'm looking forward to exploring everything on m—"

"On your own?" he asked wryly.

I laughed. "It would be more fun with you."

"It's just a couple of days. I'll be home Monday night."

The phone rang, forestalling my reply.

"Well, something works anyway," J.X. said as I went to answer it.

"You want me to drive you to the airport?"

He shook his head. "I'll take my car."

I picked the phone up. "Hello?"

"Christopher," came the not-so-dulcet, semi-British tones of my agent, Rachel. "You made it!"

"Don't sound so surprised."

"I didn't think you'd go through with it."

"Ha." I winked at J.X. I'm not really much of a winker, so it had the reverse intended effect of making him pay closer attention. He sipped his coffee, watching me over the rim of the earthenware mug.

"Have you changed your mind about the convention?"

"What in our previous acquaintanceship would lead you to believe I'd change my mind about that?"

"The fact that you're speaking to me from San Francisco."

"Aside from that."

"Christopher, your career is in a delicately-balanced position right now."

I couldn't hide my weariness. It leaked out in a long sigh. "When is it not?"

"You can't afford to go off the grid again. We have to talk, *really talk* about your future, and it makes sense to do it at the convention."

"Probably not. Since I won't be there."

She made an exasperated sound. I get that a lot from the women in my life. Not that there are a lot of women in my life.

"This is no time for a midlife crisis."

"I agree. That was so last year."

"Christopher! I've had an idea…" she burbled on, but half my attention was on J.X. who set his coffee cup in the sink and came over to me.

He said quietly, "Honey, I've got to go."

I nodded politely, which was not the right response, as I could tell from the way his brows drew together. He leaned in, and I leaned in, and somehow the phone was in the way—where did all that cord come from?—our mouths latched on—mostly. It was a fleeting kiss, tasting of coffee and toothpaste on his end, and coffee and exasperation on mine.

"I'll call you when I get to the hotel," he whispered.

"…dragon tattoo," Rachel said.

"I am *not* getting a tattoo," I said. "Thanks to you, I already have two piercings in my ear and a wardrobe that looks like the Hollywood version of what writers wear—which, incidentally, I still haven't finished paying for." I nodded enthusiastically to J.X. so he could see I was listening to him.

"Have you heard a word I said?" Rachel demanded.

"I love you," J.X. said.

"I heard you," I said shortly.

Rachel's silence and J.X.'s expression seemed equally taken aback.

"Love you too," I said hastily to J.X.

He smiled uncertainly. My smile was equally doubtful.

"Christopher?" Rachel inquired. "Are you still there? *Christopher?*"

"I'm here," I said automatically, as J.X. raised his hand in a final farewell and disappeared into the hall.

A few moments later, and from what felt like a long way away, I heard the front door close. This was followed by the distinct sound of a key turning in the lock.

So much for milestones and relationship markers. *Love you too.*

Love. You. Too.

Somehow I had intended the first time I managed to say the words to J.X. to be a little more…meaningful.

CHAPTER TWO

In New York publishing circles Rachel Ving is known as Ving the Merciless.

With reason. She's a good agent and we've been through a few things together—including a murder investigation. There's nothing like a little unplanned homicide to show you who your real friends are. I liked Rachel and I respected her—and I didn't blame my currently floundering writing career on anything she had or hadn't done for me—up to and including dragging me into that previously mentioned murder investigation. That said, not all her ideas are good ones.

"Scandinavian crime fiction," she was still jabbering as J.X. walked out of our new house. "I keep waiting for someone to send me another boy in the suitcase."

I tuned back in with difficulty. "Huh?"

"*The Boy in the Suitcase* by Lene Kaaberbøl and Agnete Friis. We should have thought of it before. Have you read Jo Nesbø? You must have. Harry Hole?"

"Hairy... What the hell are you talking about?"

"I'm talking about saving your career."

"Yeah, well I'm not sure I—" I stopped cold. What? *What?*

If Rachel heard that revealing start and stop, she didn't acknowledge it. "This isn't just about you, you know. You're my biggest client. When you don't earn money, don't earn money."

"I understand that, Rachel. But."

But what? I stared, frowning, at the glass-enclosed breakfast nook and the pretty garden outside. More weathered brick, more topiaries. Rococo patio furniture? In robin's egg blue, no less. Did people really sit on those uncomfortable-looking chairs? It did not look like the garden of anywhere I had ever lived. Or would live. There was a pool at least. Somewhere. Somewhere behind the tiny terraces and low hedges was a small, secluded, kidney-shaped pool. That had been one of my stipulations for the house hunting. Must have pool. And separate offices. And a fireplace in the master bedroom. And gardens, front and back. And a skylight. An older home in a quiet neighborhood. But with a fully modern kitchen. In case I ever wanted to cook something.

Somehow I had expected it to take J.X. longer to find such a place. Let alone shove it through escrow at light speed. But no. Four months after our trip to Connecticut, here we were, setting up house together.

Rachel was still delivering her pep talk in a tone eerily reminiscent of Margaret Thatcher readying the troops to take back the Falklands. "I know what I'm talking about. The only way to shake off this writer's block is to go in a completely different direction."

"Painting, maybe? Look, I don't have writer's block. I just don't feel like working at the moment. There's a lot going on in my life."

"Christopher, you have to get back on that horse."

Only this horse was looking more and more like a Shetland pony.

"What horse? I'm not Scandinavian, if that's where you're headed. The answer is no." The only boy with a suitcase I cared about was on his way to San Francisco International Airport. Why did he have to throw the words out like that? And why had I not answered with more…attention to detail? Not that it was the first time J.X. had used the L-word. But it was the first time in our new home, in our new situation, in our new life together, and I had wanted to… What? I was probably overthinking this.

Rachel said patiently, "Of course you are. Your mother is Swedish, right?"

"Swiss. Not. She's American. My grandmother was Swiss. That doesn't qualify me to write Scandinavian crime fiction."

"You don't have to be Scandinavian to write Scandinavian crime fiction."

"You have to have read some of it though. I've never read a word. I saw *Girl with the Dragon Tattoo.* Okay, the version with subtitles. But that's the closest I got."

Rachel made a tsking sound. "Then do your homework. Start researching. Just as you do for Miss Butterwith. Only *not* Miss Butterwith. It's time for a breakthrough book, Christopher. You know what that means."

I swallowed. Oh yes. I knew.

Standalone.

Something dark and edgy and psychological. Ideally, a little twisted. Random violence. Grisly murders. Calculated violence. Torture. Maybe some child molestation, if I could work it in. I groaned. "It would be easier to write Scandinavian."

"Exactly. Especially since you *are* Scandinavian."

"I'm beginning to think that's code for something else."

Rachel chuckled evilly. "So. The convention? Are you reconsidering?"

"No. For the last time, no. I've got to go buy a sprinkler head. But say hi to my—J.X. when you see him."

* * * * *

The problem with moving to a new city that you never wanted to live in, is you don't know where to find the best place to have brunch—or where the nearest home improvement store is. But I don't write mysteries for nothing, and I soon managed to locate a Lowe's on Bayshore Boulevard.

See, that's the nice thing about chains. You always know what you're getting. Zuppa Toscana soup at Olive Garden or Rust-Oleum paint at Lowe's, there are no surprises and no disappointments. This is why I prefer chains over indies. You're not supposed to admit that though.

I wandered aisles wide and mostly empty on a Thursday morning, checking out lighting fixtures and lawn furniture. They had a magnificent selection of garden hoses. Once upon a time, the word *kinks* was synonymous in my mind with garden hoses. I lingered, fondly considering lengths and widths. I mean, as crazy and inconvenient as this was—my situation, not the home improvement center—I couldn't help feeling a little chuffed that I *was* doing it. Doubts and misgivings notwithstanding, I was starting a new life with J.X.

Anywho. My new home and garden center was well organized, and it didn't take long to choose a sprinkler head: stationary pop-up in a half-circle design. Some things in life are simple.

"Oh my God," someone said from behind me.

I glanced over my shoulder. There was an attractive guy about my age—average height, slender, curly dark hair, blue eyes—staring straight at me over the forest of plants stacked on his trolley.

I nodded politely. Possibly discouragingly.

"It is you, right?" he said.

This time I glanced around, just to make sure he *was* actually addressing me.

"It was this morning."

His blue eyes were wide with disbelief verging on shock. "Christopher Holmes? It *is* you?"

"Yeah." I unbent enough to say, "I'm sorry. Do I know you?"

"Oh God. Jerry Knight. You won't remember me. We met years ago at Murder in Midtown. The one in DC."

Ten years ago. That was the convention after I'd found out David, my ex, was cheating on me. It was the convention where I'd met J.X. So, yes, a lot had been going on at that conference, and it was safe to say I barely remembered the event, let alone Jerry Knight.

"That was a great conference," I said.

"Meeting you was the highlight. You are my all time favorite writer."

I laughed self-consciously. "Or at least your favorite of all the writers shopping in Lowe's this morning."

Jerry laughed too, rolling his trolley forward and offering his hand. "No, but seriously. I love your books. I've got every single thing you've written. Even the Japanese edition of *Miss Butterwith Plants a Clue*. I'm your biggest fan."

He had a firm handshake. Any clamminess could be put down to the metal handlebar he had been tightly gripping. That and the fact that it was like a rain forest in the garden center. Even now mist was rolling out through the open doors.

"Thank you," I said. I can't deny that it was heartwarming hearing this, especially on a morning when I was feeling a little...okay, a long way from home.

"I had you sign five of my books." His smile was sheepish.

"*Now* it's coming back to me," I joked, but really that wasn't all that unusual. The only genuinely unusual signing request I'd ever had was to sign someone *else's* books—and that had happened twice from two different readers. Oh, and the reader who had asked me to sign her naked breast. That was one for the scrapbook.

Jerry asked, "Is it true you're done with the Miss Butterwith series?"

"Uh...well, it's not official or anything. I just think maybe the series has...run its course." I listened to the echo of these words and waited to feel the reverberating shock of my final acknowledgment of a fact I had avoided facing for so long. But I felt...nothing. No sadness, no regret. No relief or happiness either. Nothing.

Jerry looked disappointed but understanding. "They're such great characters, Miss B. and Mr. Pinkerton. And of course Inspector Appleby." He smiled and I smiled because Inspector Appleby was pretty darned appealing, if I did say so myself.

"So what are you working on now?"

I held up the sprinkler head and we both laughed.

"No gardener?"

"Gardener?"

"I guess I always picture big name authors like you living in a mansion with a drawing room and a butler and a private secretary. Cocktails at five and holidays at St. Moritz or the French Riviera. That kind of thing."

It took a few seconds for all the words that followed *big name authors like you* to sink in. And then I hated to destroy the illusion. Technically, the house on Chestnut Lane wasn't a mansion, but three thousand square feet was plenty big for two people. Was it big enough? That remained to be seen.

I said, "Ha. Don't you believe it. Most writers I know have to keep their day jobs. Anyway, we'll hire someone to take care of the yard, I'm sure." Of that, I had no doubt. The front yard was pretty, but the Tommy Church back garden was one of the house's major selling points. Church is regarded as the father of modern landscape architecture. In fact, he's credited with the concept of "garden rooms," a quintessentially Californian notion, if there ever was one. No way was I going to risk lowering our resale value by doing something destructive like planting the wrong roses or moving the tall stone urns out of alignment.

"We just moved in," I added with uncharacteristic forthcomingness. "This morning was the baptism." I held up the sprinkler head.

Jerry looked interested and surprised. "Really? You're new to the area?"

I'm not the chatty type, so it had to just be feeling like a stranger in a strange land that caused me to pop out with, "Yeah. Well, my uh...he's from up here. We just bought a place on Chestnut Lane. In Russian Hill."

"Right. Right, because I *thought* you were based in Southern California. Russian Hill is a nice area. Pretty views and beautiful old houses and cute little cafes and shops. You'll love it."

"Yeah. It's nice. I'm sure it's going to be great."

"Are you going to be doing any signings or book events up here?"

"I don't know. Maybe. I don't do a lot of signings."

"I noticed!" He was still smiling though. "Well, I'm on your mailing list, so I guess you'll let us know."

"Yep. I will definitely keep you posted." I began to sidle away down the aisle, away from the registers as Jerry pushed his trolley forward. I was ready to check out too, but I wasn't sure I wanted to stand in line chatting with Jerry. He seemed like a nice guy, but sociable was not my default. Actually, default was my default.

"It was so great meeting you," Jerry called. "You made my day."

I waved my sprinkler head in farewell.

I spent a few minutes browsing hummingbird feeders and then thought to pick up a couple of bags of picture hooks before heading to the checkout counter.

I paid for my purchases and left the store. As I approached my car I spotted Jerry loading plants into a minivan parked beside my BMW.

He looked up and his frown reversed itself into a bright smile. "Hello again!"

"Hi."

"I promise I'm not stalking you."

"No, I know." I said, "At this point it looks like I'm stalking you."

He laughed as though that was really funny, and pushed his empty trolley to the cart return area.

I unlocked my car, tossed the plastic bag with my purchases in the passenger seat, got in and was just starting to reverse when there was a tap, tap, tap on the passenger side window. I braked. Jerry was smiling tentatively through the tinted glass.

I pressed the button to lower the window a crack.

His mouth formed the words, "Hi again."

I relented and lowered the window all the way. "Hi."

I could see my lack of enthusiasm was making Jerry rethink whatever impulse had led him to stop me mid-getaway. He forged bravely on. "Er, I know you must be busy and I don't want to seem pushy or anything, but I would love to buy my favorite author a cup of coffee. Just to thank you for years of great reading and to welcome you to the neighborhood." Red-faced but hopeful, he gazed at me. The hand gripping the window sill of the door was white-knuckled.

Oh God. Being the socially backward type myself, I knew only too well how excruciating this was for him. And I did not want to crush him with a refusal. If only I was J.X. who was perfectly capable of accepting spontaneous invitations. In fact, he was always doing stuff like that: going off with readers for dinner after a book signing or attending book club luncheons. But I was me, and I had already exhausted my daily allotment of social niceties. I just wanted to go home. And failing that, get back to the house on Chestnut Lane and start unpacking all those boxes and crates.

"That's really nice of you, Jerry. It's just…there's so much to do right now. Moving in, you know. Nothing is unpacked. I couldn't even find the toaster this morning. There are people coming to hook up. I mean, to hook things up. You know. You know how it is." I was starting to babble in my own discomfort.

"Yeah, of course." Jerry looked crestfallen.

I made an effort. "But it's been really nice meeting you. I don't get a lot of opportunities to talk to readers." In the back of my mind I could hear J.X. and Rachel chorusing that if I'd ever go to conferences I could meet all the readers I wanted. What they failed to understand was that was *already* the case.

"No, I totally understand," he said. "It was a dumb idea."

"No! It was very thoughtful. I appreciate it. It's just…you know. Another time."

"Right. Sure." He smiled sadly and I smiled too brightly, and threw the car into reverse again. He stepped hastily out of range of my tires.

I stopped at a market on my way back to Chestnut Lane and stocked up on a few essentials like frozen pizzas, frozen fried chicken, frozen pot pies, frozen egg rolls, frozen lasagna, frozen burritos, beer, frozen popcorn shrimp, chocolate muffins and ice cream. Also a bag of limes, a bag of pre-washed romaine lettuce and two bottles of sparkling mineral water. After J.X. and I had started seeing each other more regularly, I had tried to make a conscious effort to eat better and exercise more. There's nothing like having to get naked with someone younger and trimmer to make you start worrying about dimples where there should be none. I'd lost a few pounds and toned a few muscles. But whether it was stress or the fact that J.X. and his sleek, taut body would be out of sight for a few days, I found myself *craving* cardboard-flavored pizza.

My hunting and gathering finished, I headed back to the house. It took about five minutes to replace the sprinkler head. I showered downstairs and considered my plan of attack as I ate my pizza.

Should I start with the front room, to give a semblance of order to the house? It would be time-consuming but pretty simple. Just shelving the boxes and boxes *and boxes* of books we both owned would go a long way toward making this feel more like a home and less like a publisher's warehouse.

Or did it make more sense to start with the kitchen? It would be nice to be able to cook a real breakfast or wash a dish. But how we organized the kitchen was something J.X. and I should probably figure out together. I could start with my office.

No.

Definitely not.

Maybe the bedroom. But then again, might as well wait until the new bedroom suite was delivered that afternoon.

I ate the last piece of pizza and considered my unusual lethargy. Of course part of it was probably just lack of sleep and the previous day's nine-hour drive. Not to mention the exhaustion of trying to get my entire life packed and moved over the last few weeks. I mulled over the idea of having a beer and cooking the fried chicken. It was past noon, after all. Time for lunch.

I had the freezer door open and was contemplating the fine layer of frost that had already formed over the box of chicken when the kitchen phone rang, startling me.

I answered cautiously.

J.X. said, "Hey, it's me. I'm at the hotel. How's it going?"

The sound of his voice had an unexpected effect. All at once I felt both cheerful and calmer. My overstrung nerves unclenched, released, smoothed out. The knot in my gut eased. Or perhaps that was the pizza inching toward the next phase of digestion. Whatever, I was happy to hear his voice.

"It's good. The sprinkler is repaired and I'm unpacking...everything. How was your flight?"

"I spent longer getting through security than in the air. Did you have trouble..." His voice seemed to dip and then I heard female laughter and noise in the background. J.X. said distantly, "Very funny, give me my phone, Samantha."

Ah, yes. Conferences. Networking. Socializing. Shenanigans. And more shenanigans. Shenanigans were how J.X. and I had met. Funny to think that it could have been Jerry Knight I met that weekend.

"Sorry about that." His voice came back on, loud and clear. "Kit, I got a call from Nina. She sounded upset but I couldn't understand what the problem was. I was thinking maybe if you went over there?"

My moment of serenity deflated like a runaway balloon pricked by the point of a weathervane.

"If I went over there...where? *What?* Where there are you talking about?"

"To Nina's house. To see her. To see her and Gage."

Nina was J.X.'s ex-wife. Gage was his nephew. J.X. had married Nina, his younger brother's pregnant girlfriend, after Alex died in Iraq. He had done this for the sake of his very conservative family and her equally conservative family and the unborn kid. It was noble in a soap-opera-ish way, but it wasn't the kind of nobility that I understood or approved of.

Also, though the gesture had been quixotic and J.X.'s feelings for Nina were platonic, the one time I'd met her—over Christmas turkey—had convinced me that Nina's feelings were not so clear cut. Maybe not clear cut at all. She didn't like me. J.X.'s parents didn't like me either. Possibly for the same reason. And the kid, Gage, disliked me with all his little heart.

"And I would do that...why?"

"Because I can't and you're family. And..."

"And what?"

"And this would be a good chance for you to get to know them."

I laughed, though it came out sounding slightly hysterical. "I hope you're kidding because there is no way in hell I'm going over there. They can't stand me. None of your family can stand me, and the last thing Nina wants is your gay boyfriend showing up."

J.X. made an exasperated sound. "Kit, you're *family* now. That's important. A lot more important than whatever it is you're thinking at this moment. I know it's inconvenient and maybe a little awkward, but it's also a perfect opportunity."

I cannot pretend this little speech of J.X.'s, particularly the phrase *a lot more important than whatever it is you're thinking*, did not irk the living hell out of me. So much so that I actually couldn't speak for a few seconds.

"Kit?"

I managed to choke down my anger before I expired on the spot. "Putting aside my thoughts—and feelings—for a second, I am up to my ears in boxes. Yours included. We've got the furniture company delivering the bedroom suite this afternoon. We've got the satellite dish people arriving any minute. There is no food in this fucking house. So whatever this unspecified emergency is with your ex—"

"She's not my ex."

"Yeah, actually she is. And if she can't spell out what the problem is for you, it's a good bet *I* can't solve it for her. Even if I had the time—or inclination—which I don't."

There was a pause before J.X. said grimly, "That's pretty blunt."

"Not really. Blunt would be to point out that we're *not* family. We're living together. And it may or may not work out."

I'm not sure what his response was—I'm sure he had one. I'd never known him to let me have the last word. But I got it through tactical superiority that time. I hung up.

Then I tottered over to the nearest stool—J.X.'s contribution to our kitchen furnishings were tall, bachelor pad bar stools of leather and steel—before my knees gave out. I was shaking with a crazy rush of anger and adrenaline and alarm.

Also shame. I was too old to be hanging up on people like an angry and inarticulate teenager.

Not my finest hour. Or even my finest one and a half minutes. But this was what I had been afraid of from the first. That we were going to commit to this madness and it wasn't going to work out.

Of course it wasn't going to work out! How could it possibly work out? We barely knew each other. And we didn't always like the us we did know.

But it *had* to work out. There was already an offer on my former home. It was too late to turn back now.

I waited for J.X. to phone back. When he didn't, I told myself I was relieved. I wasn't sure. I hated arguing. I hated confrontation. But I hated cold silence worse. One thing about David, he had not been the strong, silent type. Far from it. He had been the yelling and shouting and punching and breaking things—inanimate things—type. Which had generally led to my yelling and shouting too. But I still preferred explosions to cold silence.

To keep from thinking, I began emptying the boxes in the kitchen. What was the alternative? No, J.X. and I were both tired. Short on sleep and stressed. We *had* committed to this course, and there wasn't any retreat. That I could think of.

I dumped silverware in drawers, placed glasses on shelves, located J.X.'s toaster, and opened a box of little jars of spices I had never heard of. What was Tajin? What was Egyptian dukkah? Did we even eat the same food?

On the bright side, the mountain of boxes eventually dwindled to a mole-hill, speeded by my decision not to wash anything because it had all been packed in bubble wrap for less than 48 hours. The less-than-48-hours-in-bubble-wrap rule was well known in Southern California. And if it wasn't equally well known in Northern California, J.X. could wash any mug he liked.

I came across the gin and tonic and the day looked a little less grim. And, to give J.X. his due, his refrigerator was much better at making ice than mine. The cubes in my glass crackled musically as the tonic fizzed over them.

Refreshed, I got my second wind and started stacking dishes on shelves. Plain white plates. Plain white saucers. Plain white cups, plain white bowls. I opened another box. Plain white *square* plates. Okay. That was a relief. I was beginning to think my true love was stuck in a rut. I put all the square white plates and bowls away. I opened another box.

Plain white plates.

All the dishes seemed to be J.X.'s. Where were my dishes? Down in the basement with my fridge?

Irritated all over again, I opened the door to the basement and started down the steps. I'd never lived in a house that had a basement before. This one was supposed to function as storage and laundry room. And we were certainly getting our money's worth of storage. There were a ton of boxes down here—not to mention my sofa. And who had decided *that*?

Now thoroughly pissed off, I began to explore. On the bright side, the basement was immaculate. Not a cobweb in sight. Not even much in the way of dust. A couple of throw rugs and it could probably double as an additional room. Or a hideout. My TV was probably already down here. Possibly my stereo system.

Except…that smell. What *was* that? Whatever it was, it had to go. Backed-up plumbing? Overflowing garbage bins? Ye gods. I started looking for the source, and tracked it to a large wooden crate marked CHINA. My crate.

What the hell? Had the moving company helpfully decided to move my rotting garbage?

The lid had been hastily and none too securely hammered down, but it was anchored enough to resist my half-hearted efforts to raise it. I went back upstairs, located the fireplace hardware in the parlor, and returned to the basement with the poker. J.X.'s poker, for the record.

I levered the poker beneath the wooden lid and pried until it gave with a cracking sound.

I covered my mouth and nose with the crook of my arm as white bits of biodegradable popcorn floated up along with that ghastly odor. Sure enough I spotted a black trash bag. Instead of Oma's vintage pale green china with gold trim, those lunatics had packed my garbage bags.

That's what I was trying to tell myself. But I knew. Of course I knew. I was a mystery writer. No moving crew was *that* crazy. This could only be one thing. One terrible thing.

Carefully, gingerly, I reached out and pulled back the corner of the trash bag. A lifeless, dull eye gazed up at me.

CHAPTER THREE

I'm not afraid of death. I just don't want to be there when it happens. To anyone.

That said, I've had some experience with people purchasing one-way tickets to the Great Beyond. Take it from me, it doesn't get easier. For any-body. But fortunately there are rules and rituals which help us all. Funerals, sure, but there are others. Like the time-honored ritual for finding a dead body. It begins with calling the police.

Which is what I did, just as fast as my wobbly legs could carry me upstairs.

Unlike when you're complaining about loud music, the cops come a lot faster when you're reporting a dead body. In this case, the uniforms arrived first to "secure the scene," and take my initial statement. Then came Homicide—which would have made a nice book title, if I was still writing mysteries instead of living them.

As the introductions were made, Inspector Ishwar Jones of SFPD's Investigative Bureau—Homicide Detail—stared at me with consternation.

"*J.X.'s* Christopher Holmes?"

"J.X.'s Izzie Jones?" I returned with equal astonishment.

Once upon a time Inspector Ishwar Jones had walked the streets of San Francisco with a bright, ambitious young cop by the name of Julian Xavier Moriarity. Moriarity had quit the police force to become a bestselling writer of crime novels and thrillers, and to eventually buy a house with another crime writer who just happened to be a magnet for murder.

Me.

Anyway, that was *his* problem. My problem was the being-a-magnet-for-murder thing.

On those rare occasions when I had pictured meeting J.X.'s friends and colleagues, the introductions didn't take place at crime scenes. To be honest, they didn't take place at all, although I knew in my heart that J.X. was a social animal and would expect me to behave sociably when required. Which would have been bad enough.

The social awkwardness of Inspector Jones' astonished, "*J.X.'s* Christopher Holmes?" left me blushing as guiltily as if I really was responsible for the body in our basement.

Jones was big and bald and had a very definite Kojak vibe—the Ving Rhames Kojak not the Telly Savalas Kojak. He put a courteous hand on my shoulder, steering me out of the way of the crime scene personnel trooping in and out the door leading to the basement stairs. "Is there some place we can speak privately, Christopher?"

I led the way through the kitchen and out through the French doors of the breakfast nook to the back garden. All the while, Jones spoke quietly and pleasantly, no doubt assuming that finding a dead guy would be a distressing experience for most homeowners. And it was. Certainly. But it was not a new experience for me, as J.X. could—and probably had—informed him.

"And where is J.X.?" Jones asked as we sat down on the excruciatingly uncomfortable patio chairs. It was about the only thing he'd said so far that actually sank in.

"He's in Vegas. At a convention."

"*Ah.*" Somehow with that single syllable Jones seemed to convey an understanding of my entire relationship with J.X.—up to and including our argument a couple of hours previously. "Of course. He does a lot of book tours and signings. I saw his picture in *People* magazine."

"Yes. They reviewed his latest book." Gushingly.

"That conference was good timing on his part." His brief, white smile invited me to share the small joke, but my heart wasn't in it.

"Yes."

"Okay, Christopher, being a crime writer, you know how this works." He offered another reassuring flash of teeth. "I have your initial statement, but I need to ask you a few questions. Like you writers always say in your books, it's just routine."

"Right. I know. Fire away."

"Did you recognize the victim?"

"No."

"Did you get a good look at him though?"

Right there, I gave Inspector Jones credit because he was perfectly correct. I had taken one horrified peek at the grisly discovery in the packing crate and I had been out the door and up the stairs like a shot. I had no idea of hair or skin color or build or facial structure. His eyes had been blue. And filmed over. That I remembered.

I shuddered. "Enough, I think."

Jones nodded, reserving judgment on that point.

"How do you think he got into one of your moving boxes?"

I had been thinking about that too. "The moving van broke down twice on the way here. They had to replace the water pump in Barstow. That took several hours. So unless the movers packed him up themselves—and why would they?—it must have happened then, though I don't know how it could have. The lid was hammered down. And whoever put him in there would have had to do something with the china that was already there. And dumping a crate of dishes would be noisy. I assume the truck was in a garage with mechanics and people all around. Anyway, they didn't arrive here until after midnight. And it took the movers a couple of hours to unload everything."

Jones nodded thoughtfully. He took down the name and details of the moving company. "You never dealt with this company before?"

"No."

"What made you choose..." He glanced at his notes. "Movers and Shakers Relocation Company?"

I groaned. "Pricing, mostly." Indifference, really. I had stalled until the last possible moment and then I'd snatched at the first company available for the job.

"Sure. Makes sense. Did you follow the moving van? Did you stop in Barstow?"

"No. I drove on ahead."

He thought it over without comment.

My nerves got the better of me, and I burst out, "You can't think I had anything to do with this. In the first place, the movers packed everything. Almost everything. In the second place, if I had killed somebody, I wouldn't hide his body in one of the boxes going in my own moving van."

Jones looked interested. "No? What would you do?"

"I'd take that particular box in my own car, and somewhere along the way I'd make a detour, drive off into the desert and dump the body as far away from the main highway as I could."

Jones raised his eyebrows. "Well, that would certainly be a more practical approach."

"It would make no sense for me to cart that body up here. And even less sense to pretend to discover it in my own basement and go out of my way to bring in the police."

"I agree," he said. Two little words which went a long way to calming me down. Then he had to spoil it by saying, "Of course, someone could argue that being a mystery writer, you might be prone to coming up with convoluted plots."

J.X. for one. That sounded exactly like the kind of thing he'd say.

I must have looked dismayed because Jones laughed. "I don't think that's what happened. Like you say, that would be a pretty dumb plan, and I can't see J.X. saddling himself with a dummy."

"Thanks." It wasn't exactly delivered as a compliment, but I was willing to take what I could get. In this case, a Not Guilty verdict.

"You seem to attract trouble, I gotta say."

I threw him a glum look.

"Is there anything else you can think of that might be of help?"

I moved my head in negation. "How did he die? Do you know yet? Is it possible he climbed into the crate himself and maybe smothered?"

Yeah, right. Dumped out a serving set for twenty, jumped into a trash bag, and climbed into the crate? Oh, and nailed down the lid from inside? It was a silly suggestion, but Jones didn't retract his previous "you're no dummy" comment.

"We don't have the coroner's verdict yet, obviously, but it looks to me like someone stabbed him in the heart." He punched himself lightly in the solar plexus, which is why I guess police departments hire medical examiners instead of relying on officers for the science stuff. Jones studied me. "I've got to go back inside. Do you have some place to stay tonight?"

"I'll get a hotel room."

He said that sounded like a good idea, and disappeared through the French doors. I stared up at the sunny sky. Such a pretty day. Birds singing, flowers blooming. Sun shining. A good day to be alive and not dead in a crate in a stranger's basement. I pulled my phone out. After I'd called the police, I had phoned J.X. But he hadn't picked up. I tried him again.

And once more the call went to message.

Maybe he was busy. Maybe he wasn't taking my phone calls. I did an internal taste test as I considered that possibility. The flavor was bitter.

Anyway, this was not news I wanted to leave in a message. I disconnected and began to search for a place to spend the night. Was it insensitive to splurge on a really nice hotel? I began to surf hotel sites.

The Suites at Fisherman's Wharf sounded pretty good: dining area, living room, and a kitchenette offering a 2-burner stovetop and dishwasher. 42-inch flat-screen cable TV and free Wi-Fi, and decorated with floral patterns and beige accents. Maybe I could just move in there and J.X. could come and visit on weekends.

I sighed and changed my search criteria to "very nice hotel." I felt in urgent need of some *very nice* right about then. Vaguely, I was aware of the crime scene folks continuing to mill through the house. Lots of vehicles and plenty of personnel in attendance when someone dies a violent death. No privacy or dignity for the dead. Or the living.

"Yoo-hoo! Yoo-hoo!" called a familiar voice.

I looked around, but saw no one. I rose and finally pinpointed the yoo-hooing to the other side of a four-foot-tall hedge that divided our property from Emmaline Bloodworth's. I could see her coolie hat floating just over the edge like a flying saucer looking for a safe place to land.

"Christopher? Hellooo?"

I walked up a couple of small terraces and leaned across the perfectly clean-shaven expanse of twigs and leaves. Emmaline's bright blue eyes blinked up at me.

"What's happened? I was afraid you'd had some kind of accident."

"Not me. Not this time." I explained as succinctly as possible what had happened.

"Good heavens. Are you all right?" She seemed genuinely concerned, which was nice. And there's no better security system than nosey neighbors.

"Yes. Fine." That probably sounded heartless, but if I told her it wasn't my first murder, she would need some kind of explanation, and I really didn't have the energy. I said off-handedly, "It's just the shock of it."

"I should think so. *Murder*," she breathed. "Do they—?"

"It didn't happen here," I tried to reassure her. "He must have been dead when he arr—a while."

Truthfully, I had no idea how long he'd been dead. It did seem to me that for a stabbing, there had been relatively little blood. Nothing had leaked out of the crate. That I'd seen, anyway. My stomach gave a queasy shudder. As frozen pizza toppings go, murder is the least appetizing.

"Will they let you back in the house?" Emmaline asked.

"Once they finish processing the crime scene."

"How long does that take?"

I shook my head. From our vantage point between the two houses we watched as the satellite dish people arrived—late as usual—and were turned away. They were just disappearing from view when the furniture delivery people arrived and were also declined entrance.

"Oh dear," Emmaline said. "Don't you think you should talk to them? Set up another delivery time?"

"Probably." But I made no move. Sometimes you have to consider that maybe the cosmos is trying to tell you something.

"Is it possible the crate wasn't one of yours?"

"No. It had my name on it. And I remember seeing them packing my china."

"I wonder where your china is."

"Good question." That china had traveled all the way from Switzerland, and though it was not something I would have chosen for myself, it was mine and I wanted it back, down to the very last saucer.

Eventually Emmaline's feet began to hurt and she excused herself with an invitation to drop by anytime, unless I ended up being arrested.

I thanked her and continued to hover at the side of the house, watching uneasily as the coroner's van arrived and was loaded up and sent on its merry way.

Inspector Jones came outside again and located me lurking in the hydrangeas.

"Hey there, Christopher."

"Oh, there you are," I said.

"The good news is the ME is sure that the vic was killed offsite. The bad news is we're not going to finish processing the crime scene tonight. But you should be back home by—at the latest—end of day tomorrow."

He gazed at me expectantly. I realized that because of my connection to J.X., I had been bumped from coach to first class, and they had even thrown in complimentary champagne. All this speed and sensitivity in a preliminary homicide investigation was *not* business as normal. Heaven and earth was being moved to return me to safe haven as soon as reasonably possible.

"That's...I don't know what to say. Thank you. All of you. I appreciate it."

Jones winked. "Nothing's too good for J.X. Man, we had some times together."

"I can imagine."

"Did he tell you about that time we chased that dumbass junkie up to Coit Tower?"

No. J.X. had not told me about that time. Or about almost any other time when he'd been on the force. Possibly because we were always too busy with my latest drama.

I said, "I think he's always using that stuff in his books."

"You know it," Jones laughed. "You *know* it."

Reporters crowded the sidewalk when I finally flung open the front gate and departed 321 Chestnut Lane. Maybe it was a slow day for news in The

City. Fortunately they didn't seem to know who I was, beyond the unlucky homeowner, and I ignored the clicking cameras and questions thrown my way. I tossed my laptop and leather carryall in the back seat, jumped in my car, and sped away to the Fairmont hotel.

The Fairmont is a San Francisco icon. It's on Nob Hill, no less, and the cheapest room is $549. A night. Worth every penny, in my opinion. It was just what my shattered nerves needed. I checked in, had a G&T in the Laurel Court bar while I booked myself an in-room massage. Then I had another G&T before I trudged up to my room in time to take a hot shower before the masseuse arrived.

My room was on the seventh floor and it was lovely. Quiet and comfortable with a pillow-top bed, a marble bath, flat screen TV and Keurig coffee maker. What more could a lost and lonely wayfarer require? A minibar? It had that too. The décor was in soothing tones of platinum and pewter with royal-blue accents. The carpet was a tone-on-tone floral paisley pattern. How sad was it that I felt more at home in a hotel room than I did in my nice, new house?

The massage was heavenly, the nap that followed even better. When I woke up, I ordered room service: the citrus-charred breast of organic chicken and—because any entrée with the word "organic" in it grants you permission to have dessert—the lemon and mixed berry cheesecake. After verifying that J.X. had still not left word, I ordered another gin and tonic.

Clearly I had crossed a line from which there was no coming back. Which is what I had expected from the first, though not quite this soon. I'd expected enough time to organize my half of the medicine cabinet before the wrecking ball fell.

Or maybe he was just…busy. Conventions did keep you…busy. We had kept each other busy that first convention.

That didn't make me feel a whole hell of a lot better. But sitting around thinking about it wasn't going to help. While I waited for my dinner to arrive, I got out my laptop, and reluctantly checked my email. Rachel had sent me three notes. The first two urged me to grab the first plane out to Las Vegas. The third requested a genealogical search of my Swiss heritage. I sighed.

Nothing from J.X., but getting an email rather than a phone call from him right now would only have increased my anxiety.

Dear Christopher,

It has come to our attention that as boy-friends go, you leave a lot to be desired.

Yours Truly,
Your Soon-to-be Next Ex

No, I could do without that. I signed out of email and did some online shopping, downloading a couple of bestselling Scandinavian crime fiction titles, including *The Boy in the Suitcase, The Keeper of Lost Causes, The Dinosaur Feather, Death Angels,* and *The Devil's Star.* Danish, Danish, Danish, Norwegian, Swedish. That was a pretty good sampling, and a couple of Glass Key Award winners to boot.

When in doubt, work. That had been my mantra for most of my life, and it had never failed me yet. Of course, if I was being strictly accurate, it hadn't done me a lot of good in the affairs of the heart department. But if there was one thing I had learned over the years, relationships came and went. Work remained constant. Work was my pole star.

Not that I had any intention of writing Nordic noir, or whatever the hell it was Rachel wanted me to crank out this month, but it couldn't hurt to see what the kids in the winter parkas were writing.

Lene and Agnete led off: *Holding the glass door open with her hip, she dragged the suitcase into the stairwell leading down to the underground parking lot.*

I skipped ahead and yes, a boy in a suitcase. Alive. Which made a nice change. I would wait till after I had my dinner to see if he stayed that way.

Jussi wrote: *She scratched her fingertips on the smooth walls until they bled, and pounded her fists on the thick panes until she could no longer feel her hands.*

Right. Well, that was marriage for you.

Next S.J. Gazan's *The Dinosaur Feather. This sounded promising: Anna Bella Nor was dreaming she had unearthed Archaeopteryx, the earliest and most primitive bird known.* Very good. An intellectual puzzle. I much preferred not to start out with people in agony, at least not until I was sure my hotel room minibar was stocked to see me through to the end.

I clicked out of the other books and settled down to read *The Dinosaur Feather*. Room service arrived and carried in my supper. I scribbled my signature, closed the door firmly, and returned to my book and dinner. Lost china, dead bodies, and even the house on Chestnut Lane seemed a long way away now.

The next time I looked at the bedside clock it was nine. Only nine o'clock? I could hardly keep my eyes open. I wanted nothing more than to crawl between the sheets, bury my head in the pillows and lose myself in deep, deep sleep. But that had to be the strain of the last few days, not the book.

> *Clive gave Fjeldberg a horrified look.*
> *"Parasites?"*
> *"Yes, his body was supposedly riddled with them," Fjeldberg*
> *snorted.*

Or maybe it was the book.

Someone was knocking on the table next to my head. I could just make out the tap-tap-tap in the great distance beyond the rushing wind of my snores. I snapped my mouth shut, unstuck my eyelids, and listened doubtfully. There was something distinctly *police-open-up!* about that knock.

Shit. My cell phone was on vibrate. I tore off my sleep mask, flung myself over, knocking the glass of melted ice water to the plush carpet, and grabbed my phone. Even in the gloom of the room I could make out the outline of J.X.'s fuzzy photo. I clicked to accept the call and before I could croak out anything resembling words, J.X. roared, *"Where the hell are you?"*

I fumbled my glasses on, threw a hasty look at the shadowy interior of the room, and said, "The Fairmont."

"The Fairmont? The fucking *Fairmont?*"

"It's actually really nice."

I was verbally treading water, stalling, not giving him a serious answer, and certainly not intending to be a smartass, but that was my mistake because he *needed* a serious answer. There followed a torrent of words unlike any I had previously heard from J.X.—and with that kind of breath control he was probably an amazing long distance swimmer. The gist of his "argument"—though brawl-with-broken-beer-bottles—might be a better word for it—was his sincere bewilderment that I had not called him the previous day. He made this point several times, though the volume faded with each repetition as he grew hoarser and hoarser.

When he'd finally worn himself out and I could wedge in a word, I said, "I tried calling you. You didn't pick up."

From the sounds on the other end he was either spluttering his disbelief or suffering what my grandmother used to quaintly call "a conniption." Finally he managed a strangled, "*Kit.* Why didn't you leave a *message?*"

"You must admit that's not an easy message to leave on voice mail."

More spluttering. He wasn't usually so inarticulate. I deduced he was short on sleep and probably hungover from discussing fine literature into the wee hours.

"Well, why the hell didn't you call *me?*" I demanded. My own grievances kicking in.

"I did! I phoned *the house* four times. Because you never answer your goddamned cell phone. You never even have it on."

"Well, I *did* have it on."

"I had to hear from Izzie Jones that you found a body. In our *home!*"

"In a moving crate, but yes."

"And I called your cell. How do you think we're talking right now? You sure as hell didn't call me. I must have phoned you six times last night. If your goddamned cell was on how could you not pick up? I was starting to think something happened to you."

There was a note in his voice... I realized this was about him being scared not about him being inconvenienced.

I automatically clicked over to check if he had left messages and, not being all that familiar with my cell phone—as J.X. would have been the first to point out—disconnected the call.

CHAPTER FOUR

"**O**h *shit.*"

Worse yet, J.X. had called *eight* times last night. I stared in horror at that long list of missed calls, panicked, and began scrolling through contacts for his number. Somehow the damn phone had scooped up all the names and addresses from my email and dumped them into my contacts list. When had that happened? *How* had that happened? Everyone I had ever emailed seemed to be listed as a contact.

"No, no. Please, please. Where *are* you—"

The phone vibrated again, nearly jumping out of my hand with the ferocity of that ring. Or maybe it was just that my palms were starting to sweat. A lot. In fact, my glasses were fogging. I think my eyeballs were sweating too.

I clicked to answer. "Sorry," I gulped. "Sorry about that."

I could hear him heavy-breathing on the other end. But those years of police training stood him in good stead.

"Kit." He got the syllable out with great control.

"I know. God. I'm so sorry. I didn't mean to hang up on you. This time. Yesterday I was mad, I admit it. But just now, that was an accident. And if I'd heard the phone last night, I'd have answered. I have the damned thing on vibrate, and I guess I didn't hear the first…few times you called. I took a sleeping pill."

And slept like a baby, but it didn't seem tactful to mention it.

"Look, I'm going to try and get a flight back this afternoon."

Yes. I felt weak with relief. That was *exactly* what I felt he should do. No way should I have to be dealing with this myself.

But contrariwise, dealing with what? I'd had an unpleasant experience, yes, but it was all over now except for the shouting. And we'd nearly finished the shouting. In fact, all that was left was fumigating the basement. What was J.X. going to do other than lend moral support? It wasn't like I was involved in an actual murder investigation, and even if I had been, it wasn't like I hadn't been through *that* a time or two before. The police didn't really think I was involved, and dragging J.X. away from his conference was just…cowardly.

I said sturdily, "No. Come on. There's no need for that."

"No need? You found a body in our house!"

"In a moving crate. It doesn't have anything to do with us. You're at the convention for a reason, right? So let's stick to the plan. You come home on Monday after the signing at Cloak and Dagger."

"You're joking."

"No. I'm not. I'm serious. And sober. Which right there should tell you something. Because I wasn't last night."

"I don't feel right about this, Kit. I feel like I need to be there."

"Now listen. You're the one who said it was important for you to attend this conference. So if it was important yesterday, it's still important today, right?"

"It's not more important than you."

It was the way he said it. So staunch and unhesitating, like he'd never have to think twice about it. Not a compliment, not making nice after a spat, just the way J.X. saw it. It was unexpected and it closed my throat for a second.

"Well, okay," I said gruffly. "But it's not either or. I grant you, I was kind of freaked out yesterday. But I had a good night's sleep and I'm okay. Seriously. It was just a gruesome coincidence. It's over and done and you should carefully consider how much you'll regret the decision to come home once you're stuck with unpacking two hundred boxes of books."

He made a semi-amused sound, but his voice was still troubled as he said, "It's your call, I guess. I do have a couple of meetings set up with my agent, and my editor, and my publicist and some power bloggers. I don't want to miss them if I don't have to. But—"

"But nothing. It's fine. I wouldn't say it, if I didn't mean it. Right?"

He said honestly, "I'm not sure. I think you might."

That made me laugh. "Call me tonight. Okay? I promise to take your calls from now on."

"All right. But if something happens—"

"What else could happen? A major earthquake followed by raging fire? Wait. I'm in San Francisco now. Forget I said that."

J.X.'s laugh was more natural that time. "At least we know our house managed to survive the last major earthquake followed by raging fire. Okay. Then if you're really sure about this, I'll talk to you tonight."

I started to click off, but he hadn't disconnected yet, seemed to be waiting for something, and I realized I couldn't leave things the way they were. Or the way they weren't.

"J.X.?"

"Yes?" He sounded a little wary.

"Look. What I said yesterday. I shouldn't have. It was uncalled for. And I definitely shouldn't have hung up on you."

J.X. drew a sharp breath and I knew my instinct had been right. "It's my fault. I pushed too hard. It's just that I want us…"

"I want us too," I said. I wasn't sure if it was true or not, but I knew in that moment I wanted it to be true.

"I want us to be a family, want you to be part of the rest of my family. I know you think they don't accept you, don't like you, but it's just they don't know you yet."

"Yeah. Well."

"And I honestly really feel like this is the perfect opportunity for you. It's a chance to get to know Nina and Gage without me around, to do something for them, to wi—" He caught himself.

"Win them over?" I asked.

"To bond with them."

"Mmhm." I called upon my inner resources. Surely I still had some vital elements left? A little sodium. Probably some sulfur. "Does she, Nina, still need…something?"

"Maybe if you could call her and ask? If you could just make that first gesture, Kit."

I closed my eyes. Opened them. "What's her number again?"

I felt worse after I listened to J.X.'s progressively worried and angry messages.

He'd had a couple of drinks by the last one, placed at 1:15 in the morning. It got a little confessional in tone and I turned cold listening to it. "Kit, if you're deliberately not taking my calls, if you're this childish, this selfish, this heartless... I don't know where we go from here."

It wasn't that I didn't see it from his perspective. I did. After an afternoon of phone calls, I didn't blame him for being upset. He'd stayed calm a lot longer than I would have. But that peek into his uncensored brain made it clear he too realized there was a good chance things weren't going to work out for us, that the idea of it not working out was already in his mind, and in some corner of his heart he was already preparing for it.

And since I was already preparing to prepare for it too, I'm not sure why it made me so sad. But it did. It was like someone cut my lifeline. I sat on the edge of the unmade bed in my hotel room and I replayed the message a couple of times, and on each replay J.X. sounded more tired and more...done.

I deleted his messages, wiped my eyes, and used the hotel phone to call down for breakfast, which arrived as I was shaving.

The Fairmont did not let me down. Breakfast consisted of the house granola—almonds, mixed oats, seeds, vanilla yogurt, and fruit compote— coffee, juice and an omelet of free range eggs, smoked chicken sausage and cheddar cheese. Having waived the temptations of pastries, cappuccino, and breakfast potatoes, I felt quite virtuous as I nerved myself to call Nina.

She answered on the third ring, just as I was starting to hope my call would go safely to message.

"Hello?" She sounded soft and sleepy at ten in the morning, which was unlikely for a young woman with a small child to care for.

I said briskly, "Hi, Nina. This is Christopher. J.X.'s, um. J.X. got your call, but he's out of town right now and he asked me to contact you." *Contact you?* That certainly sounded businesslike. I tried to sound less like a coworker and more like a caring family member. "Is everything okay? Do you need something?"

Please say no. Please have mercy.

"J.X. is out of town?"

"Yes, he's in Las Vegas at a mystery fiction convention. But I'm here getting the house ready, so if you need something…"

There was a pause and she said, "My ring went down the sink."

"Your ring?"

"My wedding ring."

Oh right. *That* ring. "That's… Did you call a plumber?"

She said tearfully, "I don't have money for a plumber! I don't even know who to call. J.X. always handles this kind of thing."

Of course. Of course he did. Because he was a glutton for punishment. Which was how we got together in the first place.

"Do you want me to…?"

She said nothing to fill my awkward pause.

"Should I come over there?" I asked, and if she couldn't hear the reluctance dragging on every word I spoke, she was tone deaf.

Nina said with equal reluctance, "If J.X. isn't there, I guess you have to." Which was about as faulty reasoning as it got, but I was not moderating her debate performance, I was bonding with her. And so far it was going brilliantly.

You know what? Fine. What the hell ever. I couldn't go back to Chestnut Lane till the police sounded the All Clear, and I didn't want to sit in a hotel room—even a nice hotel room—reading about parasites and professors and people who hated their parents. I said, "Okay. Sure. What's the address?"

They say when you marry someone, you also marry their family.

For me and David that had been irrelevant. I liked my family—when taken at the required minimum dosage—whereas he didn't get along with his relatives at all. So there was never any hassle of trying to split holidays fairly or making time for monthly visits to the in-laws.

J.X., however, was part of a closely-knit family. He spent holidays with his kinfolk and even visited them between official three-day weekends. He was crazy about his nephew and made the effort to see him a couple of times a week.

All of which I liked and respected about him. So long as it didn't involve me.

But it did involve me now.

And I honestly wasn't sure how that was going to work out.

It took me forever to find the house. I got lost twice trying to locate Capitol Avenue. And then I got lost again trying to find a place to park. But eventually I arrived at a small, stucco Spanish/Mediterranean home with an attached one-car garage—that alone put the property beyond price in this parking hell of a city.

There was a security screen in front of the heavy dark wood door and an even more powerful protective measure behind the heavy dark wood door: Laura Moriarity—J.X.'s mother. I deduced Nina had rung her up in a panic after talking to me. Was Laura supposed to be chaperone or moral support or simply outside observer?

Whichever, whatever, the sight of her triggered my own panic attack, which as usual resulted in the immediate flapping of my mouth. "Somebody call a plumber?" I asked brightly. I don't do "brightly" very well, so it mostly sounded desperate. Less like a question and more like a plugged-up sink crying for a doctor.

"Mr. Holmes," Laura said forbiddingly. She was a tall and chilly blue-eyed blonde. Castilian Spanish, according to J.X. who got his own warm coloring from his "Black Irish" father. If Laura ever got tired of terrorizing in-laws, she could always find work as a butler, scaring tradesman away from the front entrance of Persnickety Manor.

"Mrs. Moriarity. I understand there's a plumbing emergency." Now I sounded equally grave. The specialist flown in from Zurich for consultation. *Code Blue! Code Blue! Find me a plunger STAT!*

Without wasting time on chitchat, she led the way into the house. I had a quick impression of tidy, sunny rooms and hardwood floors. Nothing fancy but well-kept and cozy. There were several framed photos of a handsome, young, blond man in military uniform.

Nina was waiting in the den. There were toys at her feet, but I assumed they were not hers. She did look very young. Small and plump and pretty. She had big brown eyes and shiny dark hair. She rose as I followed Laura into the room, gazing up at me with eyes as wide and worried as something caught in a trap.

"Hi," I said.

"Hi," she replied.

I waited, but it did not seem to be a through street. I reversed and turned to Laura. Nina might be genuinely helpless, but Laura wasn't. I wondered why she hadn't simply summoned a plumber herself. Why again was I here?

Laura met my gaze coolly. In fact, they both seemed to be watching me with an expectancy that reminded me of lionesses contemplating zebras at a watering hole.

"So you lost your ring down the sink?" I prompted, turning back to Nina. "Which sink?"

"The bathroom. The main bathroom."

"Would you like me to call someone?"

"J.X. just usually takes care of it himself."

"It's happened before?"

"Twice." She looked sadly down at her bare left hand. "My ring is a little big. He bought it when I was pregnant."

"Couldn't you have it resized?"

"That's how J.X. bought it."

Was there sentimental value in having a ring in the wrong size? Wasn't it more likely that a ring that wouldn't stay on your finger was a bad omen?

Nina said, "J.X. usually just takes the sink apart. I know to turn the water off now."

Now. J.X. really was up for sainthood. Me, I'd have summoned a plumber on her behalf. There are some things worth paying for. But Laura and Nina continued to watch me with those intent, unreadable expressions, so maybe this was some kind of a test? It seemed to be a test as far as J.X. was concerned.

I said, "Well, if it's just a matter of removing the P-trap, I can do that. I mean, assuming you've got a wrench or a pair of pliers."

"J.X. leaves his tools here." There was a hint of a challenge in the way Nina said that, so yes, this was probably some kind of territorial thing. And maybe me demonstrating acceptance of her boundaries would help? Or would I look weak? The zebra with the bad limp?

I was just glad she hadn't dropped her ring down the bath drain because clearly nothing less than shifting the tub would do, and with my bad back, I'd probably have ended up writhing on the floor beneath their pitiless gaze while they drew straws on who would put me out of their misery.

"Lead on, Mac-er-Ma'am," I said.

Nina did the honors, leading the way to the garage where a plastic bucket sat with a wrench and a pair of rubber gloves inside. So yes, apparently this was not an uncommon occurrence. What did she have against drain guards? Or was I missing the point of this exercise?

I picked the bucket up and Nina said, "The bathroom's this way."

We returned inside, Nina pointed out the bathroom, and withdrew a safe distance to the den.

It had been twenty years since I'd had to dismantle a drain pipe. The last time, my mother had dropped a diamond earring down the kitchen sink. It was one of a pair my father had bought her on their tenth wedding anniversary, and though my father was out of favor, she still loved the earrings.

Anyway, I had been successful that time, and hopefully I would triumph here too. I needed a little triumph this morning.

Laura and Nina spoke quietly, in Spanish, in the front room. It would be childish to let that bother me, right? They were probably not talking about me. They were probably discussing the Giants' scores or what to do about the Middle East.

I placed the bucket directly beneath the P-trap to capture whatever lovely goop fell out after I removed the trap. I sat down on the bathroom floor and used the wrench to loosen the P-trap's slip nuts.

A floorboard squeaked. I glanced around and the kid, Gage, poked his head around the door frame. He had been four at Christmas, and I had the vague idea there had been a birthday since then, so he was a brown and skinny five-year-old with eyes like Bambi and a perpetual frown. Or maybe the frown was only perpetual around me. Judging by appearances, he'd been playing outside. Or possibly mud wrestling.

"Hi," I said.

He ducked away, but a couple of minutes later he was back. This time he stuck his tongue out.

I ignored him.

He departed once more, only to return in a minute or so, stepping boldly into the doorway. He put his hands on his non-existent hips and stuck his tongue out again.

"You know, I see you," I said. The slip nuts were loose enough that I could now unscrew them the rest of the way by hand.

Gage stuck his tongue out again.

"That's not very nice."

"You're not my friend," he said.

"I'd like to be."

This was trespassing. He scowled, looking uncomfortably like J.X. in his less charming moments. The dirt on his little face even suggested the shadow of a beard. "I don't like you."

I don't like you either, you little shit. But to my surprise I heard myself say calmly, "That makes me sad. And I know it makes your uncle sad."

His brows drew together. He opened his mouth, but before he could respond, Nina yelled from the other room, "Gage! Come in here now. Stop bothering Mr. Holmes."

"He's fine," I called. Maybe they didn't hear. There was no response.

Gage scampered away on muddy, soundless feet.

My phone vibrated suddenly and I jumped, nearly braining myself on the underside of the sink basin. I got to my knees, fumbled my cell out of my pocket. I didn't recognize the number. But I had learned my lesson. I answered. It was Inspector Izzie Jones telling me I could go back home any-time I chose.

I reached over and swung the bathroom door shut. "Was there any iden-tification on the body?"

"No, but we know who he is."

"You do?"

"I recognized him the minute I saw him," Jones said cheerfully.

I thought over our two conversations the day before. He sure as hell hadn't given any indication at the time he knew who the victim was. So the inspector hadn't been quite as blasé and trusting as he'd seemed. Cynicism. I liked that in a man.

"Who is he?"

"His name is Elijah Ladas. We've been looking for him in connection with a robbery homicide at a gallery in Sausalito."

"A gallery? You mean an art gallery?"

"Arts and antiques."

"What would an art thief be doing in my moving van?" Come to think of it, what would an art thief be doing in Barstow, assuming Barstow was where he'd joined the safari? Was there any art worth stealing in Barstow? Was there any art in Barstow at all? Not counting Paint-by-Number kits.

"That's something we'd certainly like to know."

I said, "Unless someone is after my Dell mapbacks or my Criterion DVD collection, there was no reason to target me."

"Yeah, well, we think it wasn't targeting so much as innocent-bystandering."

That was a relief. "Do you have any suspects?"

"The usual," Jones said, and I wasn't sure if he was pulling my leg or not. He promised to keep us posted and bade me adieu.

I undid the final nuts, freed the trap, and a dank-smelling watery sludge slopped into the bucket.

Nice.

I tugged the plastic gloves on and began sifting through the muck, wondering if I was still in bed at the Fairmont having some weird, psychologically significant dream about searching for J.X.'s ex-wife's wedding ring? Because it was hard to believe I was doing this in real life.

A gleam of gold shot through a hairy green lump. I dug out the ring—a plain gold band—wiped it off with a handful of toilet paper, and squinted at the engraving inside the band. It was just a date, which was sort of a relief.

An expensive wedding ring or a tender inscription would have bothered me more than I wanted to admit.

I dumped the dirty water down the toilet, replaced the P-trap, fastened it, turned the valves back on, rinsed the ring and carried it out to Nina, who was still talking quietly with Laura. Nina looked up, her eyes red as though she had been crying.

I said awkwardly, "Here you go. Good as new."

"Thank you," she said huskily, taking the ring and not looking at me. She slipped it on her left hand.

Laura rose. "I'll see you out," she said.

I'll. See. You. Out. Wow. Didn't they have a footman for that? But maybe it was just the uncomfortableness of the situation because at the front door she unbent enough to say, "Thank you for coming over here this morning. It was very kind of you...Christopher."

"I'm glad I could help."

Gage, who had been playing with a couple of Tonka Gear Jammer Big Rigs in the front hall, joined Laura at the door to give me one final view of his—in my opinion, unnaturally elongated—tongue. I raised a hand in farewell.

Back on Chestnut Lane, everything looked pretty much as usual, not counting the news van from independent television station KAKE parked out front. A slim, dark-haired woman in a pale pink trench coat jumped out of the passenger side as I approached the gate. The driver was slowed down by his camera.

"Mr. Holmes? Sydney Nightingale, *Baywatch News.* I just have a few questions."

I snorted at the idea of "Baywatch News," put my head down and kept walking. Nightingale trotted alongside me, her tan kitten heels making a clip-pity-clop sound on the bricks.

"Is it true you found the body of notorious art thief Elijah Ladas buried beneath your basement?"

"No."

"You didn't?" She sounded startled, so her source at Police HQ must have been generally infallible. "Whose body did you find?"

"This is private property," I said.

She wore her dark hair in a stylish flip. Her blue eyes were made up to give them a cat's eye tilt. She had a cute spattering of freckles across her nose. "Was there or was there not a body in your basement, Mr. Holmes?"

I reached the front porch, got my key in the lock. The wrong key as it turned out.

"Can you confirm your relationship to crime writer J.X. Moriarity?"

I found the right key, turned the lock and opened the door.

"Any comment? Any comment at all, Mr. Holmes?"

I stepped inside and closed the door in Nightingale's pretty face.

A woman was speaking loudly from the kitchen. More cops? More reporters? I charged down the box-strewn hall to do battle, but realized I was listening to Rina, my Southern California realtor, leaving a message.

"...your decision, but it's a good offer. I really think we should take it. Either way, we have to tell them *something.*"

I stopped in the doorway, listening. Rina was right, of course. We did have to tell the buyers something. I wasn't sure why I was hesitating. But I was, and I continued to hesitate as she finished her message and hung up.

I poured myself a glass of water. As I drank the water I studied the remaining boxes in the kitchen. I'd made more progress than I'd realized the day before. I was all the way down to pot holders, dish towels and oddball kitchen utensils like meat skewers, baster sets and a tenderizer hammer. That final one, now that I thought about it, made a nice little murder weapon.

I was slapping the hammer experimentally against my palm when the doorbell rang.

I charged down the hall, flung open the door—and my mouth—all primed and ready to deliver a blistering, "If you're not off my property in thirty seconds, I'm going to call the police." But it was not intrepid girl reporter Sydney Nightingale from *Baywatch News,* blighting the beauty of the June afternoon.

Jerry Knight stood on the porch. He smiled broadly, held up an enormous picnic basket, and caroled, "Surprise!"

CHAPTER FIVE

I don't like surprises. And I'm not that good at hiding my feelings.

"Uh…" I said. Actually that *was* me trying to hide my feelings. The inward dialog went more like *Are you fucking kidding me?*

Jerry's smile fell. He looked at the dumpster-sized basket. He looked at me. His arms trembled as he tried to unburden himself.

I automatically reached for the basket, then realized what I was doing and tried to press it back on him. He put his hands up as though we were playing a game of Baby, Baby, Who's Got the Baby?—or Who's Got the Live Grenade?—taking a step back.

"Really," I said. "I can't." I pushed the bassinet into his arms, which automatically closed around it. He nearly overbalanced but steadied.

"I just thought—I saw you on the news last night and I thought—"

What? That I might be in the mood for a picnic? How long had he been parked on my street waiting for me to come home?

"It's very kind of you. It's very thoughtful. But I can't."

He looked bewildered. "Why?"

"Because…"

The truth was not an acceptable answer. Unlike Jerry's gesture, the truth was not kind. That except in cases of flood, fire, famine—and winning raffle tickets—strangers did not bring other strangers picnic baskets.

Jerry wasn't waiting for my explanation. He was ready with his own. "You had a horrible experience and I thought you probably didn't have a chance to cook. And I wanted to welcome you to the city but you didn't have time for coffee. I remember reading in an interview that you liked lemon meringue pie, so there's a lemon meringue from my favorite bakery. And cold roast beef sandwiches. And dandelion bacon salad like in *Dead Weights for Miss Butterwith*." It came out in a jumbled rush. I got the gist of it though. He had done something very nice and generous, and I was being a jerk. So what else was new?

I said weakly, "You went to too much trouble, Jerry. And expense."

"I wanted to. You've given me so many hours of pleasure with your books."

"But it's just…that's my job."

"And it's my job as your number one fan to let you know how much we readers appreciate it." He smiled tentatively.

"Well, thank you. It's really kind." I hesitated. Appearances to the contrary, I didn't *want* to be unkind. Or ungracious. But I also didn't want to encourage, well, the wrong thing. You're not supposed to accept expensive presents from strangers. That's the rule.

Jerry continued to watch me with those sad-hopeful eyes.

Okay, maybe it's more of a guideline.

I think what ultimately decided me in Jerry's favor was the memory of finding the body of Elijah Ladas in the basement. That had been pretty damned unsettling, and even though, if I looked at it logically, *I* was inadvertently responsible for the body showing up at 321 Chestnut Lane, it was going to be a while before I could comfortably walk downstairs. In fact, I kept getting the persistent, uncomfortable feeling that someone was standing in another room listening to us. It was a big, empty house, and, chicken or not, I didn't want to be here by myself.

I asked, "Would you like to come in for a cup of coffee?"

Jerry's face lit up. "Yes!"

I held the door wide, and Jerry stepped inside. *"Wow."* He stared around himself.

"I know. Mostly books," I said. "Between me and J.X., we could start a used book store."

"No, I mean the house. *Wow.* It's so beautiful. I love old houses!" Jerry tipped his head back, studying the ceiling. "That skylight. Is that original to the house?"

"No. That was put in a couple of renovations back."

Jerry beamed at me. "It's exactly the kind of place I pictured you'd live in."

"It is?"

He nodded eagerly. "It's you. It's exactly you."

Doubtfully, I tried to view the foyer from Jerry's perspective. I kind of thought "exactly me" was more like a sprawling California ranch style with a leaky bathroom tap and a wasp nest in the tree shading the pool.

"Is that chandelier original?"

"I don't know."

"It's beautiful."

He was right. All the fixtures were beautiful. All the little details were perfect. As in perfectly suited to the house.

"And hardwood floors. I *love* hardwood floors."

"Yes. They're very nice."

"You can always tell whether they're real or laminate."

"I guess so. True."

"They take a bit of upkeep though. You do have a lot of boxes, that's for sure!" Jerry nodded at the tenderizer hammer I still held, and grinned. "Was that for that reporter?"

"Oh. I forgot." I held it up. "I'm trying out for Thor."

Jerry laughed as though that was brilliant. He was a good audience. I had to give him that.

"Is Lois Lane still out there?" I asked.

"No. They drove away while I was ringing the doorbell."

"Good. Maybe some actual news happened somewhere." I led the way to the kitchen, and Jerry followed, still toting the giant picnic basket which he dropped with noticeable relief on the kitchen table.

While Jerry continued to admire the appliances and floors and windows, I set about making coffee and unpacking the picnic basket. There was an embarrassment of riches. Or, more exactly, an embarrassment of munchies.

"Those are from *Sweet, Sweet Sorrow for Miss Butterwith*," Jerry said as I held up a jar of pralines. "And there's a jar of maple butter like in *Miss Butterwith's Sticky Wicket*."

"You really *have* read everything."

"Every single thing you've written. Even the short stories. *Miss Butterwith's Suite Sixteen*. Although I don't *usually* like short stories."

"Thanks. I appreciate that."

"I would have put a bottle of wine in, but I read somewhere you're allergic to it."

"I don't think this basket could have contained one more item."

I divvied up the cold roast beef sandwiches, poured the coffee, and Jerry and I chatted and ate. Or, more exactly, I ate and Jerry chatted. He asked a lot of in-depth questions about the Butterwith books and characters, and eventually I was cornered. I was forced to admit I didn't really remember a lot of the stories.

That shocked him.

"How could you not remember?" He seemed genuinely bothered by my inability to recall things like the vicar's name in *Miss Butterwith and the Holy Terror* or the number of flower girls in *Miss Butterwith Takes the Veil*.

"I remember the important stuff." I tried lamely to excuse my failings. "I remember who did it in every book. Go ahead. You can test me. I remember all my killers."

"But it's *all* important."

"Not really. I mean, yes. Of course. But a lot of information goes into every single book. A ton of research and imagination and…words. I can't retain everything. I'm not a computer."

I could see this greatly disappointed Jerry, and to give him time to recover I went to play the messages on the answering machine. J.X. had not been exaggerating about leaving a number of calls.

"Kit? Are you still there? Can you pick up?"

I hit fast forward.

"Are you okay? Kit? Are you there?"

I gave Jerry an apologetic smile and moved to the next message.

"Kit? *Christopher?*"

Christopher? He really was mad. By the next message he'd probably started using my middle name. *Christopher Andrew Holmes! I'm speaking to you!* I sped through the rest of the messages. Poor J.X. He'd been rattled, no question. But in fairness, if anyone should have realized I wouldn't— couldn't—still be at the house, it was him. And the complaint about me not answering my cell phone wasn't accurate either. I'd been trying to use the damn thing more often. And if I could ever get it off vibrate, I'd probably even answer it more often.

Jerry asked, "So you really are living here with J.X. Moriarity?"

"Yes." I waited to see Jerry's reaction to this. I was pretty sure he was gay, but you can't make assumptions about readers. Plenty of straight guys enjoy cozy mysteries about old ladies and their cats.

"I wouldn't have thought—" He stopped himself.

I asked unwillingly, "What?"

"I just wouldn't have thought he was really your type. I mean, no offense, but his stuff is pretty unrealistic."

I relaxed. Different sub-genres? That I could live with. "Well, actually he had a lot of experience as a cop. And he's pretty thorough about his research. He's even got a research assistant to help him out."

Jerry curled his lip. "His work is too obvious. Too much sex. Too much swearing. And the violence is over the top."

I can't deny I felt a flash of petty satisfaction at hearing this. J.X. had given me plenty of grief over the Miss Butterwith books, so it was refreshing to hear from someone who actually preferred my stories. But it would have been disloyal to admit. Instead I said, "Have you read his standalone? It's really good. Brilliant, in fact."

"I don't read him anymore," Jerry said curtly.

I decided to leave that alone and played an earlier call from my realtor.

Same message as before. Were we going to accept the offer on my house or not?

"Do they know who killed that man in your basement?" Jerry asked, interrupting my thoughts. If you could call the endless spinning of a solitary jack, *thoughts*.

"I think the police have a list of suspects, but they're not going to confide in me, obviously."

"They should," Jerry said. "You have a brilliant criminal mind. Plus you've already solved two murders."

Yeah, well. Not so much. Anyway, what did *brilliant criminal mind* mean? I was ruminating over that when Jerry asked if I had any idea where my china might have ended up.

"No. That's a good question." I decided to find out what garage repaired the moving van and see if they had a lead on my china. Twenty-piece place settings didn't just vanish into thin air.

"I could help you look for it," Jerry suggested.

"What? No. No, thank you."

"But really, it'd be my pleasure."

"That's very kind, but I'm not even sure where to start looking yet."

"If we put our heads together—"

"Honestly, I've got so much to do here right now, finding that china is not a big priority."

He glanced meaningfully around the kitchen. "Okay. How about if I lend you a hand with the house? You sure could use some help unpacking everything."

This is why you don't invite strangers in for coffee and sandwiches. Then they feel like they owe you. And you feel like the bad guy for not wanting their help.

I said, "The thing is, Jerry, I'm a complete control freak. You really do not want to be around me when I'm in the midst of organizing everything. Or anything."

Jerry said earnestly, "But I really do. I would really, really like to help you." He smiled. "The faster it's done, the faster you can get back to writing, right?"

I said forbiddingly, "I'm on sabbatical."

"Oh. But still. You want to be moved in and comfy ASAP, right? Let me help."

"Thank you. No."

"But there's so much stuff here. It'll take you forever."

I opened my mouth, but Jerry was saved by the bell. Or, to be precise, the ring of the kitchen phone.

I answered and immediately recognized the din of background noise. Was J.X. spending every spare minute in the bar? Couldn't he ever call me from the privacy of his hotel room, some place where we could truly talk?

"Kit, Nina called." J.X.'s voice was considerably warmer than the last couple of times we'd spoken. "That was a really nice thing you did this morning. Thank you."

"It's okay." I felt compelled to add, "She needs to get that ring resized."

"I think sometimes she gets lonely and needs a little attention. She misses Alex. She's just a kid herself, really."

I sighed.

"Anyway, how are you doing?"

"Making headway."

"Izzie told me they'd finished with the house. You're sure you're okay staying there on your own?"

I thought longingly of the Fairmont's masseuse and minibar. "Of course."

"Because it's only Friday and you could be here by this evening. The conference has barely started. Tomorrow night is the awards banquet."

"I thought this was settled."

"It is. But it feels weird to be here without you." He said softly, "I miss you."

Aware of Jerry's alert silence, I cleared my throat. "Me too. But that's not practical."

J.X.'s voice resumed its normal level. "I guess. I just know it would be nice to sit through one of these dinners with you sometime."

"Misery loves company. Especially where rubber chicken is involved." I felt a stab of guilt though. J.X. was up for a Mean Streets award this year. It hadn't even crossed my mind that he might want someone to hold his hand. Or, in his case, his program while he went up and accepted the award. Which was the most likely outcome.

Not one to hold a grudge, he had already moved on to other news. "Also, I don't want to upset you, but I'm hearing a lot of talk about Anna. Her death was a shock obviously, and…” His tone became careful. “The fact that you declined to speak at a fan convention tribute is causing some speculation.”

“I’m not there. Did they want to do it via speaker phone? Anyway, authors were lining up to speak at that thing. They didn’t need me.”

“True. But you’re *you*. You’re Anna’s most famous protégé.”

I said bitterly, “You can tell anyone who asks that Anna had no doubt of my feelings for her when she died.”

“That’s pretty much the line I’m taking.”

“It’s nobody’s goddamned business.”

“I know. I know, honey. People talk. That’s all. They’ve got to have their little gossip.”

“Is Rudolph speaking at the memorial? Or tribute? Whatever.” Roast might be appropriate, given the circumstances. Especially if it was being held in Hell.

“He’s not here. He cancelled.”

“Exactly!”

J.X. probably couldn’t help his irritating tendency to view both sides objectively. “But he did write a very nice obit for *Publisher’s Weekly*.”

“Just tell anybody who asks that I don’t go to conferences anymore. Tell ‘em I’m a recluse now.”

I’d forgotten about Jerry until I heard the gasp of dismay behind me. I glanced around, covered the handset mouthpiece and said, “I’m just mouthing off, don’t take it seriously.”

“Oh.” Jerry smiled uncertainly.

“Who’s there?” J.X. asked. “Who are you talking to?”

“Uh, Jerry Knight. I met him yesterday at Lowe’s.”

I could hear the frown in J.X.’s voice. You could take the boy out of the police force, but you could not take the police force out of the boy. “Who’s Jerry Knight?”

“A reader, actually.” It was kind of hard to explain with Jerry sitting right there. “He brought us a very nice picnic basket as a welcome to the neighborhood gesture.”

Jerry smiled broadly and said, “I brought it for *you*.”

"Oh, so he's a neighbor?" J.X.'s voice changed. "Damn. I've got to go. My panel is about to start. I'll call you again tonight."

"I'm not changing my mind."

"I know, Kit. There are other reasons for calling, right? I *like* to talk to you."

My face warmed. "Oh, right. I like to talk to you too." I said in my best British accent, "I shall inform the exchange that your trunk call is to be put through *immedjetly.*"

J.X. laughed. "Lunatic." He disconnected.

I was still smiling as I replaced the handset. Jerry said, "That was him? J.X. Moriarity?"

"Yes."

He raised his eyebrows. It was an irritating expression. The expression of someone who knows something you don't, but is holding their tongue out of respect. "You've been together a long time."

"Well, we've known each other a long time."

"Yep. Since that DC Murder in Midtown ten years ago."

"Yes." I studied him in surprise. "That's right, you were there too."

Jerry gave a sheepish smile. "Yep. I was there too, and I could see there was a-a spark. He was like a puppy following you around all the time. He was nobody then."

He was never nobody. Not to me.

But I didn't say it. You don't say those kinds of things to strangers.

"That really was a long time ago."

"Was he talking to you about Anna Hitchcock? That was a terrible tragedy."

"It was."

"She was so brilliant. I have all her books too. And you were there when it happened." Jerry looked sad and worried on my behalf.

"No. We'd left by then." I took a deep breath. "Anyway, this has been such a pleasant break, but I really have to get back to work now."

"Are you sure I can't help?"

I hoped my smile wasn't starting to twitch. "Really. No."

"There's just so much to do here, and seeing that *he* left it all on you—"

This time the bell did save him. The doorbell. The silvery chimes rolled through the house and I put down the tenderizer hammer and headed for the hall. I said tersely, "Excuse me."

CHAPTER SIX

Emmaline stood on the porch holding a casserole dish.

She raised the large white dish like a priestess offering the gods their main entrée, and the delicious fragrance of ham, onions and paprika wafted up. "Scalloped potatoes and ham. Don't worry, I won't come in," she said. "I saw you were back and I thought you'd probably be in the mood for a home-cooked meal about now."

"No, please come in," I said. *"Please."*

"But I know you must have—" She gave up as I tugged her through the doors and into the hall. "Oh my!" She stared at the obstacle course of boxes in all shapes and sizes.

"I know. But I am making progress."

"Is your partner h—" She broke off as I shepherded her down the hall and into the kitchen where she spotted Jerry.

"This is Jerry. He was just going," I said.

"No, no. Not on my account," Emmaline said. "I can only stay a minute."

Jerry smiled, shook hands and sat back down at the table. I put my hand to my eyebrow to stop the incipient tic.

"You look familiar," Emmaline said. "Have we met?"

Jerry thought Emmaline looked familiar too and they began to bounce theories on prior acquaintanceship back and forth. I watched, mesmerized.

"Where did you go to school?" Emmaline asked finally.

But no, that wasn't it either. I was about to drop my head on my folded arms and cry myself to sleep when Emmaline suddenly wearied of the chase and turned to me.

"I saw on the news that the dead man you found was a notorious art thief."

"As crazy as it sounds, that seems to be the case," I admitted.

"Elijah Ladas," Jerry supplied. "Just that name sends a shiver down your spine." I must have looked surprised because he added, "It sounds foreign."

"Oh?"

"Sinister."

I nodded noncommittally.

Emmaline asked, "Do the police consider you a suspect?"

"No."

Jerry said grimly, "You can't be sure about that. The police could be trying to lull you into a false sense of security. SFPD are completely corrupt."

I resented that on J.X.'s behalf, although I had no idea if it was true or not. "What false sense of security? I had nothing to do with his death."

To Emmaline, Jerry said, "The dead man was in the crate Christopher's china should have been in."

"Isn't that something," Emmaline said politely, having already heard this from me the day before. "Then where's your china, Christopher?"

I shook my head. "Somewhere in the middle of the desert a coyote is probably serving brunch."

Jerry guffawed.

"That cute little girl on KAKE was saying Mr. Ladas was a suspect in a murder," Emmaline said.

"Certainly a victim."

"I told Christopher he should offer to consult with the police," Jerry said.

"Oh, I didn't realize," Emmaline said. "I thought you and your partner were authors."

"We are. And no, I don't consult with the police." Like all honest people I preferred to avoid the police as much as possible.

"But you should," Jerry said. "You have a brilliant criminal mind."

I tried to hang onto my smile, but it was probably looking frayed around the edges. "I'm not even sure what that means, Jerry."

Jerry smiled fondly and then he and Emmaline proceeded to rehash the meager facts of the case. When no solution was forthcoming, she departed.

Jerry was still sitting in the kitchen when I returned, and I prepared to become extremely inhospitable.

Whatever Jerry read in my face had him smiling cheerfully. "She's just like Miss Butterwith. She's exactly like her."

"Well, she's not *exactly* like her."

"She's exactly how I picture her."

Of course, Jerry had a right to picture Miss Butterwith however he liked. That's part of the pleasure of reading versus watching a film or TV show—the reader is free to exercise his own imagination. But he was wrong. Emmaline was not exactly like Miss Butterwith. In fact, the only thing they had in common was they were both sprightly old ladies. I ought to know. I created Miss Butterwith. She was British, so right there. Obviously not *exactly* alike.

It would have been childish to argue the point. Instead, I smiled politely. "Is she?"

"*Exactly.* Does she have a cat like Mr. Pinkerton?"

"I don't know. I only met her yesterday morning. I don't know about her pets yet."

"You only met her yesterday? That is so *uncanny.*"

"Yeah, isn't it? But yes. I never saw the woman before yesterday. Anyway, I hate to end such a pleasant afternoon, but I really do have a lot to get done." I tried to look apologetic rather than frantic, which was how I was starting to feel.

Jerry rose at once. "Wow. Is that the time? I've got to get going. I can't believe I spent my whole afternoon here!"

He didn't sound accusatory exactly, but yet managed to give the impression my siren song had lured him from much more important matters. However, as I led the way down the hall, he observed sympathetically yet again, "Poor you. There's so much to do."

"True. But it'll go fast once I get moving."

"And you have a bad back."

I stared at him. "How did you know that?"

"You did an interview for *Mystery Scene* a few years ago. You'd just had back surgery."

"My back's okay." Actually I did have a bad back. And I'd broken my collar bone a few months earlier too. But I didn't care if I was aching from head to toe by the time I finished the day's unpacking, I was going to do it without Jerry's help.

As he was going out the door, Jerry said, "If you need my help, Christopher, just give me a call. I left my number next to your phone."

"Thank you, I will." I closed the door firmly. Then I locked it. If I'd had nails and a hammer handy, I'd have sealed myself in.

The rest of the afternoon passed in blood, sweat and tears. Okay, mostly sweat—although I did feel like crying by the twentieth time I had to climb the stairs to deliver another armload of J.X.'s seemingly infinite wardrobe. There was no blood loss, even if I did feel pretty damned drained by the time I collapsed on the mattress in the front room with a book and a plate of the best scalloped potatoes and ham I ever ate in my life.

But I felt good too as I raised my weary head to study the room. I'd shifted some of the furniture around and I'd started filling up the book cases. I'd emptied a number of containers and found places for our junk—er—*objets d'art.* There were still an unreasonable number of boxes, but as I'd discovered, a lot of them were only partially filled.

Tomorrow our new bed would be delivered, and tomorrow night I would be sleeping on a real mattress in our own bedroom. I liked that idea.

In fact, as I ate my supper and read the next title in my Nordic noir research, I felt almost content.

Tonight's book was *The Keeper of Lost Causes.* This one had to do with a renegade police detective and his idiosyncratic assistant, investigating the cold case disappearance of a female politician. There was a film version of it too, and I resolved to check Netflix for it. I liked Jussi Adler-Olsen's book much better than *The Dinosaur Feather* though it had some of the same depressing themes and motifs. Were there any cozy Scandinavian mysteries or was that out of the question? Did living in one of those lands of midnight sun result in a naturally dark outlook?

At some point I put the book aside and got up to brush my teeth and turn on the security system. On my way back to the front parlor, I turned out all the lights except for the lamp on the floor beside the mattress. I settled down once more, bunching the pillows behind my head. J.X.'s pillow still carried the scent of his shampoo.

The last line I remember reading was: *"You're aware that Uffe saw his father and mother die, right?" she asked.*

I let my eyelids fall closed.

I was having a nice dream about J.X. He was not mad at me or disappointed or hurt. We were playing some kind of a kissing game—which even in my dream seemed unlikely—and he was laughing at my objections. His dark eyes were warm and shining in that way they got when he was happy.

"Every time you say the word 'no,' I get to kiss you," he was saying.

I scoffed, "No wa—" and his lips stopped the words.

The shriek of an alarm tore through the night, the earsplitting sound ricocheting off hardwood floors and windows. I ripped off the sleep mask and sat bolt upright, heart skittering in panic inside my chest. The rush of adrenaline landed me on my feet before I was fully awake, and the first thing I did was charge into the fireplace.

The arched screen went over with a clatter, followed by the crash of the tool set—which reminded me that the poker was still downstairs in the basement. Somehow grabbing the miniature broom just didn't seem as effective a defense.

Motion detector lights had flashed on outside the house, the harsh white glare repelling the darkness, but it was still black as pitch indoors, and an unfamiliar room crowded with unknown objects became an obstacle course as I proceeded to fall over boxes, books and pretty much everything else as I stumbled toward the kitchen and the phone.

I felt my way around the long dining room table, managed not to fall over anything else before I reached the kitchen. I had a clear view of the glassed-in breakfast nook. My heart seemed to shudder to a stop. There, illuminated in the blaze of light, stood a man, hands framing his face, as he peered through the glass, trying to see into the dark rooms. I froze in my tracks, watching him.

Could he see me? I wasn't sure. I didn't think so, but I didn't know. He didn't seem to care if anyone saw him or not. Could he be a neighbor? He wasn't dressed like a burglar. He wore jeans and motorcycle boots. No shirt. His hair was very short and pale. It was molded to his head like a silver helmet. He looked like a bodybuilder. Or a character in anime. His muscular torso was covered in swirling dark patterns. Body hair? No. Tattoos. I couldn't make them out without moving closer to the breakfast nook, and that was not going to happen. Nor could I see his face, cupped as it was by his hands.

The phone next to me began to ring and I jumped, my heart zapped back into frantic life. I grabbed for it and a crisp female voice said, "This is Bayshore Security. We've just received—"

"Hurry up and send someone," I gulped out. "There's an intruder."

"The police have already been dispatched, Mr. Moriarity. Is the intruder in the house?"

"No."

"Is he trying to break in?"

"No. Yes. I'm not sure. He's standing right there staring through the window. He's not running. I'm not sure what he's doing."

"Is the intruder known to you? Can you describe him?"

"No. I mean, no, he's not known to me. He's big." That much was for sure. With my free hand, I felt around for the nearest drawer, rifled through the silverware and pulled out...a butter knife. Great. I could make toast while I waited for rescue. That flimsy utensil would probably bounce off his pecs like a rubber prop. Where the hell had I put the butcher block with the real knives? Come to think of it, somewhere in this kitchen there were *two* butcher blocks with enough stainless steel to slice and dice a whole gang of prowlers.

The security company operator was still talking and I was still answering, though I had no idea what either of us was saying. I couldn't tear my gaze from the giant peering in through the window. I felt like a goldfish swimming in a very tiny bowl beneath the gaze of a very large cat. My fins were shaking.

As I watched, the prowler slammed the window with his enormous palm. The wall of glass seemed to ripple, but it did not shatter. In fact, the blow didn't seem to be a serious attempt at entry so much as an expression of frustration.

The next instant the man was gone. He sprinted across the brick terrace, jumped over one of the low hedges and merged with the deep shadows.

Over the thudding in my ears I heard a siren baying in the night as it chased up the winding, climbing streets to Chestnut Lane.

"They're here," I told the dispatcher and hung up. I tottered over to the security pad and punched in the numbers. The electronic protest cut off mid-howl.

Sleep that knits up the ravelled sleave of care, Shakespeare said, and needless to say it was all unravelling and very little knitting once the police arrived at 321 Chestnut Lane. God knows I felt about as lively as a pile of yarn once they departed with a final cheery whoop of their siren.

I'd probably have done better to pull the covers over my head and stay in bed.

Well, no. That wasn't fair. The officers gave it their best shot, wandering around the front and back gardens with flashlight beams probing every nook and cranny—and raising irate comments from resident birds.

"Long gone, whoever he was. It sounds like a kid maybe. Or a stoner," one of the officers said when they finally reported back.

"That was no kid."

The officer conceded this with a shrug. "This house has been empty for a while, so I'm guessing your prowler didn't expect to find anyone home."

Maybe. It didn't make sense though, and I wanted it to make sense. I wanted to feel reassured that this had been a fluke. Kids fooling around. I liked that idea a lot. But no one familiar with the neighborhood would make the mistake of thinking the house was still empty. At the same time, anyone watching the house, like a burglar, would have to know that cops had been crawling all over for two days.

So maybe the officer was right. Maybe my midnight prowler had just been a drug-addled wanderer.

"He wasn't just a drug-addled wanderer," Izzie Jones said when he dropped by the next morning for coffee and a cup of bad news. "In fact, from the description you gave the officers last night, I think your prowler sounds a lot like Beck Ladas. Elijah's little brother."

"*Little* brother?"

"Younger brother. Although if you think Beck is big, you should have seen Elijah."

Well, I had seen Elijah, but he hadn't been at his best, granted.

"Great. Beck does know his brother isn't still here, right?"

Izzie—we were on first-name basis now—chuckled. "He's not the sharpest crayon in the box, but I'm sure he's figured that much out. So he must be looking for something else."

I stared. "Like what?"

Izzie shook his head.

I suddenly wished I had paid more attention to the news coverage my gruesome discovery had received. "You said Elijah Ladas was involved in the robbery of an art gallery. When was that?"

Izzie hesitated before answering. "Two weeks ago. We didn't have proof of his involvement. We just wanted him for questioning. The robbery had his MO all over it—barring the murder of the gallery owner. Homicide was never Ladas' style."

"Getting bumped off was probably never his style either."

Izzie grinned. "No. It's an interesting development."

"And a lousy career move." This reminded me. "Do you have the name of the garage that serviced the moving van? At the risk of seeming self-absorbed, I'm kind of hoping my china might still be out there somewhere."

"They didn't take the van to a garage," Izzie said. "They ordered a replacement part from a place in Mojave that services big rigs, and made the repair themselves. The truck was parked in a diner parking lot right off the freeway for a few hours. Part of that time, probably a lot longer than they'll admit to, your three movers and shakers were sitting in the diner. The back of the truck was padlocked, but when I questioned them, the driver admitted noticing the lock was broken when he came back out after lunch."

"They sure didn't mention that to me."

"No. You have 48 hours to make a claim, and they were hoping if something was missing, you wouldn't notice till after the 48 hours was up."

"Nice!" I held up the coffee pot and Izzie nodded. I topped him up. "Any theory on how Ladas ended up inside the truck?"

"We think there are three possible scenarios. The first is that Ladas was at the diner to meet someone and that someone killed him and hid his body. The second is that Ladas was in the nearby town of Wooster for some unknown reason, and again, someone killed him and hid his body in the moving van."

"Then where's his car?" I asked. "Unless he and his killer drove together, his car would either be at the diner or in town somewhere. And if they drove together, why pick Wooster or that diner to do away with Ladas? That doesn't seem very likely."

"I agree with you. I can't see any reason for Ladas to be in Wooster. There are no pawn shops or antique barns or jewelry marts. There isn't even a bank. And he'd have less reason to be in that diner. The food is lousy, the coffee is worse, and it's too far off the beaten track to be of any use to a guy like Ladas."

I considered that. Off the beaten track might be useful if you were meeting up with people you shouldn't be seen with. But "off the beaten track" in a city the size of Barstow was a lot more private than "off the beaten track" in a diner out in the middle of nowhere. In the middle of nowhere people noticed you.

"What's the third scenario?"

"Judging by the rate of decomposition, the ME believes Ladas had been dead at least eight hours before he went into the back of the moving truck. As crazy as it sounds, I think someone was driving along, looking for a place to dump Ladas' body, and hit on the idea of using a broken-down moving van."

"It's nearly six hours from Frisco to Barstow. Driving six hours with a dead body? Why not just dump him into San Francisco bay?"

"Because he would be found and identified? Not sure, but that's the scenario we're running with. It was very important to someone that Ladas not be found or identified, and they were willing to drive to Los Angeles to get rid of him."

"Why didn't they chop him into bits and dump him into the bay?"

Izzie, coffee cup halfway to his mouth, paused and gave me a contemplative look.

I said, "Sorry. That's the mystery writer talking."

"The fact is, most homicides aren't committed by hardened criminals. And even hardened criminals can be squeamish."

"Right." I said slowly, "And why would it be so important to someone that Ladas not be found or identified?"

Izzie hesitated.

I said, "Uh-oh. Beck. Am I right? Baby brother Beck?"

Izzie nodded. "Beck is—was—what you might call devoted to Ladas. And, like I said, he's not exactly a Fulbright Scholar."

"This just keeps getting better and better."

I was not reassured when Izzie didn't offer an immediate pep talk. In fact, I now had a good idea why he'd popped over first thing on a Saturday morning when everyone, including the sun, was rolling over and going back to sleep. He said instead, "When does J.X. get back?"

"He's flying in Monday night."

Izzie nodded thoughtfully, but whatever he was thinking he kept to himself. All he said was, "Well, we're trying to bring Ladas in for questioning, but he's been avoiding his usual hangouts. If you do see him again, don't confront him. Just give us a call."

"Confront him?" I repeated in astonishment. *"Me?"*

CHAPTER SEVEN

After Jones finished spreading good cheer and glad tidings all over the place, he departed, but before he left I got the phone number of the diner near Wooster where Mr. Ladas had likely joined the wagon train. I gave the diner a call and asked if anyone had noticed any suspicious looking china loitering about the premises. The hostess admitted they had noticed broken china out by the dumpster and alerted Cindy Spann of Dolls and Doodads. Cindy had salvaged what she could for her shop. They kindly gave me Cindy's phone number and I called Dolls and Doodads. Cindy, who sounded about the size of a Thumbelina, informed me she had almost ten complete sets of china left and was willing to let me have the entire lot for a reasonable price.

"Well, I appreciate that, but you do realize it's my china?"

She chirped, "That's why I'm giving you such a good deal on it."

We smacked the birdie back and forth a few times, but it was clear Cindy was a descendent of those ancient desert tribes that eke their meager living by luring lost caravans off the map with promises of blue slushies and clean restrooms. She would not budge and I hate to haggle, and in the end I agreed to buy back Oma's china at what was, Cindy assured me, a steal.

If J.X. had been driving back from L.A., he could have stopped and picked up the china for me. Instead, I'd have to also pay Cindy to ship it and hope she packed better than she reasoned. Although, seeing that I was paying exactly what she wanted, maybe it was my reasoning at fault.

The satellite dish people arrived and went around hooking up our TVs and DVD players and Xboxes, of which we had an embarrassing plethora. It was like a home for wayward lonely guys.

"Do you need me for anything?" I asked the techs and they laughed heartily.

They were clomping around on the roof when Rachel phoned.

"How is your research coming? What was your grandmother's maiden name?" she demanded before I could even get out a greeting.

"The secret password is Zwyssig. Hello to you too."

She was unabashed, but then you don't get far as a literary agent if you're the bashful kind. "That's bloody awful. Readers will never be able to look that up. No. Sorry. That won't do. What was *her* mother's maiden name?"

I gazed out at the fog winding its sinuous way around the tall urns, meandering through the brick patios and terraces. Was that going to burn off? "Wölfli. Why are you so interested in my grandmothers?"

"Wolfi?" she mused. "That might work. That's rather adorable in fact."

"Wölfli. *Li.* Wölf*li*. And I repeat, why are so interested in my grandmothers?"

"Christopher, have you listened to a word I've said to you over the past two days? I'm pitching your new book to Wheaton and Woodhouse this afternoon. We have to settle on the details. Such as your new pen name."

"What? What new pen name? I don't want a new pen name! And I don't want to write for Wheaton and Woodhouse again. I'm still mad at them for dropping me the first time."

Rachel tsk-tsked at this. "That was just business, Christopher. You know that."

"Yes. I know that after sixteen years, eleven New York Times bestsellers, and twenty awards—some of them actually legit—they dumped me like some indie writer they found shivering in the slush pile."

She made shushing noises. "Don't say anything against indies. They're very sensitive. One hint of elitism and they'll be organizing a twitcott. Anyway, the *point* is, W&W is aggressively acquiring Scandinavian crime fiction."

"I don't want to write Scandinavian crime fiction. There are too many neo-Nazis and hangings in churches. And I don't like snow. Unless it's in a snow globe."

I might as well have been talking to myself. "What about the name Petra? It's pretty, isn't it? I think it's Swiss."

"It's Greek, Rachel. And I hope you're not thinking I'm going to write under a female pen name."

Her tone grew chiding. Or chidinger. "Women do very well in Scandinavian crime fiction. And we have to reinvent you. You know how it works. A blank slate is better than a downward trend."

That flicked me on a very raw patch. "Hey, I'm still a bestseller, you know! In some places. Probably in Barstow."

"But you're trending downward."

"I sure am now."

"Chin up! How's it going there, by the way? All unpacked?"

"All un..." I couldn't even finish that. "You do know I found a body in the basement, correct? I did tell you that?"

"I know you've told me everything but what I need to hear. Christopher, we *must* focus. *You* must focus."

"Okay. Focus on this, Rachel. I don't *want* to be reinvented. Or reincarnated. Or regurgitated. I'm not going to be named Petra or Paula or Patricia or anything else."

"My God," she said wearily. "Right-o. Have it your way. You can stay a bloody male if it means so much to you."

"I *am* a bloody male. Of course it means that much!"

Sarcasm was wasted on her. It was like water off a Mandarin duck's back. "What about Peder?"

"Nice. I can hear it now. Pederphile. No."

"You're being difficult, Christopher. What about Adrian?"

"God no."

"Werner? Wilhelm? Wolfgang? Stop me when you hear something you like."

"I haven't heard anything I liked since I picked up the phone." I started to laugh. "Wolfgang Wölfli. That's it. Why the hell not?"

We were not amused. Well, I was, but the Regent of Rejections was not.

"What you're failing to realize is this new writing identity gives you an opportunity to explore themes and leitmotifs in a way you've never experienced before."

"Wearing pantyhose apparently."

"Instead of being dismissive, you might have done as I asked and researched the genre. You'd see that Scandinavian crime fiction deals with all kinds of issues that are contemporary and important. Xenophobia, homophobia—"

"Agoraphobia."

The doorbell rang. I said, "Sorry. I've got to go, Rachel. I'll talk to you later. Please. I beg of you. Don't turn me into Ariadne Oliver."

"That name is familiar. Who represents her?"

I left her speculating and strategizing.

This time the bell tolled for the furniture company. I led the way, realizing that in all my trips upstairs, I'd barely noticed these rooms. I'd been too busy lurching back and forth with armloads of towels and linens destined for hall cupboards, or lugging armloads of clothes, mostly J.X.'s, to the floor-to-ceiling closets in the master bedroom. It seemed you could never have too many tailored white shirts or pairs of black jeans.

I watched nervously from the landing while the delivery men maneuvered a ponderous armoire entertainment center up the staircase, and when I couldn't take it any longer, I went to make sure the bedroom was ready to receive company.

The master bedroom was at the rear of the house. The newly hooked-up electronics and J.X.'s valet stand were currently the only pieces of furniture, and it was the perfect opportunity to admire the elegant bones of the architecture. It was a large and airy space featuring a fireplace, a pretty little deck that faced Coit Tower, and a separate dressing area with those impressive closets lining one side.

As I gazed around myself, I realized that it truly was a beautiful room. The morning light would be beautiful. Heck, the morning fog was beautiful from up here. The walls were painted the palest and warmest of blues, like a hand-tinted photograph of a vintage holiday by the sea. The moldings were a silvery white, like sea foam. The long flowing drapes were gauzy ivory, the large nubby rug was also a restful eggshell white.

I walked out onto the balcony and remembered what Jones had said about him and J.X. once chasing a junkie up to Coit Tower. Someday I wanted to hear the story of what had happened when they caught him. Or her.

I turned as the delivery men finally shoved the armoire through the bedroom door and departed, perspiring and muttering, to cart the rest of the suite upstairs. There seemed to be a lot of it. This again was something I'd left up to J.X., and I wondered now if my lack of input had seemed easy-going or just indifferent?

The delivery men unwrapped the furniture from its plastic and protective coverings. Twin highboys, twin bedside tables, a large bed. The wood even darker than the floor and straight, clean lines. Masculine but elegant. They pushed the furniture around as requested, set up the bed and left.

After I locked the door behind them, I hiked back upstairs and studied the room. Our bedroom.

I realized I was smiling. I wasn't even sure why.

It took me a while to find the framed painting I'd bought for J.X. as a housewarming gift. I'd regretted the purchase almost immediately as a silly extravagance, but now...now I thought maybe it had been a good idea after all. Allan P. Friedlander's *A Good Year*. Wine country in tones of old gold and ripe yellows and rich greens. A remembrance of our own adventure, an acknowledgement of where it had all started. Again.

I hung it over the fireplace. Then I found a pair of my own soft 1500-plus-thread sheets in a cool, creamy yellow. I may not care about clothes, but I care about comfort, and anyone who tells you there's no difference between 800-plus thread count and 1500-plus thread count isn't sleeping on 1500-plus thread count. I made the bed, topping it with the raw ivory silk comforter J.X. had purchased. Then I carried up a couple of alabaster table lamps and a tall floor lamp with bronze acanthus leaves and an amber shade.

I was studying the final results with satisfaction when I realized J.X. hadn't called the night before. In fact, he hadn't called all day. I glanced at the clock on the fireplace mantel. It was already six, which meant he'd be sitting down to his awards banquet. I could always call him, of course, but he'd be busy schmoozing.

He'll be gone to greener pastures as soon as the novelty wears off, as soon as it becomes clear to him that your careers—your lives—are going in two different directions.

I could still hear the ghostly echo of that prophecy. Add in a wicked witch cackle, and the scary home movie would be ready for the nightly screening room in my brain. Not a word of it had faded from my memory. But I wasn't going to let someone else's warped and poisonous world view dictate my future with J.X. I trusted him.

That wasn't to say I was sure we'd make it as a couple, but I did believe it wouldn't be for lack of trying on J.X.'s part.

I defrosted the fried chicken and ate dinner at my laptop, which was how I spent most of my meals. Although, I guessed that would be changing once J.X. got home. Out of curiosity, I tried to find out what I could about the gallery robbery in Sausalito. Only one incident popped up, but it appeared in a number of online articles. Quercus Gallery had been robbed early Sunday morning in late May. The thieves had cut a hole in the roof of the one-story building and lowered themselves inside. Ignoring the tempting display of paintings and sketches, they'd headed straight for the exhibition of rare Scandinavian coins on loan from local collector Alan Lorenson. Ten million dollars worth of Scandinavian coins.

I nearly swallowed a chicken bone.

The two thieves wore gloves and ski masks, and once inside the store had immediately disabled the security cameras. The existing footage amounted to a short and grainy replay of two very large and fuzzy figures in black, descending from the ceiling of the gallery on ropes. They dropped to the floor, moving with efficient speed, each man knowing his job. One figure loomed up into the lens of the camera. Cold, colorless eyes stared straight at me. Then the camera went black.

Unbeknownst to the intruders, John Cantrell, the gallery owner, had been working late. There was no video record of his encounter with the thieves, but he had been left dead on the floor of his private exhibition room. His neck had been broken.

My stomach knotted reading that.

The break-in and murder had taken less than ten minutes. By the time the police had arrived, the intruders were long gone—and with them a Viking's hoard of old silver and gold coins, including a Swedish 1632 Gustav II Adolf gold dukat, two 1898 Swiss Helvetica coins, and nearly 1,000 coins from the 1060s, mostly German, English and Danish. Some of the coins were only worth a few hundred dollars. A handful of them were worth a million each.

Thanks to *Miss Butterwith Shows Uncommon Cents*, I knew a little about rare coins. Well, not so much about coins as coin collecting. Along with artwork and wine, rare coins were very popular with investors in the new economy, skyrocketing a staggering 248 percent in value over the past ten years. A handful of legendary coins like the Brasher Doubloons broke records every time they came up for auction.

Some investors considered coins and other collectibles safer than stocks, although "treasure assets" were speculative and therefore risky. Their only value was the hope of a future sale to another collector at a still higher price, and in a troubled economy that was a bigger gamble than usual. Plus the market was unregulated. Rare coins could be traded or purchased from individuals, dealers or auction houses, which left a lot of room for fraud. And fraud was rampant. There was also the problem of theft. Even in a plastic protective case, coins were small and easily pocketed.

On the other hand, rare coins received favorable tax treatment. As capital assets, no tax was imposed as the coins appreciated in value until the point of sale, and once the coins were sold, the tax rate was significantly lower than the highest individual tax rate.

But collecting was never just about tax savings and investments. Collecting was an emotional thing. Coins were beautiful and interesting and rich with history. To handle an old coin was to touch the past.

Ten million dollars worth of past in this case. Viking treasure to boot.

And every penny of it still missing.

What the articles did not say was that Elijah Ladas—and possibly his industrial-sized brother—were suspected of the theft. There was no mention of Ladas at all. In fact, the investigating detectives had only vouchsafed that they had a suspect and hoped to make an arrest soon.

By nine o'clock J.X. still hadn't phoned. Celebrating in the host hotel bar, no doubt. I'd been there and done that myself a few times. I didn't begrudge him.

But I felt restless. Uneasy.

I wandered around the house, but I didn't feel like unpacking any more boxes. Every time I saw the door to the cellar, a shivery sensation crept down my spine.

Though the house was beginning to feel familiar during the daylight hours, at night it grew foreign and unknown once more. The pretty rooms turned to sharp angles and dim corners and the uneasy suspicion that something important was missing—or worse, that someone was watching.

Welcome to a writer's imagination. The gift of being able to scare yourself silly behind your own locked doors. Although in all honesty, it wasn't so much the fear of intruders or physical danger that had me wandering from room to room like a lost soul. No, it was the second thoughts, the second guesses, the coulda-shoulda-wouldas that turned a home into a foreign landscape.

Maybe some fresh air was in order. I decided to take a turn around the garden, walking out through the breakfast nook doors. The city lights glittered beneath a crescent moon hanging low in the purple-black sky. Ornamental grasses threw sharp and spiky shadows across the still-warm bricks. The night air felt satiny and smelled of the city and mysterious flowers.

At the back end of the garden, there was a tall and dense hedge. Behind the hedge, the property line dropped away to a series of steep hillside terraces belonging to the houses behind Chestnut Lane. Not inaccessible, but definitely a hike. Reassured, I turned away and wandered up a series of small patios to where the pool was tucked away. The lights were on and the turquoise water looked crystal clear and inviting. It was almost warm enough for night swimming. Did J.X. like night swimming? I had no idea. There was so much we didn't know about each other.

I stepped closer, and as I did, I spied movement out of the corner of my eye.

Something rose up from the shade of a tall urn. My heart stuttered in fright and tried to crawl out through my ribcage. My first horrible suspicion was that Jerry Knight was sneaking around my backyard. That was followed by the more horrible—and more likely suspicion—that Beck Ladas had returned.

But a girl's voice exclaimed, "Oh! You startled me." She sounded both shaken and mildly outraged.

I quit clutching my chest and glared, though it's hard to glare effectively in the dark. "I startled *you*? You nearly gave me a heart attack."

Astonishingly, she shot back, "You'd have to have a heart for that."

"Excuse me?" I knew that voice. I peered more closely at her. She stared warily back. "You're that reporter. Something Nightingale from KAKE."

I could see her chin lift defiantly. "Yes. Sydney Nightingale."

"Ms. Nightingale, what the hell are you doing skulking in my backyard? What part of no comment do you not get?"

"All of it," she said impatiently. "I'm only asking for a few words. What's so hard about that? Why are you being so mysterious?"

"I'm not being mysterious. I don't like being hounded."

"Hounded! Well, if you weren't acting like you had something to hide—"

"Wait a minute. The fact that you're crawling around in my backyard is *my* fault?"

"Kind of! Yes. My editor sent me out here for a story. All I need are the answers to a few simple questions. And maybe a photo of the crime scene."

"Go." I pointed like Death in a Bergman film to the street beyond. "Leave. Now."

I would have to work on my silent menace because she didn't so much as waver. Like a good general, she did change tactics. "Mr. Holmes, I'm sorry I said you were hiding something. And I'm sorry to be a nuisance. Honestly. But you don't understand how it is for me. For any woman journalist these days. We've got to comp—"

"I feel for you, Nellie Bly," I interrupted. "But there's no story here."

"You found a body in your basement. How can there not be a story there? Even if you weren't a famous crime writer, there's a story."

Famous crime writer. I tried not to soften. Anyway, she probably had me confused with J.X.

"I'm just looking for a little human interest angle, that's all. How can you be a writer and not want publicity for your books?"

Oh, *touché*. Or *ouché*. I could practically see Rachel's scolding image materializing behind her, taking me to task for missing this golden opportunity to promote myself and my work.

"Because this is the wrong kind of publicity," I said to both Rachel and Sydney.

Sydney shot that feeble protest down like someone picking off pop-up ducks in a shooting gallery. "There's no such thing. There's no such thing as bad publicity. Believe me, I've covered enough of people's embarrassing moments to know. You're a mystery writer involved in a real life mystery. That's *great* publicity."

"I'm not involved in a mystery," I protested. "I found a body. That's not the same thing. I didn't know him. I have no connection to him. He just happened to end up in my house. Which was unfortunate for both of us."

"Ten minutes. That's all I'm asking." She held out a card.

I stared at the pale square for a moment. The crescent moon slipped shyly behind the pewter-edged clouds and there was only darkness and silence. And the gurgle of the pool pump.

Reluctantly, I took the card. "I'll think about it."

Her smile glimmered. "You won't regret it, Mr. Holmes."

I said gloomily, "Sydney, they *all* say that."

CHAPTER EIGHT

"...worry about that. Just call when you—"

J.X. was leaving a message on the answering machine when I came through the breakfast nook doors, and I knocked over a kitchen chair in my haste to get to the phone before he hung up. I'd have been willing to crawl across the dining room table after our last round of phone tag.

I snatched the receiver off the hook. "Here! I'm here!" I gulped. "It's me. Present and accounted for."

"Hey! I thought I'd missed you." J.X.'s voice was warm and cheerful. "Sorry for not calling earlier. It seems like every time I start to phone you, there's some interruption."

"I know how that goes," I said. And I sort of did.

"How's everything there?"

I said at the same time, "I guess congratulations are in order?"

"Oh." His laugh was a little strained. "I didn't win."

"What? Those *bastards*." I was only half kidding. I actually did feel an unfamiliar surge of protective anger on J.X.'s part. "Who won?"

"Crais."

"Oh." It was hard to get too riled up because, well, Robert Crais. But still. I said, "Good. I'm still a couple of awards ahead then. That's a relief."

He joked, "How is it you always know to say the right thing?"

"My next project will be a book on etiquette for writers. I believe Rachel is selling Swedish translation rights this very minute."

J.X. made an amused sound. But he sounded serious when he said, "I wish you were here."

I was surprised by how much I wished I was there too. Not that he really needed me there, but if it would have helped? Yes. Because he *was* disappointed. I knew him well enough now to hear that infinitesimal huskiness in his voice.

An idea flashed across the arid landscape of my brain. "Hey, what if I drive down to L.A. and meet you for your signing at Cloak and Dagger? We could come back together. Kind of a mini road trip."

"Are you serious?"

"Yes. I am. Would you like that? Can you get your plane ticket changed?"

"I don't care if I can change it or not. Hell yeah, I'd like that. But are you sure? You just made that drive a couple of days ago."

My back winced in anticipation of another nine hours behind the steering wheel. "I know. Crazy, right? I guess I miss you or something."

He made a sound. Not exactly a laugh. More like...I don't know. Like I had caught him off guard. It was such a small sound, but somehow revealing. It actually closed my own throat for a second. Did it mean that much to him?

"Well, if you're really willing to do that, I'll book us a room somewhere nice for Monday night. Adrien invited me out to dinner after the signing. I know he'd love you to come."

"Sure. That sounds fine. I remember Adrien." Who didn't remember Adrien English after the thing with Paul Kane? Not that it was an isolated incident. Crime writers experienced their share of violence like everybody else. Sometimes they were the victims. Sometimes, like Anne Perry or Richard Klinkhamer, not. The only difference was, for us crime was just work experience. Grist for the mill.

J.X. said wryly, "You're sure this isn't all a clever ruse to sneak back into Southern California?"

"Nope. I mean, yep. I'm sure."

"How are you? Is everything okay?"

I opened my mouth to tell him about last night's intruder, but it was just going to worry him. It wasn't like he could do anything. "I'm fine. The house is fine. The bed is set up and rarin' to go."

He said in a deep, sexy voice, "I like the sound of that."

I did too. But there was no point in getting ourselves worked up. "It's a beautiful house," I said instead. "I don't think I made that clear. But I know you tried hard to find the right place and I think this is it."

His laugh was a little self-conscious. "Now I *know* you feel sorry for me not winning."

I laughed too, but I saw suddenly how it probably felt to him when he was trying to be serious and I made a joke. "Anyway, despite everything—including reporters skulking in the garden—things are coming along nicely."

J.X.'s voice changed. "Are reporters skulking in the garden?"

"I just ran one off a few minutes ago. I'm trying to look at it as a promo op. Make sure you share that with Rachel when you see her."

"I don't like the sound of that."

That made two of us. If girl reporter Sydney Nightingale could slink around the garden undetected at night, what was to keep even less appealing characters from finding their way to my back door?

"I know. Maybe we should electrify the front gate."

J.X. chuckled, imagining I was kidding. "Speaking of Rachel, did you tell her you were working on a thriller set in Switzerland?"

"It's a long story."

"About 80K?"

"About, yeah. The Swiss Miss Cocoa Girl retires, buys a cat named Olaf, and with the help of a handsome Interpol agent solves a series of grisly Alpine crimes."

He was further amused. We chatted a little more before I said, "I guess I better let you go. Have fun. But not too much fun. Don't do anything I wouldn't do."

"You mean like attend a convention?" J.X. teased.

It had been a long day. I set the alarms and headed upstairs. I took a quick shower, then crawled into bed with my laptop. From the bed I had a nice view of both the Friedlander painting over the fireplace and the balcony. Stars above and city lights below. The night breeze stirred the gauzy draperies.

I turned on my laptop and did a Web search for Sydney Nightingale. I'd seen her sitting in a news van, so I knew in all likelihood she was legitimate, but suspicion is part of the mystery writer's makeup.

My suspicion was unfounded. Sydney was indeed a reporter for *Baywatch News*. In fact, she had covered the original robbery, looking a little green around the gills but still spunky as she stood in front of Quercus Gallery and gave out the details of the robbery and murder for the at-home viewers.

Feeling stalkerish myself, I did a little more searching. Sydney was thirty-two and a former model. She had graduated to doing the weather for *Gateway News* and then eventually landed the reporter gig at *Baywatch*.

So she was legitimate. That didn't mean I wanted to spill out my life story to her. Okay, in fairness, she hadn't asked for my life story. But what was there to say about finding a body? Yes, there was potential irony—at least coincidence—in a mystery writer finding a dead body in his own home, but that really wasn't much of a story.

Still, I knew what Rachel would say and I knew I was probably going to give Ms. Nightingale a call.

On impulse I did a search for Elijah Ladas. To my surprise he popped up all over the Web. In fact, he seemed to have been some sort of underworld celebrity. Even I had to grant that he had one of the most attractive mug shots I'd ever seen. He was a big man, ruggedly handsome with pale blue eyes and silvery fair hair. Well, the silver hair had probably been gray by those later photos because Ladas had to have been at least in his forties by the time he died.

A large part of his fame seemed to originate with his co-writing credit on a series of pulpy thrillers about a gentleman thief cum adventurer by the name of Lazlo Ender. His co-writer, Richard Cortez, had passed away in the late nineties, and the series had died with him. But apparently the books had been quite popular in their day and Ladas had shamelessly worked that popularity to his own advantage. He had gained entry to the homes and art collections of San Francisco society—and then had turned around and robbed a number of his social acquaintances. Well, to be accurate, he was only suspected of robbing his wealthy friends, but there was most definitely an alarming pattern. That pattern had eventually made Ladas persona non grata with the Nob Hill set.

Even so, he still showed up at the occasional movie premiere or yacht club event, squiring some pretty young thing trying to build her street cred or bolster her edgy image in the media.

As far as I could tell, he hadn't been arrested in recent years, though his kid brother Beck had been nicked—as Inspector Appleby might have put it—for a number of ill-conceived and mundane burglaries.

The Lazlo books were not available in digital, so I ordered a copy of an old print edition of the first title through AbeBooks.

So what had brought Ladas out of comfortable retirement? Because that's how it seemed to me. Had he run short of funds? Had he grown bored with the straight and narrow? Was it simply the lure of Viking treasure? Or... or...had baby brother come up with a plan to rob Quercus Gallery and needed Ladas to pull it off? The gallery job was much more Ladas' style than Beck's, but Ladas was getting a little long in the tooth for that kind of job, surely?

It was interesting—from a purely academic standpoint.

For sure, things had not gone according to plan.

I took my glasses off, wiped my eyes. But it was no use, I couldn't stay awake. I put my laptop aside, climbed out of bed and locked the bedroom door and then closed and locked the door to the balcony. I wondered if Izzie had managed to bring Beck in for questioning or if Ladas Jr. was still running from the law. So long as he wasn't planning on paying me another midnight visit, I didn't much care.

Sunday was beautiful. Yes, even I, professional, full-time curmudgeon had to award the fresh and sparkling morning full marks. It was like the week had been practicing every day to get to this perfect moment. I had my coffee and toast out on the terrace. The air was sweet and clear, the butter-soft sunshine warmed the bricks beneath my bare feet. A couple of hummingbirds duked it out over blue-eyed grass—*sisyrinchium bellum*, Miss Butterwith would have said. I sighed. I missed Miss B. and it troubled me that I seemed to have nothing else to write about.

Maybe once I was settled.

This morning that actually felt reasonable. Maybe even likely. I sipped my coffee and considered my kingdom with a benevolent eye. We'd have to see about hiring someone to mow the grass and another someone to take care of the pool. Maybe get a third someone in a couple of times a month to dust and scrub the toilets. Yes, even with all these someones running around underfoot, the place had possibilities.

When I finished my coffee, I went inside, phoned Rina, my realtor. I told her to accept the offer on my former home.

*　*　*　*　*

I decided that maybe it would be easier on my back—and I'd be better able to concentrate on J.X.—if I split up the drive and left that afternoon, stayed overnight somewhere on the way, and arrived in Los Angeles in time to sign papers for Rina.

Once I'd settled on my plan of action, I went next door to speak to Emmaline.

"On the run from the law?" she inquired sweetly, before inviting me inside for a cup of tea.

"Ha." I declined the tea, but accepted her invitation to step inside, pausing to examine a series of watercolor botanical studies in the front hall. Her house was similar in layout to ours, minus the Corinthian porch and with the charming addition of stained-glass windows in the foyer. "These are nice."

Emmaline's cheeks pinked. "Thank you! I did those. Years ago."

"They're really good. Then you're an artist?"

She chuckled at the idea. "No. I'm a retired teacher. I used to teach high school. Science, actually. Biology, environmental studies, botany."

"Botany?"

She raised her eyebrows. "Why? Is there something wrong with botany?"

"No. Not at all."

"It's one of the oldest branches of science."

"I know. In fact, I used to write a mystery series about a botanist."

"Isn't that interesting!"

"Yes. Well, she was English."

Emmaline was still smiling, but something in her eyes changed. A look of...discomfort? fleeted across her rosy face. "As a matter of fact, I think I may have had your friend in one of my classes."

"J.X.?"

"No, no. Your other friend. Jerry."

"He's more of an acquaintance," I said.

"Then you haven't known him long?"

"No. I met him Thursday in Lowe's. Or actually, I guess we'd met at a conference a few years ago. But I don't know him really."

"Well." She stopped right there and I felt a little prickle go down my spine.

"Was he a good student?" I asked tentatively.

"I think he was." Her smile was almost apologetic.

"But what?"

"That's the reason I'm hesitant to say anything. I taught so many young people. Hundreds. Thousands. To be honest, the faces blur after a time. Once in a while a student stands out, sometimes for the wrong reasons."

"And you remember Jerry for the wrong reasons?"

"That's just it. I'm not sure that I'm thinking of the right boy. He looks like a lot of people."

"Supposing that Jerry is the boy you were thinking of? Was there something I should know about him?"

There was no sign of a twinkle in her blue eyes now, no hint of dimples. "That's the second problem. I'm not sure I remember the story correctly."

I tried to control my nervous impatience. I respected that she didn't want to say horrible things about Jerry if he'd never been guilty of more than being the normal obnoxious teenager. I even agreed with her in theory. But I couldn't really view my safety and well-being in theoretical terms.

"Then I'll take whatever you tell me with a grain of salt."

She thought it over. "*If* this is the same boy, he formed an attachment to a classmate, a girl. Well, teens do. They're so emotional, so intense at that age. But he hounded this poor little thing until she had some kind of a breakdown.

I think she tried to kill herself. Her parents threatened to sue the school, but I don't believe anything ever came of it."

"What happened to him?"

She made an exasperated sound. "I'm not sure. I think his parents moved him to another school."

I weighed that information. Frankly, it sounded sort of innocuous—I'd been thinking in terms of bloody valentines—although being a mystery writer I could expand on the idea of "hounded" in all kinds of alarming ways. But then Emmaline was playing it down too. I could tell by the way her gaze kept flickering from mine.

"I'm pretty sure Jerry is gay," I said.

"I'm probably thinking of a completely different boy."

"Probably. But I appreciate the heads-up." It was easy from there to segue into letting her know I would be out of town and asking her to call the police if anyone suspicious showed up at the house.

Emmaline gave a ladylike sniff. "It seems to me all you have are suspicious people showing up!"

"I think the delivery men would resent that remark. Not to mention the police." I reached down to pet a giant gray tabby cat winding itself around my shins. It opened its pink mouth and meowed loudly, showing all its pointy teeth.

"Now Pinky," Emmaline said.

I looked up, startled. "P-Pinky?"

"That's his name."

"*Pinky?* Is that short for anything?"

"Like what?"

"Mr. Pinkerton?"

Emmaline chortled. "What kind of a name is that for a cat?"

"True." I smiled feebly and straightened. I glanced down at the cat. I could have sworn it winked at me.

I gave her my cell number and the general details of my trip, and then Emmaline saw me to the door. "You must come and see my garden another time. It was also designed by Church. I'll have you and Mr. Moriarity to dinner one night. How does that sound?"

I said agreeable noncommittal things, she closed the door, and I headed back up the sidewalk to 321.

The warm air was slightly humid, fragrant with flowery scents. Bees hummed and somewhere nearby a radio was playing a Jack Johnson song I recognized: "Better Together."

A shadow fell across the pavement. I looked up and felt my smile fade.

Speak of the devil. Jerry was walking toward me. He wore sunglasses and a wide smile. He carried a large box wrapped in silver paper with a large white bow.

"Surprise!"

I was getting to hate that word. Among other things.

I rummaged around for a polite smile, but I seemed to be running low. I could only come up with a strained grimace. "Jerry!"

"How's my favorite mystery writer this beautiful morning?"

I ignored that, eyes trained on the parcel he held. I'm sure my dismay showed. "Is that—?"

"It's for you, silly!"

"But you already brought me that picnic basket."

"That was just a welcome to the neighborhood. This is a housewarming gift."

"Jerry, that's really nice of you. Really nice. But I..." my voice petered away in the face of his open disappointment. Made more unnerving by the fact that I couldn't see his eyes. Twin reflections of my own worried expression gazed back at me.

In fairness—or unfairness—Emmaline's story had predisposed me to view any further overtures from Jerry with dark suspicion. Although, in fairness—and unfairness—I was already headed that way.

"I just don't think I can accept this," I said firmly. "I'm sorry."

At first I thought he didn't hear me. He stood there, his face immobile behind the mask of his sunglasses. The sunlight glinted off the metallic paper. I couldn't help thinking of tinfoil hats. Then he frowned. "Christopher, maybe you're getting the wrong idea," he said. "It's not like I'm a celebrity stalker."

"No. I don't think that at all," I said quickly.

"Even if you *were* a celebrity."

"I know. But I feel uncomfortable accepting this many presents from… you."

Jerry was still frowning. "You're my favorite writer, yes, but I don't think you're perfect. Not at all. I've written you some really bad reviews."

"You wrote me bad reviews?"

He shrugged. "You needed to know."

I stared in wonder. "What did I need to know?"

"That you made a mistake."

"What mistake?" I wasn't arguing. Of course I made mistakes. Everyone made mistakes.

His forehead wrinkled as he thought about it. "Well, for one thing, I didn't like how you ended *Miss Butterwith and the Kernel of Truth*. Inspector Appleby should have ended up with Robin Cloud. It was fine that he let him get away with killing Ira Pogue. Pogue needed killing. But Robin shouldn't have had to leave. He was perfect for Inspector Appleby."

"But Inspector Appleby isn't gay."

Jerry laughed very hard at this.

"He's not gay," I insisted. "I invented him. I get to say whether he's gay or not."

"Who's he dating? Miss Butterwith?"

I opened my mouth and then closed it.

"Anyway, that was a two-star review. And I also didn't like the plot of *Miss Butterwith Sees Stars*. I don't like anything to do with astrology."

"It was astronomy."

"Or astronomy. They're both boring. That was a one-star because the book was also too short."

He handed the package to me and I took it automatically. "Okay," I said. I pushed through the front gate to my yard and started for the porch. I said over my shoulder, "Well. Thank you, Jerry. I'm just going to put this inside. I'm actually on my way to run a few errands."

"You're not going to open it?"

"I…"

I should not have looked back. It is always a mistake to look back. Just ask Orpheus. Only in this case Eurydice was still on my heels, looking both stubborn and self-deprecating. "I was kind of hoping to see your face when you opened it."

"Oh. Well, it'll look like it does now, only happier."

Jerry laughed and punched my arm. "You've got such a great sense of humor. It's in all your books."

I smiled weakly. Jerry wasn't budging. "I guess I could open it now."

I was rewarded by a blazing smile.

We went up the steps. I unlocked the doors and held the nearest one for Jerry. He took his sunglasses off and looked around the foyer in amazement. "Wow! This is great. I can't believe how much you got done in a couple of days."

"Yes. Thanks. I'm keeping busy."

I started to carry the package into the kitchen, but Jerry said, "Christopher, I don't want to intrude. But could I take a peek in your office? It would mean a lot to see the place where the magic happens."

"My office isn't set up," I said. "It's just boxes and furniture. No magic has ever happened in there." Even I could hear how forbidding my tone was. I tried to put a humorous spin on it. "Seriously. It's a disaster area." That came out sounding like I was leading the Hazmat team. *Yes, your shoes too! Everything must be burned!*

"Right. Right." Jerry held up his hands. "Genius at work. I shouldn't have asked."

"No, it's—" I gave up. He wasn't listening anyway as he peeked around the corner of the first doorway. "Look at this! Your living room looks like you're all moved in."

"Technically I think it's a large parlor. But yeah, we're…"

Jerry vanished inside the parlor. I followed him, silently berating myself for letting him through the front doors. Never again. What was the matter with me? Next I'd be letting in people selling vacuums and solar panels.

Jerry went straight to the wall of bookcases. As he scanned the shelves, his expression of eagerness changed to shock. "None of your books are here!"

"Not here. I keep copies in my office. Or I will, once it's set up."

"You should have them out where people can see them."

I had no response to that. Or rather, my response would have been *Why?* Shouldn't my shelves more accurately represent what *I* read?

Jerry examined our shelves with the attentiveness of the devoted reader and I uncomfortably shifted the wrapped box. It felt heavy. It felt expensive. It felt like too much. Whatever it was, it was too much.

And yet readers sent J.X. wonderful and amazing gifts—first editions and aged whisky and art prints. He got gift baskets like readers feared he was running out of food stamps. One reader had painted a gorgeous book map of every place in San Francisco where one of J.X.'s stories took place. Another had sent him a quilt made from images of his book covers. And there was nothing peculiar or uncomfortable about any of it. J.X. was happy and appreciative and nobody tried to get a peek at his office or his anything else.

"Your boyfriend reads some weird stuff." Jerry was holding my 1989 copy of *How to Read Faces* by Dr. Li Tao. It *was* a weird book and it probably belonged on my reference shelf, except it was so entertainingly kooky. It had been one of the sources for *Miss Butterwith Faces Trouble,* but I wasn't going to share that with Jerry. No more sharing with Jerry. Period.

Jerry finally finished his scrutiny of our books and turned to me. He nodded at the parcel. "Aren't you going to open it?"

"Yes. Right." I sat down in the nearest chair and undid the wide silk ribbon, pulled the paper apart and studied the Levenger box. Of course it was bound to be something nice if it was from Levenger's and I swallowed. Probably not a pen.

Jerry came over to stand beside me. "What do you think it is?"

"I don't know."

"Try to guess."

"A vase?"

His brows drew together. "From Levenger's?"

"I don't know, Jerry. Maybe a bookend?"

His face fell.

"I love their bookends," I said quickly. "That would be a great gift." I lifted the lid, and sure enough there were a pair of those whimsical Levenger Reading Bear bookends. "I love them!" I said.

"Are you sure? Because I could get you something different."

"No. These are perfect. I—we—will cherish them."

"They could go right on that bookshelf." He pointed to the nearest one. "Once you get your own books on there."

"That's a nice idea." I set the box aside. "You're such a thoughtful person and I really appreciate your kindness. I wish we could chat a little longer, but I really do have a bunch of errands to run."

His smile faded. He said sadly, "Oh, sure."

But better men than Jerry had tried to guilt me and failed. Including my mom. Ruthlessly, apologizing all the way, I hustled him to the front doors and tried to give him the old heave-ho.

He dug his heels in on the threshold. "Christopher, I was hoping you might be willing to sign some of my books if I brought them by one day."

"Sure," I said recklessly. By then I'd have said anything to get him over the doorsill. "I can do that. You can email me through my website and we'll set something up."

"It's okay, I have your phone number." He smiled kindly, patted my arm, and went out the door.

CHAPTER NINE

When I returned from running my errands, I found a young woman sitting on the steps of my porch.

I could smell her perfume, something spicy and confusing, from down the walk. She was a tall, gangly girl with a lot of blond hair tied up in one of those misleadingly casual knots. She wore sandals, a denim skirt, short white blouse and primrose sweater—the kind of thing that is meant to look like it was purchased at a thrift store but costs a fortune. I should know. I had a whole wardrobe full of stuff like that, bought at Rachel's insistence when she'd decided I needed a makeover.

Well, when I say "a wardrobe full of stuff like that," I don't actually mean skirts and blouses, but I had an awful lot of ripped jeans and baggy cashmere sweaters and T-shirts with trendy slogans that frankly might just as well have been in hieroglyphics as far as meaning anything to me. I mean, seriously. *Fierce?* In relation to me? It was like hearing a kitten's mew coming from the MGM lion.

"Can I help you?" I called.

She rose—she was taller than me—and offered her hand. "Hello. Mr. Holmes?"

"Yes?"

"I'm Ingrid Edwards."

I shook hands with her. Her fingers were ice cold, which I figured was either extreme nervousness or she'd planted an empty Frappuccino cup in my begonias. "How can I help you?"

"This is going to sound very strange."

"You don't know the day I've had," I told her. "But take your best shot."

"I'm Alan Lorenson's granddaughter." Her wide blue eyes studied me, waiting for my reaction.

Lorenson. Where had I heard that name before? "I see," I said, though it was probably obvious I didn't.

"My grandfather is a rare coin collector. Well known in numismatical circles." She paused to give me another chance to say *Ah ha!* But I wasn't having an *ah ha* moment. I was having a *hmmm* moment.

I nodded encouragingly. Not that I wanted to encourage her. I just wanted to get this encounter over with so I could hit the road.

"Grandpa loaned his entire coin collection to Quercus Gallery. The dead man that you found in your basement two days ago was suspected of stealing that same collection from the gallery."

That was my *Ah ha!* moment, but I kept it to myself. "The police mentioned something about it. The gallery owner was murdered during the robbery?"

Ingrid bit her lip. "Mr. Cantrell, yes. That was terrible. He was an old friend of my grandfather's."

"I'm sorry."

"Although the man who robbed the gallery is dead, the coins are still missing. There were over a thousand individual pieces."

"Right. Elijah Ladas," I said. That much was now public knowledge. "He had a partner. I'm guessing his brother."

She looked flabbergasted. "Mr. Holmes, how do you know that?"

It was so tempting to pull an *Elementary, my deah lady!* moment. But I refrained. "I saw the videotape of the break-in online. There were two men."

"Oh. Of course. I didn't realize you were following the case."

"I'm not. But the police think Ladas' brother showed up here the other night."

"Showed up *here*?" Ingrid's eyes went still wider. She glanced past me as though expecting to see Beck charging around the corner of the house even as we spoke. "Then maybe my idea isn't so strange."

I asked uneasily, "What's your idea?"

The words seemed to burst out of her. "What if Ladas hid the coins somewhere in the moving van before he was murdered? What if the coins are in one of your boxes?"

I stared at her. I wasn't positive how much information the police had released about the crime, but I sure as hell did not want anyone hanging onto the mistaken idea that ten million dollars worth of rare coins were somewhere in this house.

"That's not possible," I said. "A thousand coins? However small the coins are, put them together and they're going to take up some serious space. For another thing, the ME believes Ladas was dead before he was placed in the moving van. Probably for several hours."

"They can't be sure."

Clearly not a fan of mysteries, Ingrid. "Actually, they can," I said. "There are all kinds of things that happen to the body once you die, and those things help determine how long you've been dead—as well as where you died and how."

She shivered. "But there must be room for error."

"There is, but even so. Besides, the police went through everything in the moving van."

That wasn't exactly true. The police had looked through a number of containers while searching for the murder weapon, but they hadn't been through every single crate and box. Which didn't change the fact that there was no way anyone could have hidden a thousand coins without me having found them by now. With the exception of the boxes in the basement and J.X.'s office stuff and my own, I *had* been through every container.

"They might have missed something though."

I shook my head. I wasn't trying to be defeatist or obstructionist, let alone unkind. But what she was suggesting wasn't feasible. A thousand coins hidden...where?

To my horror, tears filled her eyes. She whispered, "I don't know what to do."

"Well, but Ladas is dead and the police will be—I'm guessing, I'm not in their confidence—investigating every part of his life. I'm sure the coins will show up. Don't you think?"

"No."

"Unless," I was thinking aloud—always a mistake, "he'd already sold them before he was killed."

"Or hid them." She continued to stare at me with those big, mournful eyes. Big, mournful and stubborn eyes.

"Ingrid…"

A lone tear trickled down her cheek.

I sighed. Maybe it would help if she could see what I meant. "All right."

Her smile blazed through her tears. "Oh, thank you! I knew from your books you must be a kind person."

"You've read my books?" I unbent, despite myself.

"Er, no. But my grandpa is your biggest fan. You write about the old lady gardener and her cat, right?"

"High-octane-edge-of-your-seat-roller-coaster thrillers about old ladies and their cats, yep. That's me."

"And I know from those cute covers, you'd have to be nice."

Hadn't she ever heard the one about not judging an author by his covers? Anyway, resistance was futile. I knew that.

"Come on," I said. "Let me show you what you're up against."

I won't deny that it was kind of a comfort to have someone with me the first time I unsealed the basement door post police investigation. It wasn't logical—there was nothing left in the basement but a bad memory and, more faintly, a bad smell. Mostly, the bad smell had to do with the chemicals used to process a crime scene.

Ingrid's blue gaze fixed on the crate marked CHINA. Her throat moved. Her voice was barely more than a whisper as she said, "Do you think he… suffered?"

"Probably. Depending on the type of knife, the depth of penetration and where he was hit in the heart. It could have taken a minute or a few hours. He'd likely have long enough to know what happened and that would be the suffering part, I think."

I glanced at her face and wished I'd kept my mouth shut. I cleared my throat. "But on the bright side, wherever it happened, he was already dead when they put him in the crate. So at least..." Yeah. I shut up.

She went to the crate, still draped in yellow-and-black crime scene tape. "Is it okay to look through this?"

"Uh, if you want to. The crime scene people were all through there."

I could have saved my breath. She sifted through the blood-browned popcorn and then straightened. She looked at me. I said, "Go ahead and look in any box you like. The police have been through everything down here, but if it will make you feel better, see for yourself."

She did. She went through every single box. She checked the washing machine and dryer (not mine, but I didn't have the heart to tell her) and the empty refrigerator musing quietly to itself in the corner. She was swift and she was thorough. She was also sweaty and pale by the time she finished.

Ingrid joined me on the sofa and put her face in her hands. She wasn't crying. She was just...spent.

From behind her hands she said, "I don't know what we're going to do."

"Was the collection insured?"

She shook her head.

I hadn't thought it would be. It was hard to get insurance for a coin collection, not least because collections were fluid, their owners buying and selling items constantly.

"I can't believe it's all gone."

"It may not be," I said. "Ladas might have sold some of the coins, but then again he might not have. Scandinavian coins are going to get a pretty close look from any potential buyer right now because of the murder of the gallery owner. Plus a couple of those coins are just too well known. A Gustav II Adolf gold dukat doesn't just pop up on the market every day. I think there's a good chance Ladas might have stashed the whole take, planning to wait out the publicity and attention."

She lowered her hands. "Stashed them where?"

I looked at her in surprise. "I have no idea. I don't know anything about Ladas. I'm just theorizing." Putting that *brilliant criminal mind* of mine to use, as it were.

"Where would be a likely place?"

"To hide a thousand coins? I have no way of knowing. If it was me, I sure as hell wouldn't hide them in any place or building that the police could easily connect me to."

Ingrid looked thoughtful.

I said, "I don't know if it would help or not, or what your finances are, but you could hire a private investigator to check into Ladas' background. Find out where he lived, his known associates. The police will be doing the same, of course, but their focus is on solving the robbery and murder. They don't have quite the same interest in recovering the coins that your family does."

She brightened. "That's a good idea!"

"I have them occasionally." I rose. "Sorry. I hate to throw you out, but you can see how much I've still got to do to get this place ready."

"Yes. Sorry! Of course." Ingrid stood up and preceded me out of the basement and up the steps leading to the kitchen. She was silent all the way to the front door, lost in her unhappy thoughts. But as I was releasing her back into the wild, she said, "Thank you, Mr. Holmes. You've been really kind. And really helpful."

"Sorry I couldn't be more helpful," I said, and I meant it. Because until those damn coins were found and the mystery of who killed Ladas answered, I had the uncomfortable feeling I was not going to get much peace and quiet.

* * * * *

By six o'clock I was on my way back to L.A. I fed Jack Johnson's *To the Sea* in the CD player and put many miles between me and San Francisco as swiftly as the speed limit would allow.

You and your heart

Shouldn't feel so apart...

I hoped the house would be okay. I hoped Little Ladas would not break in looking for a treasure trove of old coins. I had set up timers for lamps and TVs, I had notified my nosey neighbor and the police that I was going out of town, and we had a good security system. More than that, I could not do. It was in the hands of the gods. And they probably had more important things to worry about. Like the price of gasoline on this godforsaken trek.

Highway 101 was about an hour longer than taking the I-5, but it was a little more scenic and a lot less stressful minus the big trucks and traffic once I got away from the city and surrounding environs.

A couple of hours into the trip, my back began to twinge, but I was set on making it to Paso Robles, which was about the halfway mark. I wanted to time the second half of my drive so I avoided the L.A. Monday morning work traffic.

One thing about a long drive, it gives you time to reflect, and the more I reflected on the events of the past couple of days, the more I thought there was something odd about Ingrid Edwards' visit. Not the visit itself, though that did seem a little unusual, but her reaction to the crate where Ladas had been hidden.

I liked to think I was a reasonably sensitive person, but that question about whether Ladas had suffered? In my opinion, that was the question of someone taking a personal interest.

Of course, she might just be the kind-hearted type, but Ladas had robbed her grandfather and murdered her grandfather's old friend, so her sympathy—if that had been sympathy and not morbid imagination—was unexpected.

She seemed a bit naïve, granted.

Or was that an act?

Maybe I was the naïve one, letting a strange woman in my house to poke around my basement simply because she claimed to be related to one of Ladas' victims. All because she'd sprinkled a few tears and claimed Grandpa was my biggest fan?

I hated to think what J.X. would say when he heard the details of my latest adventures in householding.

But suppose, worst case scenario, she was a not very bright confederate of Ladas and Co.? Maybe letting her in to have a look wasn't such a bad idea. Maybe allowing her to see first hand that there was no possibility the coins were in the house was the best way to take the focus off both myself and my domicile. Maybe she would report back to Beck and tell him there was no further point to lurking around 321 Chestnut Lane. Assuming he was still lurking and not on the run from the law.

Except…when I had mentioned Beck had been to the house, she'd looked genuinely frightened. Not just alarmed, which would be a normal reaction from any law-abiding person upon hearing there might be a violent criminal in the vicinity. No, I'd seen fear in her eyes.

Of course, again, she might just be the overimaginative, oversensitive type.

Or I might be.

By King City my back was starting to give me hell. Most of the time it was fine, provided I didn't lift anything too heavy or forget my stretching exercises for too long. But the last week had put a lot of strain on muscles I rarely used, and those ominous pinches up and down my spine and right leg were bad news. I started to watch the highway exits for likely-looking lodging. In the end I held out for Paso Robles and my previously booked motel, though I could barely totter from my car to the reception desk.

A quick shower, and chicken fried steak and mashed potatoes at the adjacent coffee shop revived me. And a couple of gin and tonics in the motel bar completed the restoration project. By the time I reached my room I was humming, "I left my house in San Francisco…"

I stopped humming and started swearing when I noticed J.X. had texted me.

I called him and he picked up at once, as though demonstrating how these things were properly handled.

"I'm not ignoring you. It's because it's on vibrate," I said. "I can't get it off vibrate. Obviously I would rather talk to you."

"Than vibrate on your own?" J.X. teased.

The teasing was a relief, even if he was clearly off drinking somewhere without me.

"Exactly. Where are you?" I asked.

"Exactly where am I? Vegas. Actually I'm sitting in the St. Mark's Square plaza at the Venetian with your agent and my agent. I'm looking at a beautiful, painted sunset and wishing you were here. Oh. Your agent wants to say—"

"Christopher!" shrieked Rachel, nearly piercing my eardrum. "Have you started the book yet? When can you have the proposal ready?"

"You know who you're starting to remind me of? Edna Mode. Give the phone back to J.X."

A brief commotion followed. Then came what sounded like a splash. Hilarity ensued—or possibly hysteria—before J.X. was back on the line. I could practically taste the alcohol from where I sat. Or maybe that was canal water. I sighed.

"Kit? Are you there?"

"You seem like you're having a good time." I tried not to sound grudging. After all, it had been my choice to stay home and practice becoming a recluse.

"We're celebrating. The entire Dirk Van de Meer series is going to be translated into Japanese."

"That's nice. All eighty-seven books?"

He laughed. "All ten books, yes. The entire series. I am going to take you on the nicest vacation with that fucking great advance. Just you wait."

"Yay," I said. "Please tell me none of you are driving?"

"Would you like to go to Venice? I mean the real one. Not this place."

"Sure. So how are you getting back to the hotel? I don't think the gondolas go all the way to the Marriott."

"We'll get a taxi back to the hotel. Listen, I just called to say I love you, I miss you, I can't wait to see you tomorrow."

I could hear the chorus of awwwwwws from Rachel and Simon Legre—who I liked to refer to as Simon Legree—J.X.'s agent. I started to laugh. "Likewise," I said. "I'll see you tomorrow. We'll be wearing a white gardenia in our lapel and holding a bottle of aspirin."

I think Rachel was shouting final words of career advice as I clicked off.

I woke several hours later to an unfamiliar darkness and the hair-raising certainty that someone was trying to get into my motel room.

For a few disbelieving seconds I lay still, listening to that cautious but definite shifting of the door handle.

I raised my head. Wrong door. That was it. Happens all the time. I'd been guilty of it myself.

Jesus, this guy was slow to catch on.

I pulled off my sleep mask. It didn't sound like someone was trying to slide a key card. It sounded like someone was furtively, carefully trying the handle. And there was another sound. A thin, scratching sound. Was someone trying to pick the lock?

I reached for my glasses, slid them on. Through the part in the curtains, the parking lot light threw a band of yellow across the door. I watched the latch rise and depress like a silent tongue.

Dry-mouthed, heart hammering, I sat up, feeling for the motel phone.

As I did, I heard the distinct, terrifying slide of a bolt. The door opened a crack, outlined in fuzzy yellow porch light. The cool night air, smelling of exhaust, warm rubber and chlorine bleach, swirled in.

I dropped the phone and on some instinct—the instinct that makes you grab for the remote to change the channel before you see something terrible—snatched my car keys, pressing the panic button. The BMW's car alarm blasted into the night from what sounded like a foot from the door.

The motel door dropped back into its frame, and the room was pitch black again. I scrambled out of bed and got over to the window in time to see a giant blond man running through the parking lot and crashing through a feathery white wall of Chinese fringe trees.

CHAPTER TEN

The real mystery at Cloak and Dagger Books was how they managed to stay open. A few years ago you had a better chance of marrying a terrorist than finding Adrien English behind the counter—or anywhere else in the shop.

When I arrived a little after seven, the place was already crowded with people milling through the aisles, clutching J.X.'s books in their feverish little hands.

"Oh, I know you!" a woman said as I sidled through the throng, trying to make my way to where J.X. stood talking to a dark-haired man and a woman with matching corduroy blazers. "You're…you're…"

"Agatha Christie," I replied.

I had not had a good day, although I'd have been the first to admit that I would have had a much worse day had Beck Ladas—or whoever that had been—managed to break into my room. I'd packed and left the motel within five minutes after watching the intruder disappear into the trees, and I'd driven the next few hours with one eye on my rearview mirror. I didn't think I was being followed, but what did that matter? It wasn't like Ladas didn't know where I lived.

I'd stopped for breakfast as the sun was rising and I'd phoned Izzie Jones. He had taken being woken at the crack of dawn better than I had, but he hadn't been able to offer much in the way of comfort.

"Why is this lunatic following me?" I'd demanded. "What is it he wants?"

"I don't know," Izzie said. "But if there's something you're not telling us, now would be the time to speak up."

I spoke up all right. When I stopped yelling, the terrified kitchen staff popped their heads up from behind the counter, and Izzie said, "Look, Christopher, I had to ask."

"No, you didn't, and I resent the question. Do I *look* like a criminal to you?"

"Er, no. But—"

"No. I have anxiety attacks over parking tickets. I am not the outlaw type. I'm the homesteader type. I am the circle-the-wagons-leave-me-alone type. I don't know what's going on here, but it's nothing to do with me."

And maybe if I kept saying it loudly and often enough everyone would agree and leave me alone.

Anyway, here I was, and I continued to work my way through the crowd toward J.X. He looked good. Mouthwateringly good. In a black T-shirt, black jeans and black boots, he looked both sexy and a little rough around the edges. A study in ebony and gold. The perfect subject for an updated Velázquez. *Portrait of a Successful Author.*

And he was actually moving *away* from me on a tide of admirers. I swore inwardly.

When I say *work my way*, I mean wriggle. I was not socializing. I was not in a socializing mood. I was in a who-the-hell-came-up-with-this-idiotic-plan? mood.

I bumped into an older man who did a double take. "Aren't you...?"

"Hercule Poirot," I agreed. I put my finger to my lips.

I was beginning to feel like a hapless salmon in a 7th grade science film—one of those poor fish who never make it past the grizzly bears—when J.X. suddenly looked my way. It took him a split second to recognize me—I believe my hair was in my eyes by then and my clothes were half torn off—but his face lit up. He smiled. A big, white, happy smile. He smiled as though looking across a crowded room and seeing me was the best thing that had happened all day.

He came to meet me—the crowd parted before royalty—and I said, "Hey, sorry I'm la—"

His hand landed on my shoulder, he pulled me in and his mouth covered mine. He smelled like leather, tamarind leaves and auramber. He tasted like breath mints and himself. It was not one of those civil *Darling, you made it!* kisses appropriate for meeting at public events. This was more of a *Darling, they told me you were dead!* smooch. Okay, not quite that passionate, but definitely more fervent than I was used to at a book signing. Or anywhere else outside of my bedroom. I think we may have received a round of applause.

By the time I stopped seeing stars, J.X. had shuffled us over to a little alcove by a fake fireplace. A pair of Kabuki masks smiled benignly down on us.

Actually, being Kabuki masks, the smiles were more cryptic than benign.

"Hello to you too," I said. To J.X.

"I was afraid you weren't going to make it," J.X. admitted.

That startled me. "I said I'd be here."

He smiled. It was sort of rueful and sort of affectionate. I felt an uncomfortable jab, remembering other times I'd promised to be there, but had cancelled or "forgotten" or developed a migraine midway through.

I stumbled through my explanation of the reason for driving to my realtor's first. J.X. was watching me with an oddly intent expression. I offered a lopsided smile and said, "I've accepted the offer on the house."

"You *did*?"

There it was again. There was no mistaking that look for anything but happiness. Not just happiness. Relief. I felt another twinge. Had J.X. really been willing to embark on this relationship trusting me as little as he did?

I nodded. "In for a penny. In for a pound."

"I can't wait to pound you," he said softly, meaningfully.

I swallowed the wrong way. Since I wasn't chewing or drinking, the gasping and spluttering might have seemed excessive. J.X. took it in stride. When I had recovered, he said, "While I'm thinking of it, where's your phone?"

I handed it over. He slid his thumb across the screen, clicked a couple of times, shook his head, clicked again, handed it back. "It's off vibrate, so no more excuses for not taking my calls."

"I do take your calls!"

He just shook his head, grinning at me.

A slight man with black hair and eyes the cool blue of a Siamese cat's joined us. He offered a quick, attractive smile and said apologetically, "Sorry to interrupt. J.X., would you mind if we got started?"

"Of course!" J.X. said, "Kit, you remember—"

"Adrien English," I said.

Everyone in publishing—and devoted fans of *Entertainment Tonight*—knew the story of how English actor Paul Kane had purchased the film rights to an obscure mystery by an indie bookseller because Kane was in love with Adrien English's homicide detective ex-boyfriend. It had all ended in true Hollywood fashion. Minus the big budget sequels and merchandising deals.

At the same moment I spoke, Adrien smiled more warmly, offered a hand, and said, "Christopher Holmes. This is a nice surprise."

I said, "Congratulations. You've got a full house tonight."

We shook hands. Adrien said, "I wish I'd had a heads-up. I'd have pulled some stock for you to sign."

"Strictly an interested observer this trip," I said.

He looked puzzled—what sane author ever turned down the opportunity to sign stock?—but offered another of those practiced smiles before spiriting away J.X. I remembered that ruthless charm of old.

A very pretty blonde, who looked like she'd stepped out of an Abercrombie & Fitch advertisement—miracle of miracles, Adrien actually had *two* assistants on hand that evening—offered me a tray of wine in plastic glasses. I passed, and went to find a seat in the nearly filled back row.

The store lights were lowered and J.X. began to read from his new book.

It was a very long time since I'd attended a signing that wasn't my own. It gave me an odd, uneasy feeling. It wasn't that I wished I was in J.X.'s place. No, I felt he was where he belonged and I was where I was comfortable. I was delighted that his signing was so clearly a big success. He read well—it helped that the book was so good—and during the question and answer session, he was open and affable. You'd never look at him in that milieu and think *ex-cop*. He had an effortless charisma. Star quality. I did not—never had—that, but I wasn't jealous. J.X. had worked hard to get to this point. And I felt an almost possessive pride in him that night.

But. But I also knew that a chapter had closed for me. I hadn't written in months. I had no real plans to write anything. Worse, I felt no interest in writing anything.

And if I wasn't a writer, what was I? I had spent my entire adult life earning a living through my words. If I no longer had the words, what did I have? Writing wasn't just a job description. It was a way of looking at the world, of relating to the world. For as long as I could remember, everything I experienced had been filtered through the perspective of a writer making mental notes.

Halfway through the Q&A session, a tall blond man pushed through the doors of the shop. He scanned the room, spotted Adrien and nodded gravely. Adrien smiled. That unguarded, oddly sweet grin was the reason Adrien English had once been the most hit upon bookseller in gay publishing. Also the most oblivious.

Meeting my gaze, Adrien's smile grew self-conscious.

The blond man moved quietly through the aisles of towering shelves to the other side of the bookstore. He unhooked the velvet rope and went straight upstairs, and I surmised that this was the infamous ex-LAPD officer.

It was nearly ten by the time J.X. finished signing the final book. The two shop assistants had sneaked upstairs about thirty minutes earlier. Adrien ushered the last pair of customers out the front, and closed the ornate metal gates across the entrance. He locked the glass doors and sighed. A profitable but long night.

He and J.X. briefly discussed where we could go for dinner at that time of evening, and then he said, "I'm just going to check whether Jake wants to join us." He disappeared in the darkened half of the store.

"Come here and say hello properly," J.X. murmured, tugging me over.

We said hello properly.

"You look tired," J.X. said at last. "You've got shadows under your eyes."

"Long day." His look was inquiring, and there was a lot to tell him, but I didn't want to launch into it then and there.

We fell silent listening to the voices drifting down from the other side of the shop—the tone, not the words. Even from where we waited I could hear them smiling at each other. Adrien said something and the other man, Jake, laughed. They sounded like a couple who had been together a long while, but still enjoyed each other's company, still looked forward to their time together.

They sounded like I hoped J.X. and I would sound years from now.

Adrien returned downstairs. He said cheerfully, "Jake has some paperwork to finish up."

"What does he do?" I asked.

"He's a PI. Anyway, he'll meet us over there."

A likely story, I thought, but not long after we settled at Doc and Doris's with its comfortable booths and blackened beams, and ordered our drinks, Jake strolled into the restaurant. Adrien raised his hand, Jake nodded, impassive as ever, and wandered over to our booth.

Adrien moved over and Jake slid in beside him. He stretched one arm along the top of the booth, not touching Adrien, but somehow the overall impression was of a single self-contained unit.

Adrien made the introductions, we all said hello and then we all got busy ordering our meals before the kitchen closed.

"The steak and mushroom pie is really good," Adrien said, and Jake's mouth twitched, although what was funny about steak and mushroom pie, I failed to see.

After our drinks arrived, the conversation livened up. Or I did. I related my adventures in finding Elijah Ladas' body in the basement. J.X. had heard most of this before, of course, but he looked progressively stern throughout the recital. Adrien and Jake had seen the story on the news. For some reason I hadn't been thinking it would receive more than local coverage.

"No wonder you look tired." J.X. was frowning.

"And yet I still managed to make sure the soap matches the toilet paper in the master bath. You did say peach, right?"

Jake choked on his drink.

"Anyway, there's more." I filled J.X. in on the prowler two nights earlier and then the midnight visit from Sydney Nightingale, the visit from Ingrid Edwards, and the attempt to break into my motel room.

"Beck thinks you've got the coins," Adrien said at the end of my tale.

"He can't. He has to know what his brother did with them, surely?" I looked at J.X. J.X. said nothing. His expression was not reassuring.

"Beck doesn't sound like the brightest candle on the cake," Jake said. "If you were his brother, would you have told him more than you had to?"

"But I had nothing to do with any of it. His brother was dead before I ever made his acquaintance."

"You should have told me what was happening," J.X. said flatly.

"What could you have done about it?"

"Catch the first flight home!"

I glanced at our dinner companions, who were doing their best to pretend they had never seen anything as fascinating as the restaurant décor.

"It sort of escalated," I admitted. "If I'd known at the beginning that Beck Ladas would be trying to break into my motel room, yes, I'd have asked you to come home first thing."

J.X. looked slightly appeased, but only slightly.

The second round of drinks helped us all get past the moment. From there the conversation wandered to the topic of what a pain in the ass it was to dig a writer out of a place he'd lived forever—Adrien and Jake had only recently moved in together—publishing, the book market, self-publishing, Amazon, and Scandinavian fiction.

"No more Miss Butterwith?" Adrien was smiling. "I love those books. I'm going to have a lot of very disappointed customers."

That reminded me of the one topic I'd skipped over when I was bringing J.X. up to date. Jerry Knight. But no way was I bringing that up in front of Adrien and Jake. I knew they'd be wondering what kind of idiot allowed a relationship to develop with an obvious stalker.

"Never say never," I replied. "But for now, the old girl is enjoying her retirement. What about you?" I asked. "Any more Jason Leland mysteries in the works?"

Adrien's lashes lowered, veiling his thoughts—but I knew he would be remembering Paul Kane. He reached for his glass, saying neutrally, "Maybe. We'll see."

Our meals came. Steak and mushroom pie for Adrien, burgers and fries for the rest of us.

Adrien said casually, "I have to say, I never pictured Anna Hitchcock as the type to kill herself. Was she in poor health? Nobody seems to know. You were there that weekend, right?"

That was the kind of curiosity that got cats killed, and behind Adrien's shoulder, I saw Jake's hand make a spasmodic movement. It was instant and instinctive, like he was about to grab someone teetering on the edge of a cliff. Except he didn't grab. He didn't move a muscle after that first protesting twitch, but his hazel gaze was alert and watchful as it met mine.

"We left that day. I was only there to teach a writing workshop."

"There had already been a couple of deaths earlier that weekend, hadn't there?"

"I'm a tough teacher."

Polite smiles. It wasn't funny.

J.X. said, "It was a weird place. Very hinky vibe." That was said to Jake, ex-cop to ex-cop. Jake tipped his head in acknowledgement, but said nothing.

"Hitchcock left one heck of a literary legacy," Adrien said. "That's something."

"It'll have to do."

His look was inquiring, but I wasn't about to confide any further, and he was too polite to push harder.

"You don't go to conferences do you?" I asked him suddenly. "Workshops? Conventions?"

Adrien shuddered. "No."

I delivered a pointed Told-You-So to J.X. who only shook his head.

It was a surprisingly enjoyable meal, and we had a final drink at the bar before saying our goodnights. In the parking lot outside the restaurant, J.X. and I invited Adrien and Jake to visit any time they were in San Francisco.

"I'll drive," J.X. offered as we walked to my car. "How's your back?"

I tossed the keys to him. "Horrible."

He caught the keys. "Hell," he said with genuine sympathy.

"How's your hangover?" I inquired.

"It disappeared the minute I saw you walk in tonight."

Now that was funny. "Looking harassed and aggravated?"

"A little," J.X. agreed, but his smile invited me to share his amusement. That open affection had to be what made the difference between laughing with someone and laughing at them.

As our car's headlights swept across the parking lot, I spotted Jake and Adrien standing beside a Subaru Forester. Adrien was still talking. Jake faced him, smiling, but somehow I could feel his gaze following our progress to the driveway.

* * * * *

J.X. had booked us into the Langham Huntington, which I thought was a bit extravagant, but whatever. He had that Japanese advance burning a hole in his pocket, and who was I to argue with a little pleasing and pampering?

"How was the convention?" I asked as we headed over to the hotel.

"You've been to one, you've been to them all." J.X. added, "Except the one in DC. *That* was a great convention."

I snorted, but yeah. That had been a good one.

"You should have let me know what was happening though, Kit."

"Next time a deranged psychopath fixates on me, you'll be the first to know. You have my word."

He made a sound that wasn't quite amused and wasn't quite appeased, but to my relief he changed the subject. "That's an interesting relationship."

No question whom he meant. I nodded. "They seem happy though." Maybe "happy" wasn't the right word. Happy was too fragile. What those two had was more like quiet contentment. Like soldiers at peace after a long war.

"He's had a couple of heart attacks," J.X. said. "Adrien, not Jake."

"Heart attacks? At his age? He better give up the steak pies. He was shot. I know that. Everyone in publishing knows that."

"I know he was in pretty poor health not that long ago."

"He's healthy enough now. He went sprinting up those stairs like an antelope."

"Yep, he sure did."

I could tell J.X. was losing interest in the topic of Adrien English. I was thinking though that Adrien was about J.X.'s age, give or take a couple of years. And, at a guestimate, Jake was about my age. It couldn't have been easy for him to start over, but he'd done it. And he seemed happy.

If he could do it, maybe I could too.

The Langham Huntington, which referred to itself as an "urban resort oasis" in its brochures, was nestled at the base of the blue San Gabriel mountains. Tall palm trees looked silver in the moonlight. Window lights glowed warmly in welcome as we started up the long drive. Like the Fairmont, the Langham Huntington was one of those iconic landmark hotels that take you back to another time and place. A time and a place when you didn't understand how credit card debt worked.

Our room was a spacious suite with fresh flowers, vintage-style details and a lush garden view—twenty-three acres worth of garden view—a private parlor and a four-poster bed.

In fairness, that night I was only interested in the bed, which we landed on in a breathless, naked heap within ten seconds of closing the door behind the bell boy.

"Jesus *Christ*, I missed you," J.X. muttered, covering my face with hot and hungry kisses. His mouth was sweet, his beard scratchy, his voice husky with sincerity. "This last week has been torture."

"Well, it was just a weekend, if you want to get tech—"

He shut me up with more kisses. I liked kissing. I liked it a lot. David had not been much for mouth-to-mouth, but during our brief fellowship J.X. had more than made up for it. If there was a place on my body he hadn't applied his lips to, I couldn't think what it was. Back of my knees, arch of my foot, nape of my neck, left tonsil... But mostly I liked it when he pressed his warm, open mouth to mine and we breathed in moist unison, hearts thumping against each other. Nothing so simple nor yet so intense as a kiss between lovers.

"I got you something," J.X. whispered after a time.

"Mmm?" That was the best I could offer in the interests of coherency.

He gave me a final smack and tore himself away. I made a protesting sound at the bounce of bedsprings. Or the bounce of something.

"Be right there..." he promised. I watched the long, elegant line of his back as he moved away from the bed. Wide shoulders, narrow hips, and skin as smooth and golden as good old Ricardo Montalban's Corinthian leather. I smiled, closed my eyes.

A moment later he waved something beneath my nose. I caught the faint scent of sweet almonds and anise.

I pried open my eyes. "Ah. Oil of cyanide. A favorite of mystery writers everywhere."

J.X.'s smile was very white in the perfect frame of his Van Dyke, his eyes glittered like black stars. He said in a low, almost guttural voice, "The oil warms inside your body so you'll feel everything I do to you that much more intensely."

I shivered. Oh my God, I wanted that. I wanted to feel that oil warming me, softening my resistance, readying me for him, for whatever he wanted to do, and I wanted him to do it all. Wanted J.X. to touch me, stroke me, caress me, fuck me. Yes, more than anything I wanted him to fuck me.

And at the same time I felt a flutter of alarm. *Not this again.*

I opened my mouth, but nothing came out. Nothing articulate anyway. Just a funny, squeaky sound that wasn't exactly a protest, but wasn't quite encouragement.

And yet J.X. smiled more widely still. He squirted the golden liquid onto two fingers and we both watched it drizzle down his hand and wrist like honey.

"Smells nice," I managed.

"Feels nice too. Slick and slippery—and it *is* warm. Let me show you."

I gave myself up to it, closed my eyes, moved my leg, lifted my hips, and J.X.'s oily finger pierced me with delicate deliberation. Usually he gave me a little more time, but not tonight. Tonight there was no time to think. His index finger pushed inside and my muscles clenched in instant how-very-dare-you reflex.

But of course he dared. Why wouldn't he when I was lying there, panting and shivering and waiting obediently for whatever he did next?

"Nice?" he whispered.

I nodded. It *was* nice. The oil felt heated and it tingled a little as J.X. touched me with pleasurable expertise.

"It's hard not to rush," he said. "I just want to bury myself in that sweet ass of yours. But it's got to be good for you. As good as I can make it. Every time."

I moaned. I told myself it was pain at such terrible dialog. I wanted to say something brisk and cutting like, "Do you serve wine with that cheese?" But I couldn't speak over my heart, currently lodged in my throat. Who was I kidding? I found his honesty unbearably exciting. Both his words and deeds.

"That's your sweet spot, right there." I could hear the smile in his voice as J.X. skimmed the tender bump of my prostate. Colored sparks flashed behind my eyelids like action bubbles in a comic book. ZAP! Zing! Shiver! Ka-POW! My brain was about to short out. Short out and burst into flame, and all that would be left would be a pile of gray ash and a couple of smoldering wires.

"Jesus, you handle so sweet, Kit. So quick, so responsive. I could make you come just like this...just touching you like this."

No lie. And I almost wished he would. Get it over with. Move on to the next part. The part where *he* was helpless and begging and vulnerable. Except that part never seemed to come anymore. These days it was always me dangling over the ravine. I felt a pricking behind my eyelids because it was just...difficult...to be forced to feel so much. To have all your defenses stripped away and be left with nothing but want and need and longing for another person. What could be more precarious than that?

I held him tighter, breathing in the scents of sweet oil mingled with imminent sex. I loved the smell of his hair and the taste of his skin and the ragged sound of his breath gusting against my face.

"I waited so long for you," he muttered.

I opened my eyes.

He was beautiful in the creamy light. Sleek and golden and somehow exotic. His eyes gleamed beneath the dark length of his lashes as he studied me. His mouth curved in a small, satisfied smile. *Mine. All mine.* I had to strangle the sudden and maniacal laugh that almost burst out of me at the idea. But it was true. Or at least *he* believed it was true. Which was almost the same thing.

J.X.'s lashes flicked up, catching my gaze. He whispered, "You want to ride me, Kit?"

The offer surprised me. To be honest, I wasn't sure. It seemed a little showy, a little exhibitionist, and I'd still be the guy with the cock up his ass. Changing positions didn't change who was submitting to whom. Not really. Besides which, he'd have only too clear a view of my not-washboard-like abs.

"Uh…"

"I want to see your face," J.X. said. "I want to watch you come."

What could I say to that?

We ungracefully shifted positions. That's the thing about sex. So much of it is just plain awkward, clumsy, are-you-sure-this-is-going-to-fit-I-think-they-forgot-to-include-the-washers. But we crawled around, and I straddled J.X.'s lean hips, toes digging into the mattress as I tried to get into position. Yoga? *Really?* And what the hell would you call this position?

Whatever I looked like—hair mussed and needing a shave, at the least— *he* looked beautiful, lying there gazing up from beneath his black lashes, a sensual smile on his mouth. Like Good Saint Somebody patiently waiting to be seduced.

I reached behind me for J.X.'s penis and his throat moved, he gave a little gulp as I took hold of him, guiding that suede-covered pole into my own body. *Insert Tab P into Slot A…* And where was the instruction manual when you needed it?

But we didn't need it. And he wasn't just a suede-covered pole. He was flesh and blood. Soft skin and hard muscle, his cheeks flushed and his eyes shining and his heart beating as fast as mine. He wanted me and he loved me and this wasn't a test of physical endurance, it was the manifestation of our desire and delight, our need to be one.

My thigh muscles were getting a workout as I sat slowly, lowly down. *Ouch.* An instant and clenched resistance.

J.X.'s breathing sped up and I felt him tighten and then force himself to hold absolutely still, fighting the temptation to shove in.

I panted for a second or two. There was no retreat. I didn't *want* to retreat. I wanted that painful pressure to change to the pleasure like no other, and there was only one way to get there. I sank down a little further. The pressure expanded, the pain bloomed—*not so sure about this, not so sure at all*—and then suddenly gave way, like a secret panel springing open.

"Oh *Christ*, Kit..." J.X.'s hands went to my backside, fingers digging in. "So hot. So sweet. So good like this."

Not yet. Not for me. But soon. I rose up a bit, pushed down lower and finally felt the hard muscles of his thighs against my ass. And the thrill when his cock prodded me in just the right place. There. Right *there*.

J.X.'s hips rocked. He stopped himself. His dark gaze was pinned on my face. "You okay?"

I nodded. I half rose, then lowered myself fully onto J.X.'s rigid erection. And again. Up. Down. Again. Again. It required effort. A lot of effort. Rising up, pushing down, lifting and lowering onto that scrape and burn.

"Yeah, do it, Kit," J.X. urged in a rough voice. "Fuck yourself on my cock. I want to see it."

Crude and crazy, but it did something to me. I closed my eyes and began to move, began to lose myself, leaning back, changing the angle of penetration. Up and down, rising and falling, lifting up and slamming down on him.

"I need you," I said. Cried out the words, in fact. "I need you!"

J.X.'s fingers sank bruisingly into my ass cheeks, and he began to move too, pumping his hips into me. We found a frantic, feverish rhythm.

I got so lost in it, in the rhythm of it, in J.X.'s reactions to it, my own orgasm seemed to, well, come out of nowhere. Like a cloudburst. That buzz of electricity, the crackle of lightning, the roll of thunder and suddenly the whole sky opening up, stars, planets, suns and moons yanked from their moorings, everything tearing loose and spilling out of the heavens in a hot, wet flood.

That release seemed to send J.X. right over the edge. He yelled and arched and thrust harder and faster, and the night tore free. The past was washed away and there was only the present. We were caught up together in a wild summer storm sweeping everything in its path out of the way...

CHAPTER ELEVEN

We slept late the next morning and then took turns in the Italian marble shower. As I stood beneath the beat of warm water and clouds of rich soap, I felt relaxed, almost at peace. Partly it was the physical release of tension. There were handprints on my ass. My leg muscles felt shaky, my guts trembly, my entire body felt buffeted like after a strenuous workout. But the release wasn't all physical, and I kept finding myself smiling into space like a complete goof.

As I opened the bathroom door, J.X. was saying, "Come on, *chica*. Don't start crying. I love him. You make things hard for him, you make them hard for me."

It was funny how his intonation changed, he sounded a little more Hispanic, a little more urban, a little more like someone I didn't really know yet. That was neither bad nor good, simply a reminder that he had a whole life I knew very little about.

Spotting me, he shifted the phone to his other ear and said, "I've got to go. There isn't anything more to say. I told you how it was."

Yeah, good luck with that, hombre.

But I had to give him credit. He clicked off without further apologies or explanation. He smiled ruefully at me. "Nina."

I finished toweling my hair and said mildly, "I told you."

To my surprise, he wrapped his arms around my waist pulling me down to the unmade bed with him. I admit I didn't resist much.

"She's a little confused. And," he said quickly before I could interrupt, "yes, I probably did add to her confusion by spending too much time over there giving her advice and playing handyman and generally trying to fill in for Alex."

I raised my brows and he shook his head. "Never. *Never.* And I still think marrying her was the right decision for that time, but…"

"It complicates things," I said.

He smoothed the edge of his thumb between my brows—and if he thought it was that easy to get rid of frown lines, he had some bad news coming. "It does. I don't want to hurt her or Gage. I love them. They're family."

I said, "I love my family too, but if you'll notice, I'm not setting up Fourth of July barbecues with all my aunts and uncles and cousins or asking you to check out my mom's security system or go golfing with my dad."

J.X. gave me a long, thoughtful look. "Since you brought it up, it bothers me that you haven't introduced me to your parents yet."

"It *bothers* you?"

"Of course it bothers me. It makes me feel like maybe there's a reason you don't want me to meet them."

That shocked me. I pushed up on my elbows. "What? What reason?"

He shrugged. "I don't know. I know you get along with them okay, and you considered yourself married to David, so it isn't anything to do with being gay."

"Of course it isn't. It isn't anything. I mean, there is no *it*. I just haven't got around to the introductions. Yet."

He smiled faintly. There was something self-derisive in that curve of his mouth. "Or maybe you don't think there's any point, because you don't view this relationship like you did your relationship with David."

I said bitterly, "You're right about that. *We* might actually last."

J.X. winced, like the words somehow hit him. "Poor Kit." He leaned forward, pushing me back and thoroughly kissing me. He finished by kissing the bridge of my nose. "I'm sorry that asshole hurt you so much."

"It's okay. I'm over it," I said uncomfortably.

He kissed me again, softly, tenderly.

I said, "If you want to meet my parents, we can…I don't know. Have them up to stay with us. I mean, at different times, because they hate each other and can't be in the same building. Or industrial complex. So be careful what you wish for. But I'll put something together. I didn't realize you cared. And I'm horrified you think whatever it is you've been thinking."

He studied me gravely and I gazed back at him with equal seriousness.

I reached up to tuck a strand of shiny dark hair behind his ear. "I love you," I said. "I wouldn't be doing any of this if I didn't. Selling my home. Moving across the state? You have to know me that well." I gave him a smile that was probably three parts grimace and one part total self-consciousness. "It scares the hell out of me how much I love you."

His smile seemed to stop the breath in my chest. He looked so *happy*.

"Is that true?"

"True. Truly. Truly true."

His laugh was relieved and easy. "Because I know this all happened faster than you were ready for. I know you agreed without completely realizing what you had agreed to. And I did deliberately take advantage of that."

I made a face. "I could have said no at any point. I didn't. I'm here because I want to be here with you."

"You don't have to be scared, Kit, because I'm never going to hurt you. Never going to let you down."

He meant it too. He said it with complete sincerity and it made my eyes sting because J.X. really was an idealist in a lot of ways. But we all hurt the people we love sometimes. We all let each other down sooner or later. Which is why contrition and forgiveness played a part in any relationship. Trying not to hurt each other, trying not to let each other down in the big things, that was as much as anyone could aim for.

I smiled and said, "I know."

"I'm not a player. I've never been a player," he said. "Look at my parents. They've been together forever."

"True," I said. I added mournfully, "But then again, look how your first marriage turned out."

Retaliation was swift and completely enjoyable.

We took time to have a nice lunch at the hotel before we finally hit the road. J.X. once again volunteered to drive, and I was happy to leave it to him.

"I had a feeling that second drive was going to be too much for your back," he said.

Somehow when J.X. mentioned my bad back, I didn't feel defensive as I had when Jerry brought it up. Which was funny because being the robust, virile type, it would have been reasonable for J.X. to expect—or at least wish for—the same macho behaviors out of me. But not only did he not make me feel guilty, he was easy-going about the migraines and the bad back and the various little aches and pains I entertained. He was genuinely kind.

And kindness was probably about as promising an indicator in a potential partner as you could hope for.

J.X. turned on the CD player and, as Jack Johnson once more launched into "You and Your Heart," smiled at me. The littlest things seemed to reassure him, make him happy.

I shook my head, but I could see my smiling reflection in the side window.

During the drive J.X. talked mostly about the convention. He'd had a busy and productive weekend. I listened absently. I was thinking about Ladas. Had he managed to pick my trail up after Paso Robles? Was he following our car right now? Or was he waiting for us back in San Francisco? I had no doubt that sooner or later he was going to pop up again. But to what end? What the hell did he want?

I didn't see how he could believe I had possession of the coins. On the other hand, Ingrid Edwards had thought it was a possibility. Unless she had some other reason for getting inside my house. But what other reason? The whole thing was so bizarre.

I sighed.

J.X. broke off what he was saying to ask, "Is your back hurting? You want to stop and stretch your legs?"

"Not yet. I can wait till Wooster when we stop to pick up my china."

"Something's bothering you. You've been frowning for the last twenty miles."

"This relates to another pain in the ass."

J.X. gave a half laugh. "What's that?"

"Well, I don't want to alarm you. I don't want to alarm myself. But I think there's a possibility I might have acquired a stalker."

The car swerved, righted itself. J.X. said, "A stalker as in…"

"As in, if he isn't, I'm going to feel horrible—as well as self-obsessed—for saying any of this." I proceeded to give him the whole account of my so-called relationship with Jerry Knight.

J.X. heard me out in silence. Up to the point where he said in flabbergasted tones, "You let him inside the *house*?"

"Sort of. Yes. I'm not sure how it happened really. It's not like me."

"That's an understatement. You. The guy who wanted me to tell everyone you're now officially a recluse. *You* invited him into the house? When you were there alone? When anything could have happened to you and I wouldn't have known for *days* that anything was wrong?"

"I kind of wish you wouldn't put it like that. Anyway, when I let him in the first time I wasn't afrai—" I stopped but we both heard the word I had tried not to say.

J.X. said quietly, too calmly, "What did he do that made you afraid?"

"Nothing. That was the wrong word. I'm a little uneasy, that's all. And that's probably mostly to do with all the other stuff happening. Beck Ladas. *That* guy, I'm afraid of."

J.X. said in that same ultra-restrained tone, "What did Knight do to make you so uneasy?"

"It's not any one thing. It's…"

"A pattern of behavior," he finished bleakly.

"Yeah. That's it. Any one of those encounters would be harmless, normal. But when you string them all together… But then I'm also probably influenced by what Emmaline told me. And that's really unfair because she's not sure Jerry was the kid involved—in fact, she can't even remember the entire story."

"You know how people get into trouble, Kit?" J.X. asked.

It was rhetorical. We'd had this discussion before in the context of writing realistic crime fiction, but I answered anyway. "They ignore their instincts."

"Correct. When the average citizen is confronted with a dangerous situation, he ignores the instinct telling him to flee or fight. He doesn't want to overreact and look foolish or make a scene and be embarrassed or be rude. He takes too long to process what's happening. The predator already has a plan. The victim is running to catch up from the very beginning."

"I know." That lecturing tone put my back up. But then I glanced at his hands on the steering wheel and saw that J.X. was gripping so tightly his knuckles were white. I remembered that he had firsthand knowledge of the awful things people could do to each other. Plus a writer's imagination. Probably the worst of both worlds.

I said, "Between the move and finding a body in the basement, I was off-balance. That's the only explanation I have."

"You don't have to explain." As if he hadn't been gasping a request for an explanation a couple of minutes earlier. "I should have cancelled that damn conference. I knew it wasn't fair leaving you to deal with everything."

"Come on," I said awkwardly. "Other than finding a notorious art thief dead in the basement—"

"But the next time Jerry Knight rings the doorbell, he's going to be talking to me."

I spluttered a laugh of protest. J.X. threw me another of those grim looks. "I'm serious. You don't know what you're dealing with, Kit."

"Neither do you, seeing that you haven't met him yet."

Irritatingly, he did not answer.

* * * * *

We reached Wooster about three.

Ma's Diner was of the old-fashioned truck stop variety. A low, rambling white-washed building from the 1940s, surrounded by cacti and some thirsty-looking scrub oaks. A row of dusty pickups were lined up in front of a hitching post. Several big rigs were parked in front and in back of the building.

We pulled under the meager shade of the scrawny oaks and got out. The air smelled hot and dusty.

"Not much to see," J.X. remarked as we walked around the building.

I had to agree. While the place wasn't bustling on a Tuesday afternoon, it was busy enough. It wouldn't be easy to break into anyone's vehicle without being spotted, let alone break into a padlocked big rig truck. Even parked behind the building, it was hard to see how anyone could have gotten into the back of the moving van, emptied out a crate of china—that *had* to have been a noisy process—and replaced its contents with a dead body. And no one the wiser?

Especially given the long row of picture windows along the back of the building.

Had Movers and Shakers been part of the plan after all?

"Let's go inside and ask around," J.X. said. He spoke with the assurance of a guy used to having all his questions answered. I wanted to point out that he didn't have a badge anymore, but I'd have been talking to the thin, dry air.

It was cool and noisy inside the diner. A jukebox played western music. Big ceiling fans shuffled French fry-scented air around the long rooms. A couple of cowboys sat at the lunch counter, eating pie and chatting with a waitress old enough to be Ma herself. The main room had plenty of roomy booths, a number of them filled by weary-looking men wearing baseball caps and T-shirts with slogans such as *Mother Trucker* and *18 Wheeler Heart Stealer.*

The adjoining dining room, which looked out over the back parking lot, was empty of customers and roped off.

I met J.X.'s gaze. "I guess that explains that. Plus it's noisy as hell in here. You can't hear anything from outside."

"But no one could anticipate the back room would be empty. You can't see through those windows from outside unless you walked right up to them."

"You're presupposing there was a plan."

J.X. asked, "What do you presuppose?"

"If there was a plan, it was the worst plan in the world. Which makes me think there was no plan. This person or persons unknown were just winging it."

He frowned. The concept of "winging it" was alien to his nature. Alien to mine too, but like that other Holmes fellow said: *When you have eliminated the impossible, whatever remains, however improbable, must be the truth.*

No one could have come up with a plan that bad. Therefore, there was no plan. There was only confusion and chaos. Which meant…what? I didn't know. But desperate people scrambling to save themselves was always a dangerous situation.

J.X. suggested we get something cold to drink, so we ordered the "world famous" chocolate ice cream sodas and drank them sitting at one of the gray Formica tables. Always a stickler for details, before the aged waitress walked away, J.X. confirmed that the back dining room was only open on weekends.

"Well, that's a couple of questions answered," I said.

He nodded.

"Did you like being a cop?" I asked, tearing the paper wrapper off my straw.

J.X.'s brows rose in surprise. "Yeah, at first I did. I liked thinking I was making the world a better place, a safer place."

"But?"

His mouth twisted. "It changes you. You get jaded. You see the worst of people. And not just the public, unfortunately."

"But you liked working with Izzie Jones?"

"Oh yeah. Izzie was the best partner you could ask for." He smiled reminiscently.

"Public servant. That's a tricky concept."

"It is. Yes. Unfortunately, not everyone attracted to law enforcement gets it." He was still smiling, though his gaze was curious. "What brought this on? You've never asked about my LEO background before."

"Not even when we first met?"

He shook his head, and now the curve of his mouth was definitely wry. "Definitely not then. You did *not* want to talk that weekend."

I winced inwardly. "I know why I latched onto you at that conference, but what the hell were *you* thinking?"

His attention seemed to be entirely on scooping the ice cream out of the fizzy soda. He said, "That I wanted you. More than I'd ever wanted anything or anyone in my life."

I didn't know what to say. He looked up, laughed at my expression, but it was a short laugh.

"You were still a cop. Your book wasn't out yet. *You* weren't even out yet." He met my gaze and I said, "I was paying that much attention."

J.X. nodded, conceding a point to me. He said, "The first time I saw you, you were sitting on a panel. You and Mindy Newburgh and a couple of upcoming bad boys. The debate was whether cozies or noir fiction was the more unrealistic. You were a little bit smashed, but you were skewering those hardboiled guys, and even though I was on their side, I kept laughing at every damn thing you said. So afterwards I followed you to the bar and I picked you up."

"Excuse me. I think I picked *you* up," I said.

"Exactly. And over the course of that weekend, I fell in love with you."

"More fool you," I said quietly.

"Hey." He nudged my foot with his own. "It all worked out in the end."

I smiled. "Indeed it did. Thanks largely to our no returns and no exchanges policy."

J.X. just shook his head.

After the ice cream sodas, we continued into Wooster and picked up my china at Dolls and Doodads. The helium-voiced Cindy Spann turned out to be a very tall, very thin woman in pink overalls. She helped J.X. carry the boxes of my remaining china to the car, thanked us—without any hint of irony—for our business and directed us back to the main highway.

After the revelations of the truck stop diner, I was out of chit chat. J.X. seemed to be in a reflective mood, so the next few miles passed in silence until he turned on the radio. Nine hours is a long drive. It's a long time to be stuck in a confined space with another person. J.X. and I had never spent nine hours in a car before. But I didn't mind the silence. It felt comfortable. I thought that perhaps that was one of the first tests of a relationship: the realization that you were still happy to be with someone even when you didn't have anything to say to him.

We took breaks. We stopped for more cold drinks and to stretch our legs, but after the six hour mark, my back began to make its displeasure known. It started with that too-familiar burning sensation between my shoulder blades. I shifted around and it eased up, but before long the burn was back and my right leg was starting to tingle.

When I tried to get more comfortable, it felt like all the links of my spine were being pried apart, and I sucked in a loud breath.

"You okay?" J.X. asked.

"Yep." I put my seat back as flat as I could get it.

"Should we stop somewhere? We can get a motel for the night."

"I just want to get home."

I listened to the echo of my words with surprise. *Home.* Yes, somehow the house on Chestnut Lane felt like home now. At least compared to the burnt and barren middle of I-5.

"Tell me if you need to stop."

I closed my eyes. Nodded.

I felt the car lunge ahead as J.X. pressed down on the gas. He drove fast, but he drove well. I was never nervous with him behind the wheel, which was saying a lot because following the accident in Nitchfield I had trouble getting in any car I wasn't driving.

We hadn't had a lot of sleep the night before and I managed to doze off a couple of times, but the second time I woke up, my back was spasming.

I got out, "Can we stop?"

"Yep. Hang on, honey." J.X. took the next exit. Overhead, gray twilight and a handful of faint stars swung past as he pulled onto a side road. I gritted my teeth as the car bounced over what felt like a series of potholes and patches in the asphalt. Through the side window I could see faded yellow and black cubes topped by ragged red pennants spelling out the word M.O.T.E.L. And right below, a giant red arrow with white letters reading ENTRANCE aimed skyward.

At last the car came to a stop. J.X. turned off the ignition, got out and came round, opening my door.

I said tersely, "Just…give me a minute."

He hesitated, but then walked away. I put my hands over my face and did some deep breathing. When I was sure I could get up without screaming, I grabbed the door frame and inched onto my hip, trying to lever myself out of the car without triggering another spasm.

I made it to my feet and hung on the open door. We appeared to be in the courtyard of an abandoned motel.

To my right was a closed—permanently—gas station. To my left was a crumbled white fence around an empty swimming pool. It reminded me of a dead blue whale. In the center of the courtyard was a square of dead roses and broken blue-and-orange tiles surrounding a large and very dry fountain topped by a dilapidated statue of the Virgin Mary.

My astonished gaze traveled to the buildings themselves, a two-story orange and brown L-shaped bastardized cross between 1960s Googie and the early Spanish missions.

This peculiar oasis was the only sign of civilization—I use the term facetiously—as far as the eye could see. Beyond a gnarled and crooked line of dead cypress, there was only wilderness and freeway.

A tumbleweed rolled past, then seemed to change direction as though having second thoughts.

J.X. walked over to meet me. He looked worried and I tried to smile.

The effect must have been alarming because his jaw took on a steely line. "What do you need, Kit? What will help?"

"A hot bath, a bottle of aspirin and a sharp razor blade ought to do it." At his expression, I added, "Kidding. I'm a kidder."

"You want me to get a room here?"

"Here?" I gazed in horror at the dark windows and peeling doors. "You mean it's open?"

"Yeah, it's open. Look."

I looked and a neon sign had just blinked on with the words Dew Drop Inn.

"Macabre," I said. "Very macabre."

"See? The lights are on in the front office. They're open for business."

"What business would that be? Highway robbery and murder?"

He opened his mouth and I said, "You notice there are no cars here, right? Other than ours? No cars. No lights. No humans."

"They've got a satellite dish."

"The better to radio the mother ship. No, I think not. Saddle up, amigo. My back is healed. It's a miracle." I pointed at the statue of the Blessed Mother.

It was like I was talking to myself. Per usual. J.X. was saying soothingly, "Let me get you settled and then I'll head back down the highway. I saw a drugstore a few miles back."

"Me settled and this motel are two things that don't go together. It's like vodka and Veronal. Or Neanderthals and Neiman Marcus. It's never going to end well. We saw *Vacancy*, remember? We both know what happens if we spend the night here."

J.X. gave a twisted smile, but he said, "Kit, there's no way you can take another two hours in the car. And no way I can take another two hours of watching you try to handle that much pain."

I won't deny that my stomach heaved at the thought. But I swallowed that unmanly reaction and said, "I just need to walk around a little."

"Walk around? You can't let go of the car door. I'm going to have to carry you to the room."

"Thank you, Rhett, but I'm just resting before I take my afternoon constitutional."

J.X. shook his head. "Come on. I'm sure it's not as bad as it looks."

"I'm sure it's worse. At least out here there's fresh air. Not counting the carbon monoxide drifting from the freeway. Seriously, I don't want to spend the night here. I can feel things crawling on me already."

No lie. I slapped at a mosquito.

"We don't have to spend the night. You can take a hot shower and stretch out for a bit while I get you some painkillers. And then we'll start home. How's that?"

I stared at the Dew Drop Inn sign. The first D was shorting out. *Ew.* That pretty much summed it up. But J.X. was right. I had to lie flat for a while. Not to mention, the very smell of the car interior was making me nauseous.

I said reluctantly, "I just want to wake up in my own bed tomorrow—not roasting on a spit in some half ape-creature's lair."

J.X. laughed. "Deal."

He gave my hand clutching the car door a quick, reassuring squeeze and went in to the front office to book a room.

I took a few hobbling steps around the courtyard, taking pains not to fall over any broken tiles. In the deepening gloom, the Virgin Mary's painted eyes seemed to follow me. She looked like she was trying to warn me without giving herself away to her captors.

J.X. came back with a room key—literally a metal key attached to an orange plastic tag. "We're all set," he said with what I felt was supreme obliviousness. "What do you need from the car?"

"Extreme and illegal speeds as it carries us from this place of doom. Other than that, nothing. We're not unpacking. We're not staying."

"Honey, I know. But...maybe you'd like to change your shirt or something?"

He had placed a supporting arm around my waist. I drew back to stare at him. "Change my shirt? What the hell is wrong with my shirt?"

Even in the failing light, I could see his confusion. "Nothing. I don't know. I just thought maybe you'd be more comfortable—"

"If you're hitting on me *now*, then I've got to tell you your timing has reached an all-time low. And if you're not hitting on me, remind me what division you worked for again? Fashion police?"

"No, of course not. I just don't know how—I just want you to be comfortable."

"Then hurry back and rescue me," I said tartly. "And if someone tries to tell you I checked out while you were gone, it's a damned lie. Unless by *checked out* they mean died, which will probably be true. In that case, you'll no doubt find me cocooned in the banquet hall with all the other victims. Sorry, *guests*."

I'm not sure if he was laughing or sobbing, but by the time we reached the room he seemed decidedly out of breath. He unlocked the door, turned the light on—a bulb immediately blew in the lamp by the bed.

"Oh God. J.X...."

"Here. Let's try this." J.X. flipped another switch and a light in the alcove next to the bathroom offered feeble gray illumination. I stared at our reflection in the mirror over the sink counter. My hair was standing up in tufts and my eyes looked like two black circles in my white face. Even J.X. looked a little worn around the edges.

While I hung onto the door frame for support, he went over to the single full-sized bed and yanked back the blue-and-green bedspread and the blankets. "You don't want to lie down on that. The sheets will be cleaner."

"Ha! You think people come here for *sex*?"

He went into the bathroom and I heard the protest of rarely used plumbing, followed by a burst of water.

J.X. reappeared. "Good water pressure anyway, and it's nice and hot."

I sighed and carefully, painfully began to pull up my T-shirt. He joined me, helping me wriggle out of the soft cotton.

"What kind of painkillers do you want? Is there anything you can't take?"

"No. Grab one of everything. I have a high tolerance. And if you want to get me a couple of those little ready-made cocktails, I won't object."

"Pills and booze? *I* sure as hell will object."

"Fine. Whatever. Just hurry back." I unbuttoned my jeans. I was surprised when he turned my face to his and kissed me. I was even more surprised that I felt that kiss. Felt it and was even comforted by the quick, warm press of his mouth to mine.

"I'll make it fast. Try and rest, okay?"

"Okay. But if you do love me, hurry the hell back. I am seriously freaked out about this place. Don't be misled by my brave front."

He managed not to snicker in my face.

I locked the door behind him and shuffled into the bathroom. One glimpse of the grungy green tiles and a ghastly chartreuse shower curtain that surely came from the Martha Stewart for *Psycho* Collection was all I needed. I kept my eyelids in squint position as I rinsed a couple of dead spiders down the tub drain and then painfully stepped in. The bottom of the tub was slick, though probably not from soap, and I had to keep one hand on the shower head to steady myself—a position which hurt like hell.

I swore for a couple of minutes, then I cried for a couple of minutes, and then the heat finally began to help. At last I turned the water off, shoved back the curtain and gingerly dried off using a nubby gray towel.

It hurt less putting my clothes on than it had taking them off, so that was a good sign. I hobbled over to the bed and eased myself down, lying crossways across its mushy mattress. The sheets smelled musty, though there was a faint and fond memory of bleach in the worn threads.

I closed my eyes. Not because I thought I could fall asleep. It was just easier not looking at my surroundings. To distract myself I tried to think of a single word that best described my feelings.

Poorly was too quaint. It sounded almost cozy. *Ah'm feeling poorly, could y'all make me a cup of cocoa?*

Miserable somehow seemed to carry an element of personal responsibility; like if I was miserable, I'd probably played a part in achieving that end.

Wretched. Ah. There we go. *Wretched* pretty much summed it up. Although, in fairness, the wet heat had helped and stretching out was a definite improvement.

I was just starting to drift off when the motel door burst open.

Literally burst open.

It flew off its flimsy hinges, tore the chain from the frame and fell flat like a hard welcome mat.

Beck Ladas stepped into the room.

CHAPTER TWELVE

Pain will set you free.

I don't mean agonizing-you-think-you're-dying pain. I mean the level of pain where it hurts so much you just don't care what anyone—including yourself—says or thinks or does. This was the place where Ladas found me. The place where pain-fueled anger and outrage outstripped fear and commonsense.

I shot up off the bed, shouting, "What the fuck do you *want* with me?"

But maybe this was how most people greeted Ladas, because he didn't noticeably pause—at least beyond trying to pinpoint me in the gloom of the room. He certainly didn't speak. He spotted me, charged in, and I grabbed the lamp from the bedside table and tried to hurl it at him.

It was bolted down, so that went nowhere fast.

Ladas grabbed for me, but his foot slipped on the cheap, shiny material of the spilled bedspread, and he went down on one knee. I rebounded off the other side of the bed and ran for the doorway. I was aware that Ladas jumped up after me and I heard his foot crunch through the plywood face of the fallen door. This was followed by what sounded like the crash of a sled hitting the wall of the building, so maybe Ladas was trying to get through the entrance while still wearing the door.

I didn't know, I didn't care. That initial burst of fury had faded in the face of the terrified realization that this guy was seriously nuts. I had no doubt, as I sprinted across the dusty courtyard, bare feet slapping bits of stone and broken tile, that I was running for my life.

I headed for the reception area and the front desk. People. Phones. Plus if any room in this complex had a decent lock on a decent door, it would be there. I passed the fountain and Ladas bellowed, "You fucking rabbit!"

So it could talk. It was, in theory, a sentient being.

Lights were going on around us. A couple of doors opened and then just as hastily slammed shut.

Just another night at Motel 666.

Something boomed behind me like a bolt of thunder touching down—or a house coming in for a landing. I couldn't help it. I looked over my shoulder and I saw Ladas had hurled my motel room door at me.

Happily he missed. Instead, the door hit the fountain, taking a piece out of the bowl, and crashed to the ground.

"I don't know what you want!" It's not so much that I was trying to communicate with him, as thinking aloud.

I could have saved my breath though because he wasn't into dialog. He put his head down and came after me like a linebacker hoping to make the tackle of his career.

I turned to run and, out of the corner of my eye, caught sight of a pair of swift approaching headlights. High beams swept over the courtyard, exposing the flattened door and Ladas, still coming after me, eyes shining with a crazy glitter.

That glitter was actually the glare of the headlights blinding him for a crucial couple of seconds.

My BMW screeched to a stop and there was a thud as Ladas did not do the same. I had never heard a sweeter sound in my life. I skidded to a standstill, turning in time to see him mid-bounce off the side of the car. He disappeared from view.

The driver's door flew open and J.X. jumped out.

"Kit!" He was a white form in the dusk, but even from this distance I could see the dangerous line of his body: pugnacious jaw, broad shoulders squared, hands in fists. Ready for action. Where the normal person would have been in retreat, he was preparing to charge.

I raced back to him. "Be careful," I gasped. "He's crazy. He's insane. Don't go near him."

J.X.'s hands closed on my arms. "You're okay? He didn't hurt you?"

I nodded, then shook my head, still trying to catch my breath.

J.X. tried to move me aside, putting me out of harm's way. Or trying to. I was hanging onto him for fear he'd go after Ladas. He had no idea what he was dealing with. From the far side of the BMW, Ladas stood up, shaking his head like one of those overenthusiastic bulls in a bullfight after it hits the arena wall.

He eyed us warily. I say *us*, but the wariness was all for J.X. who was playing a demented game of slaps with me as I tried to hang onto him and he tried to get free without resorting to punching me.

"Kit, stop!" Then J.X. ordered Ladas, "Stay right where you are."

Which must be code for "run like hell," because that was exactly what Ladas did. He turned and ran. Past the closed gas station, through the broken fence and into the desert.

"Call the cops," J.X. called to the skinny, elderly man in Batman boxer shorts and a half-buttoned plaid shirt who had hurried out of the reception area.

The man put his hands up as though already anticipating a frisking. "Cops! You're crazy. We don't want the cops out here!"

"For Christ's sake. The cops don't give a damn about you smoking pot—"

"No. No cops." The innkeeper was backing up into the reception area. He pulled the door closed behind him and lowered the shade. The lights went off.

"*I'm* crazy?" J.X. turned to me. "What. The. Fuck."

"We're going," I said. "We're going now."

"We can't just—"

"We can. Oh yes, we can. Because that crazy freak is going to follow us and Izzie can capture him at our house. Or shoot him. I don't care." I gestured wildly at the now dark motel. "For God's sake. Look around you. We're in Zombieville. Any minute the doors will open and they'll pour out of the building. Stop threatening to call the cops. Let's go now while we can."

"Kit."

I yelled, *"I can't take anymore!"* That was the truth, though I'd have preferred not to spell it out at the top of my lungs.

Into the reverberating hush that followed my words, the head cracked off the Virgin Mary and fell into the dry bowl of the fountain.

Wordless, J.X. stared at me, though I can't imagine I was more than a vibrating blur in the gloom. He said quietly, "All right. Get in the car. Where are your shoes?"

I said, trying hard for control though I couldn't stop my voice shaking, "I don't care about my fucking shoes. I *just* want to go home. Please."

"We're going home. Get in the car."

I crawled into the car. There was a white paper sack with a selection of pain relievers. In a few minutes the adrenaline was going to wear off and I was going to be in a huge amount of pain. I mixed and matched and then dry-swallowed. There were several other goodies: a tube of Biofreeze, a Salonpas pain patch, a jar of Capsaicin cream, and a small packet of Hershey's kisses. My throat closed. I had to press the heels of my hands to my eyes and do more deep breathing exercises.

Someone tried my door handle and I nearly hit the ceiling of the car.

"It's me, Kit," J.X. said unnecessarily. Except—clearly—it wasn't unnecessary.

I fumbled with the door lock and J.X. handed me my shoes and my glasses.

"Are you buckled in?" He ran his hand down the shoulder strap of my seatbelt, feeling for the latch plate, and I grabbed the belt and jammed it in the lock.

"Yes. Roger. All systems go. So can we? Go?"

He shut my door, went around to his side, and to my abject relief started the engine.

I could have wept with relief as the car roared into healthy life. J.X. performed a neat arc around the fountain and we bumped out of the driveway and back onto the pothole-riddled highway. In a couple of minutes we were back on the freeway. As the car picked up speed, it felt like we were flying through enemy lines making our way to safety and sanity and home.

J.X. had his cell phone out and was talking to Izzie. I heard the words, but the meaning barely registered. I kept reliving those moments when the motel room door burst open. Incredible to think that very morning we had been fooling around in that comfortable four-poster bed at the Langham Huntington. It seemed like a lifetime ago.

"He's okay. Just shaken up," J.X. said.

My stomach bubbled unhappily as the cocktail of pain relievers began to dissolve into the existing churning mess of anxiety and stress. I really hoped I wasn't going to throw up. I hated to put that in-sickness-and-in-health thing to the test so soon.

J.X. said, "Yeah. Thanks. Talk to you tomorrow."

He clicked off, dropped his phone into the empty cup holder. For a time there was only the slap of the tires and the crinkling of the paper bag of pain relievers I clutched like a talisman.

Now that there was a comfortable span of miles between us and Our Lady of the Severed Head, the silence began to prey on me. I knew what J.X. had to be thinking and I didn't blame him.

I said in a tone I wanted to sound light but came out brittle, "It's okay. I was only kidding about our return policy. I fully understand if you want a refund on your ticket."

He didn't glance away from the road. "What are you talking about?"

"I can't help it," I said. "I'm not brave, I'm not tough, I'm not like you. I'm scared out of my wits. I don't know why that maniac is chasing me. I don't know what's happening. And I'm aware—and ashamed, believe me—that I'm not dealing with it well."

J.X. made an impatient sound. What he said was, "How's your back?"

I stared at him in disbelief. "My *back*?"

"There's a rest stop in about ten minutes. Can you hold out that long?"

"Did you even hear me?"

"Kit." One word, but there seemed to be a volume of meaning in that single syllable. And what the hell was that tone? Patient, certainly—which was sort of annoying—but affectionate too. Understanding. That was it. And was there anything more aggravating than someone being understanding while you were having a nervous breakdown? And yet, somehow it wasn't aggravating. It was…okay. Maybe more than okay.

I said huffily, "Am I to understand you don't want your money back?"

J.X. laughed. "Really? With everything going on you're trying to break up with me *now*?"

"I'm not trying to break up with you. It's just that I understand if you want out."

"What did Ladas say to you?"

"Huh?"

"He must have said something when he burst in. What did he say?"

"Fee-fi-fo-fum. He didn't say anything. No, wrong. He called me a rabbit. A fucking rabbit. Those were his exact words."

"He didn't say anything else?"

"Not that I noticed."

J.X. went back to thinking whatever it was that made his profile so steely.

"I keep trying to make sense of this, but I just don't understand what's happening." It was beginning to be my theme song.

J.X. said, "I think we have to assume that neither does he."

"What?"

"Ladas. I think he's latched onto you because you're the only bit of real information he has. His brother ended up dead in our house, so you're his starting point."

"Great." I thought it over. "Then he'd have to be someone who doesn't read and has subpar comprehension skills."

"Yes. I'd say so. No disrespect to Miss Butterwith, but there are very few true criminal masterminds out there. And this guy seems dumber than most."

I said testily, "There are no criminal masterminds in the Butterwith books. For your information."

"Sorry."

"In fact, the serial killer in this last book of yours comes a lot closer to evil mastermind than anything I ever wrote."

"Ouch. You're probably right. Anyway, what you said at the hotel makes perfect sense. Ladas is fixated on you. So it makes sense to let him come after you where we—the police, I mean—can control the scenario."

"I don't think I quite put it like that," I objected. "I don't have any intention of being bait for a psycho."

J.X. said with genuine amusement, "Like I would ever allow that."

I raised my brows at the unconscious arrogance of *allow that*, but it was sort of reassuring too.

There was a catering van at the rest stop and J.X. bought an armload of ice cold water bottles. By then my back pain was like a third presence in the car, but J.X. grew so alarmed by my attempt to take more tablets, that I resolved to tough it out.

Until such time as he left me alone in the car again.

"Believe me, if I was seriously trying to kill myself, you'd know it," I groused as he smoothed a gob of Capsaicin cream over my back and then set about massaging it in. My door was open and I was seated sideways, leaning out, head in my hands, elbows on my knees, glaring at anyone who happened to wander past our car. Not that many people were wandering past at this time of night.

J.X.'s strong, capable hands finally came to a stop. He lightly squeezed my shoulders. "How's that?"

"Fine. Now if you would just tape that pain patch between my shoulder blades…"

Once again I had tapped into the wellspring of his disapproval. "You can't combine all these different things!"

"Of course I can."

"No, you sure as hell can't. Kit, do you have any idea how many people kill themselves self-medicating OTC? Do you even bother to read the labels on these medications you're popping like candy?"

"I'd have to put my glasses on." I sighed and tugged my T-shirt back into place. "I told you I have a high tolerance."

"Tell that to your liver."

"You tell it to my liver," I returned shortly, pulling my door shut. I scooted my seat backwards and gingerly leaned back. I did actually feel a little better. Or maybe I was just too tired to care anymore.

"The best thing would be for you to sleep." J.X. started the engine.

I snorted. "Believe me, I appreciate your feelings. And I'm going to do my best to accommodate. For both our sakes."

I closed my eyes.

The next time I opened them we had miraculously arrived at our home port and J.X. was trying to coax me back to consciousness.

"I'm awake, I'm awake," I said, waving him off.

He drew back. "That's a relief. I was beginning to think you ODed."

"Funny." I sat up and began the painful process of crawling out of the car. "It's better if you don't try and help," I told him as he hovered.

"I don't see how that can be true," he muttered.

"That's your LEO background talking." I got to my feet and I can't deny it was ridiculously comforting when he put his arms around me and let me lean into him. He kissed my hairline and my ear and then said in a different sort of voice, "Did you leave a light on?"

I nodded. "It's on a timer."

He relaxed and kissed me again.

But even with the preventative measures I'd taken, I was prepared for anything as J.X. unlocked the front door and we stepped inside the cheerfully lit foyer.

The chandelier sparkled overhead, lighting the polished staircase and gleaming floors. The square mirror over the half-moon table against the wall offered a glimpse of our wary faces.

But no need for wariness. The house on Chestnut Lane was just as I had left it Sunday afternoon.

"I can't believe this," J.X. said, letting go of me and walking into the front parlor. *"Kit."*

"I know. But I had to start somewhere and I figured we can change anything you don't like."

His voice floated from the next room. "No. God, no. It looks great in here. I only mean you didn't have to take all this on yourself." He reappeared in the tall doorway. "I never expected this." He looked peculiarly moved. Who knew unpacking all those boxes of books would be viewed as a declaration of devotion?

"I didn't hang any pictures. I figured we needed to do that together. Except upstairs. There's kind of a sort of present for you."

His eyes lit and I said hastily, "No, not that kind of present. Actually, it's really nothing."

But of course he went pounding up the staircase, and I had to follow, clinging to the railing and trying to get him to downsize his expectations.

"Anyway, if you don't like it, we can hang something else there." I reached the door of our bedroom to find J.X. standing in front of the fireplace, gazing at the Allan P. Friedlander painting of *A Good Year*.

He turned to smile at me and my heart jumped at the suspicious shininess in his eyes.

I said severely, "You're a very sentimental guy, you know that?"

"Me?" J.X. was still smiling as he came to meet me.

I spent most of Wednesday in bed with a heating pad and my laptop. "I'm taking a Mental Health day," I informed J.X. "For the next twenty-four hours I get to stay in bed and drive everyone else crazy."

"Are these a regular occurrence?" J.X. inquired.

"They didn't use to be. I can't speak for the future."

"I see. Do you need anything? Should I stock up on tonic water? Frozen pizzas?"

"And if you're going to be sarcastic about my medical condition you can stay the hell out of my bedroom."

"Uh…"

"Our bedroom."

He grinned. "Okay. Yell if you need anything."

"Trust me on that score."

A good night's sleep on an excellent mattress and the long, pleasurable backrub J.X. had treated me to that morning had gone a long way to restoring me to health. Not that I felt like dwelling on such unpleasantness.

I read a bit of Jo Nesbø's *The Devil's Star.*

In the gap lay a five-kroner coin bearing a profile of King Olav's head and the date: 1987, the year before it had fallen out of the carpenter's pocket. But these were the boom years; a great many attic flats had needed to be built at the drop of a hat and the carpenter had not bothered to look for it.

More coins. I sighed and clicked out of the book. Anyway, why had I bought all these books that had to be read on my laptop? I hated ebooks. They took all the romance out of reading. Except on moving day. Then they were a miracle of technology. But the rest of the time I wanted paper and pages and interesting covers. I wanted something I could drop in the bath or forget in the garden for a week without doing serious damage to my credit cards.

"What did you want for lunch?" J.X. asked when he appeared a few hours later.

"I don't care. I'm too upset to eat. What is there?" I frowned, eyeing him. "And what is so funny about that question?"

J.X. sobered. "Nothing. Are you in the mood for anything in particular?"

I gave it some thought.

He prompted kindly, "Something frozen or in a cardboard box, I assume? Given the contents of the refrigerator."

"Unfrozen and out of the cardboard box is usually preferable. Do we have any egg rolls left?"

"I'm sure that can be arranged."

I waved a vague hand. "Whatever."

That was intended as dismissal, but he came over to the bed and sat down on the side, putting a companionable arm around my shoulders. "What are you doing?"

"I am exercising my little gay cells, *mon ami*. Look. Beck Ladas has a Facebook page."

Know thy enemy. I had spent most of the morning finding out what I could about Beck. What that amounted to was the story of a not very bright guy with a history of brute violence. Aside from a shared last name, about the only thing he had in common with his older brother was their inability, or maybe simply disinterest, in earning an honest living. I gathered from a number of misspelled Facebook rants, Beck had been in and out of jail most of his life.

"If he wasn't chasing me all over the state, I'd be tempted to think he killed Elijah," I told J.X.

J.X. studied the page. "He has four hundred and fifty-two Facebook friends?"

"All female. And look at this. He got a new tattoo." I pointed to a gruesome selfie featuring a blood-dotted green snake.

J.X. did a double take and peered closer. "Wait a minute. Is that his…" His voice died and he swallowed.

"That's right, dude. He got a snake for his snake."

"*Madre mia.* That must have hurt."

"He says right here he's got plenty of ladies to kiss it better for him."

J.X.'s expression grew still more revolted.

"He likes the neo-Nazi party. Good to know. And he collects model trains. That's sort of sweet, you must admit." I glanced at him. "What have you been doing all morning?"

"Follow-up from the conference. I've got a ton of email. Setting up my office."

I grunted.

"Rachel called."

"Tell her I died."

He said after a moment, "You want to talk about it?"

"Not really."

He gave my shoulders a squeeze. "You know, there isn't any pressure on you."

"Yeah, there is."

"If there is, you're putting the pressure on yourself, Kit."

I sighed. "You don't know what you're talking about." He didn't answer, and I said, "I'm sorry, but that's the truth. We're not at the same place in our careers. You don't understand what it's like for me. Your star is rising."

"I guess what I mean is, this is your chance to decide what you really want for the future. You can write anything you want. Or nothing. You don't have to decide anything right away. I can carry us both for a while."

"I don't need you to carry me," I said shortly.

"That's not what I mean. I only mean…"

I waited and he said simply, "I just want you to be happy, Kit."

I had to look away.

He kissed the top of my head.

I said gruffly, "I am happy—about us."

I felt his smile. "Are you?"

"Hell yeah. This is me happy. Last night was me unhappy. Notice the difference? It's a lot quieter today."

"Mmhm." He gave me another kiss and rose. "You want anything from the store?"

"I'm fine."

I listened to his footsteps retreating down the staircase and I went back to finding out what I could about the principals in the case. Not that I really knew who all the principals were. There was the gallery owner, John Cantrell, but everything I'd read seemed to indicate he had simply been in the wrong place at the wrong time. There was Alan Lorenson, the owner of the coin collection, but since the collection was not insured, it was hard to see what he had to gain. There was Elijah Ladas who had come out of retirement for one last score—the score that had gotten John Cantrell killed. And then it had gotten Ladas killed. Now Elijah's village idiot of a brother was crashing around in his wake and we'd all be lucky if he didn't kill someone too.

Or, more accurately, someone *else*, because I'd have been willing to bet money, Beck, not Elijah, had killed Cantrell.

There remained at least one other principal. The person who had killed Elijah Ladas. In fact, there were probably two other unknowns because it would have been very difficult, maybe impossible, for one person to cart a corpse the size of Ladas' from car to moving van.

Stupid people committing stupid crimes. Greed and violence. That's all this amounted to. Not a real mystery at all. Miss Butterwith would be disgusted. I was disgusted on her behalf.

I must have dozed off at some point because when I woke it was two o'clock and the house felt very quiet. Listening to that deep and comfortable silence, I deduced that J.X. was still not back yet.

For a few minutes I watched the sunlight sparkling through the French doors. A blue jay landed on the balcony railing, cocked his head as he looked in at me, then flew away.

All at once, I felt much more cheerful. I threw on my bathrobe and went downstairs to find something to eat.

The coffee was perking when the phone rang. I reached for it and then stopped. The answering machine picked up and I listened to Jerry asking if he could bring books over for me to sign that afternoon.

My brief sense of well-being disappeared. Along with my appetite.

The door bell rang. I squinted through the peephole.

I was fully prepared to see Jerry standing there with a guileless expression and an armload of books, but I was wrong.

The figure was female. Dark hair and a sunny-yellow short skirt with matching jacket.

Sydney Nightingale, girl reporter.

CHAPTER THIRTEEN

I'm not sure why I opened the door.

Relief that she wasn't Jerry? Or simple boredom?

Sydney gazed at me—or rather at my sumptuous bathrobe—in surprise. "Hel—oh! I'm sorry. Are you not well?"

"Genius takes its toll. Actually, we got back late last night." I held the door for her and her face lit up in pleased surprise. She slipped inside before I could change my mind.

I shut the door and led the way to the parlor.

"This is nice!" Sydney said, gazing around the long, airy room.

"It needs pictures."

She sat down on a long, elegant sofa that I did not recognize as belonging to either J.X. or myself. When had that been delivered? She held up her phone. "Is it okay if I record our conversation?"

"Is that how it's done these days? On a phone?"

"I'll take notes too, but yes." She showed me a small purple notebook.

"Fine. Whatever." I sat down across from her. I was already regretting the impulse that had me opening the door to her.

"We could just start with something simple," Sydney said. "How do you like San Francisco?"

"I…think I'm going to like it," I said.

She put up a hand, pressed her phone. We listened to my voice repeating doubtfully, "I…think I'm going to like it."

Sydney smiled approvingly. She resumed, "Of course, finding a body wasn't the best introduction you could have had. But you're no stranger to crime. There are your Miss Buttermilk books. Forty-eight at last count."

"Butter*with*," I said.

"I'm sorry." Sydney double-checked her notes. "I have it written down as Buttermilk."

"It's Butterwith."

She made a question mark on her notes and continued blithely, "And there's your amateur sleuthing."

"I'm *not* an amateur sleuth."

"But you've solved two murder cases in the past year."

"It's not how it looks," I said firmly.

"And now you're involved in a third murder case."

"I'm not involved."

"But you did find a body in your basement. The body of the man suspected of robbing the Quercus Gallery of over ten million dollars in rare antique coins."

My gaze landed on the Levenger box with the two Reading Bear bookends, still lying where I'd left it. My stomach knotted. I said, "That was sheer happenstance."

"What did you think when you found the body of Elijah Ladas?"

"That I have terrible luck. And that he had worse luck."

Sydney's brows arched. She glanced back at her notes, "Do the police have any suspects in the case?"

"The police always have suspects."

"Have they given you a hint as to whom they're focusing on?"

"I'm not in the confidence of the police."

Sydney's look was openly skeptical. "It's hard to believe the police wouldn't be working with such a well-known amateur sleuth. On top of that, your partner, J.X. Moriarity, is a former SFPD inspector."

"It would be harder still to believe that the police would take a mystery writer into their confidence. That only happens on TV. Maybe you have me confused with Jessica Fletcher. I have better hair and I do not ride a bicycle."

"If you were working this case, how would you set about solving it?"

"Which case? The case of who killed Ladas? Or the case of the missing coins?"

"Both. Either."

"You know more about it than I do. You reported on the robbery to start with."

She gave me a surprised look. "True. Well, I can tell you what I know. Though Ladas was arrested several times in connection with stolen antiquities, he was never convicted of any crime. He was very proud of the fact that no one was ever harmed in any of his capers."

"Until John Cantrell and Quercus Gallery."

"Yes."

"But that was probably Igor."

She looked blank for a second, then she gave a short laugh. "You mean Beck? Yes. I agree. Murder was never Ladas' style. In fact, he liked posing as a gentleman thief. He had a penchant for fine living and a passion for old coins."

I sniffed. "That sounds like a press release."

"As a matter of fact, he was working on a book about his exploits."

I stared at her. "How do you know that?"

"I interviewed him about a year ago."

She said it so casually. "And he was going to confess in his memoirs to robbing people?"

"Oh well." She wrinkled her nose. "I don't believe he planned on publishing the book right away. Not until the statute of limitations had run out on some of his crimes."

I said gloomily, "It would probably be a bestseller." Sydney was watching me, apparently waiting for me to make some brilliant deduction. I asked, "When did he start working with his younger brother?"

"I don't know that he did. I thought he always worked alone, until I saw that security video tape. But he was getting on. He was in his fifties. That's—"

"Old. For that line of work."

When I didn't continue, she said, "So you must have some theories, right?"

"Wrong."

She laughed. She had a nice laugh. "Come on, Mr. Holmes. You found the body of a famous thief in your own basement. You *have* to be curious about what happened. It's meat and drink for a mystery writer, right?"

"Only if he's on a very strict diet."

"What if Beck killed his brother?"

"No," I said. "I don't buy that. Why would he?"

"Maybe they argued."

"About what?"

Sydney shrugged.

"I don't think so."

She frowned. "Why don't you think so?"

Among other reasons, because if Beck had killed his brother, I couldn't see any point in him harassing and hunting me. He would have to know that my involvement, such as it was, was incidental. But he did not seem to know this. Clearly, he believed I had information he needed. J.X. was right. I was Beck's starting point.

But I wasn't about to share that with Ms. Nightingale.

Naturally she put my reticence down to the wrong thing. "So you *are* working with the police."

"No. I'm really not. It's just that people have to have a reason for killing each other. Even crazy people believe they have a reason."

"You don't know what reason Beck might think he had."

"True."

"Maybe he thought his brother was going to cut him out of his share of their take."

"Well, maybe." That wasn't bad, actually. Except that Beck would know if he had killed his own brother. I kept coming back to that.

"There could be all kinds of reasons for thieves falling out."

"Yes. I agree."

She was frowning again. "But you don't think so."

I shrugged.

I heard the sound of a key in the front door and a moment later J.X., carrying a couple of plastic bags, walked past the doorway. A second later he stepped back into the doorway, eyeing us in surprise.

"Hey," I said.

"Hi there." He put down his bags and walked into the room.

"This is Sydney Nightingale," I said. "She works for KAKE TV."

"*Baywatch News*," J.X. said. "I recognize you. You did the reporting on those wildfires last year." He offered her the smile that launched five hundred thousand bestsellers.

Sydney smiled back as she clicked her phone off. She dropped phone and notebook in her purse, and rose offering her hand to J.X.

"Such a pleasure to meet you, Mr. Moriarity," she said to him. And to me, "See, I promised this would be painless. If you think of anything you'd like to add, you can always reach me here." She handed me her business card again. "Thank you so much for your time, Mr. Holmes. You've made my producer really happy."

"Okay. Well, thank you." I was a little surprised at how fast she had decided to wrap up the interview.

Sydney was already headed for the front door. J.X. saw her out and returned to the parlor where I was absently swinging the tassel on the end of my robe tie.

"I guess I scared her off," he said.

"She did scurry, didn't she? And she didn't bring her photographer with her, so I don't know if her producer is going to be really happy or not."

"She had to know you wouldn't let a photographer in here."

"True."

The doorbell rang. J.X. gave me a quizzical look. "Maybe she remembered something else she wanted to ask you."

I swallowed and said, "Maybe it's Jerry."

J.X.'s face hardened. "I *hope* it's Jerry."

It was not Jerry, it was a shipment from the Anna Hitchcock estate, and I knew at once it had to be the antique writing desk Anna had promised me back in February. I remembered our casual joking and my chest felt tight.

J.X. opened the door for the shipping company and two men in uniforms carried the heavy hand-carved ball and claw piece into the foyer.

J.X. called, "Where do you want this, Kit? In your office?"

"In the fireplace."

"Let's take it upstairs to the guestroom, guys."

I reached down and picked up one of the Reading Bear bookends. I could hear J.X. and the delivery men struggling not to drop the huge antique desk down the staircase.

Footsteps overhead.

Footsteps on the stairs.

The delivery men departed. I called, "I'm going to lie down."

J.X. didn't answer.

I wandered into the kitchen and poured myself a glass of water. I stared out the wall of windows of the breakfast nook.

The phone rang again. I groaned.

From behind me, J.X. said, "Go back to bed. Rest your back. I'll deal with it."

I turned and contemplated him for a long moment. "You'd better be careful, J.X."

"What's the matter?"

"If we're going to live together, you should know that I will take advantage of any and all weaknesses. You have been warned."

He grinned. "Duly noted."

The phone rang for the third time and he winked at me and picked it up. He listened for a moment or two and then said, "He's not available at the moment. Can I take a message?"

I gawked at him.

J.X. covered the mouthpiece and said, "Do you want to go to dinner at Alan Lorenson's?"

"Who?"

"You don't know him?"

I shook my head, but then I remembered. "Wait. *Lorenson?* Yes. When?"

J.X. returned to the phone. "When?" He reported back to me, "Tonight?"

"Tonight?"

"No?"

"No, yes. Yes, I mean."

"Yes?"

I nodded.

"Yes," J.X. said into the mouthpiece.

I listened to the half conversation while J.X. got details and directions. He hung up and said, "Who's Alan Lorenson and why are we having dinner with him?"

I explained who Alan Lorenson was. It took longer to explain why we were having dinner with him, and I'm not sure I convinced either of us.

"Are you sure you want to get any further involved in this?" J.X. asked.

"I think we are involved whether we want to be or not."

Depressingly, he didn't deny it.

I said, "You were gone a while."

"I met Izzie for a late lunch."

I said cautiously, "Oh yes? What did Inspector Jones have to say for himself?"

"Ladas hasn't been back to his apartment. In fact, the last time anyone saw him there was before the gallery robbery. His rent is currently two weeks past due."

"So he's been on the run ever since Cantrell was killed."

"He's been lying low, for sure. He's got a number of lady friends, but so far he hasn't shown up at any of their places."

"Lady friends? Is that official police terminology? And that means what?"

"It could mean we—I mean, SFPD—don't know all his lady friends. Or that he's living out of his car."

Or that one of those other unknown principals in this case was giving him shelter. But I understood why J.X. didn't want to suggest that idea if it hadn't yet occurred to me.

"How the hell hard can it be to catch one not very bright thug? Especially since he seems to be following me everywhere I go? He's probably sitting out front of the house right now."

"He's not sitting out front of the house right now. He's not anywhere in this neighborhood, I can tell you that much. I spent a couple of hours this morning looking for him."

"Oh."

"SFPD has a patrol car driving by every couple of hours. Okay? That alone furnishes a significant deterrent to Ladas trying to contact you again."

"You would think," I said. "I wish I was as sure."

CHAPTER FOURTEEN

Alan Lorenson lived in Oakland, which sounded lovely and rural, but…not so much.

I didn't doubt that the Lorenson mansion was considered an achievement for modern architecture though. At first glance it looked a bit like someone had transported a building from an old mining town to the top of a pristine and carefully landscaped hill. Wings of tinted concrete intersected with cedar sidings stained translucent turquoise. There were a multitude of square, severe, modern windows and coppery, clay tile roofing.

It no doubt cost a fortune and was probably frequently featured in architectural magazines, but I found it ugly and artificial. It made me appreciate the little gem of a house J.X. had found for us. I had never said the words "elegant," or "comfortable" to him. No, I had focused on things like swimming pool, fireplace in bedroom, large backyard, hardwood floors. The Lorenson house had all those things, but I'd have been distressed to find myself living there. J.X. had read between the lines and found a house I could actually love. And if that didn't demonstrate both understanding and…well, simpatico, I didn't know what did.

"What?" he said, meeting my gaze as we stood on the subtly tinted concrete doorstep of the Lorenson house, waiting for someone to answer our knock.

"Nothing."

"Come on. What did you forget?"

"Nothing. I just think you've got good taste in houses. That's all."

"*Oh.*" He reddened as though I'd paid him some extravagant compliment. "Thanks."

I nodded.

The front door opened and a woman in a conservative dark dress opened the door. Clearly a housekeeper and not the lady of the house.

"Mr. Holmes. Mr. Moriarity." There was no question. She knew who we were because only invited guests ever darkened this doorstep.

The housekeeper led the way through large rooms featuring lofty ceilings with skylights, huge windows and rough timber accents. There was what seemed to me a pretentious lack of furniture—and no books—but to each his own.

The housekeeper paused on the threshold of a spacious room and announced in modulated tones, "Mr. Holmes and Mr. Moriarity."

Everyone in the room turned our way. I had been thinking that it would just be us and Lorenson, so I was nonplussed to find a seven-member reception committee.

I spotted Ingrid sitting on the space-age sofa next to a pair of missionaries. Well, okay, that was probably unfair, but I had never seen a couple that better illustrated the term "church-goers." It's not that I don't understand that white oxfords and matching belt have their place, especially when partnering—as these were—a slim lady wearing a beige shirtwaist dress, but somehow I knew that pair had a Bible on their persons at all times. Ingrid looked different too. Her hair was slicked back in an unfrivolous ponytail and she wore a navy-blue dress that looked like the younger sister of the beige woman's ensemble.

A tall, elegant looking older man with snowy-white hair came to meet us. He took both J.X.'s hands in his. "This is a great honor, Mr. Holmes. A great honor."

J.X. looked as close to alarmed as I'd ever seen him. "I'm not Mr. Holmes, sir. *This* is Mr. Holmes."

I smiled politely at Mr. Lorenson.

I had to hand it to Lorenson. He was fast on the recovery. He gave J.X. a final, dismissing squeeze and turned to me, scooping my hands up in his paws. "Mr. Holmes. You look so much younger than I imagined. I can't tell you the joy your books give me."

"Why, thank you." I nobly refrained from looking at J.X.

"I'm so delighted you could accept my invitation. And on such short notice!"

"Well, there you go," I said with my usual *savoir faire*. This is why I don't do a lot of social events.

"Miss Butterwith is wonderful. And Mr. Pinkerton! How I laugh at his adventures." He laughed right then and there, apparently remembering some of those delightful adventures. Then he glanced at J.X. "And do you write too, Mr. Moriarity?"

"Some," J.X. admitted.

"Wonderful. Wonderful." He released my hands and turned to the watchful gathering. "You must meet my family. Not readers, I'm afraid. Not one of them can read."

A tall, blond man who looked like a younger, slimmer version of Lorenson rose. "Father, of course we can read!" He sounded exasperated. I suspected that was how he usually sounded at family gatherings. I felt an instant affinity.

"You're right, Nord," Lorenson said. "It's worse. You choose *not* to read."

Nord looked at me and rolled his eyes. "I know how to read."

"Of course," I said. We shook hands.

Lorenson made the rest of the introductions briskly. Nord was married to Judith, who was a petite and curvy red-head. "I know how to read too," she said. "I just never have time."

"It's okay," I assured her. "I'm not keeping track."

Nord and Judith had two children: Kenneth and Cynthia. Cynthia was a bored-looking college-age kid in a black shift. I recognized Kenneth immediately from a national advertising campaign for peanut butter.

"Hey, you're the 'nutter butter better' guy, right?" I said.

"How did you recognize me without the glob of peanut butter on my nose?" Kenneth replied. He looked like a younger and more handsome version of his father, which meant that he looked like a younger and still more handsome version of his grandfather. Willowy, blond, effortlessly elegant. At least when he wasn't smeared in peanut butter.

I recognized him without the peanut butter because they played those idiotic commercials relentlessly, but I was too polite to say so despite the fact that J.X. thinks I have no social skills.

The churchy couple turned out to be Karla and Lloyd. Karla bore a striking resemblance to the Lorenson men, but frankly so did Lloyd. The matter was settled by Lorenson who introduced Karla as his daughter. "And you've met Ingrid," he added.

Ingrid smiled pallidly and seemed to sink further into the sofa cushions.

Her parents studied her disapprovingly, but their expressions changed the minute Lorenson said, "I must say Ingrid has shown unusual initiative in this matter. In fact, if it had not been for little Ingrid, I'm not sure I'd have hit on this wonderful idea."

"Wonderful idea?" J.X.'s tone was polite.

"Father," Karla began.

"Be quiet, Daughter," Lorenson returned. He said it pleasantly enough, but...seriously? Karla turned pink and fell silent.

The housekeeper materialized again to announce that dinner was ready. Lorenson took me by one arm and J.X. by the other and escorted us like a genial prison guard to the long and stark dining room. The rest of the family trooped after us. They were not speaking, but I had never heard a louder silence.

The situation did improve somewhat when dinner was served. Lorenson might have had his faults—I hated to think anyone with such fine taste in literature had faults—but he knew how to put on a good spread. Well, perhaps "spread" was not accurate. The food was excellent, really excellent, but it was all in those nouvelle cuisine portions: two bites and you're on to the next course. I will say, the dishes kept a-coming, which helped a bit, though at the end of the eight courses I don't think I'd eaten as much as the usual Denny's lunch portion.

There was wine, probably very good wine, but not a lot of it. I don't like wine, so I left my thimbleful for the others to divvy up and stuck to the sparkling water. Given the meager quantities of booze, it was no surprise that there was no visible loosening up during the meal. Every time I glanced across the table at J.X., he was looking at me, and I knew he was thinking what I was: what the hell were we doing here?

"Have any of your books been optioned for film, Mr. Holmes?" Kenneth asked, while we were waiting for the plates of the third course—which had consisted of exactly two grilled shrimps—to be removed.

"It's been discussed," I said. Mainly by me at the beginning of my career, when I'd somehow imagined that having someone reinterpret your work and miscast all the characters would be a welcome thing.

"What a wonderful idea!" Lorenson exclaimed. "But what cat could ever hope to play the remarkable Mr. Pinkerton?"

"Exactly," I said. "That's the stumbling block."

Lorenson leaned toward me in his eagerness. "This is something I've often wondered. How do you come up with these amazing ideas for your stories? Do you read the newspapers and then visualize how events *should* have unfolded?"

J.X. cleared his throat. I was careful not to catch his eye. "Well, not exactly. Mostly I just make up stuff."

"Real life is frequently disappointing," Lorenson agreed. I could feel his nearest and dearest move restively, but no one contradicted him. He turned to Kenneth and said, "Where is that fiancée of yours this evening?"

"Sydney had to work, Grandfather. I told you that."

"Sydney?" I repeated.

"A charming girl," Lorenson said. "She reports the weather for a local news station."

"She hasn't been a weather girl for three years," Kenneth said. "She's a reporter."

Lorenson ignored him. "Did you always know you wanted to be a writer?"

"I did, yeah."

"And what about you, Mr. Moriarity?"

"No," J.X. said. "I wanted to be a cop. And that's what I used to be."

Ingrid knocked over her water glass. The others began mopping and moving plates and glasses. Lorenson didn't seem to notice. He smiled delightedly and said to J.X., "I'm guessing Mr. Holmes has been your inspiration and your mentor. Am I correct?"

"You could say that."

Yes, you could. But you'd be entirely wrong. I said, "Mr. Moriarity is being way too kind."

"Mr. Moriarity and Mr. Holmes! I just noticed that. How very funny. Are these your real names or pen names?"

"Moriarity not Moriarty." At Lorenson's blank expression, I gave up. "Yes, our real names."

"This goes to prove that truth is stranger than fiction."

"Well..."

But Lorenson was not listening. He said quietly, though he had to realize everyone at the table was listening to his every word, "What I was thinking, Mr. Holmes, was that perhaps you might lend that clever brain of yours to this matter of ours."

I glanced at J.X. He was watching Lorenson and his expression reminded me distinctly of the way Adrien English's Jake had looked when Adrien showed signs of interest in matters that did not concern him. I said cautiously, "Lend my brain how?"

"I'm sure if I were to speak to the police, they would be willing to give you access to their files on this case."

J.X. made a smothered sound. I didn't dare look his way.

"I honestly think your case is in the best possible hands right now," I said. "Mr. Moriarity is personally acquainted with the detective in charge of the case, and he can assure you—"

Lorenson waved this aside. "To be sure. I realize the police are doing all they can. But I'm sure they would be the first to welcome aid from such a brilliant mind."

"Uh, actually I kind of doubt that, Mr. Lorenson."

"Nonsense. Nonsense."

"Father." That was Nord.

Lorenson did not glance his way as he said, "Be silent." And Nord was silent.

"My family believes this matter concerns them. It does not," Lorenson told me.

I sipped my mineral water and did not look at the others.

"I spent a lifetime putting that collection together. It was my pride and joy. The money..." he shrugged. "A lot of money was tied up in my collection, I don't deny it. But I'm a wealthy man. I have all that I need for the remainder of my life. I'm eighty-two. What do you think of that?"

"You don't look eighty-two." I was being honest. He looked *maybe* late sixties.

"My father lived to be one hundred and two. His father lived to be one hundred and one. So I still have a few years left. But my needs are simple."

"You're fortunate."

He inclined his head. "I'm very fortunate. That's true. But losing this collection has been a great blow. I collected my first coin when I was eleven years old. It was a Danish 10 øre coin minted in 1947. I still have—had—that coin. It was part of the collection. Of course it was only worth about one hundred and fifty dollars, but still precious to me. I knew *every single coin* in that collection."

"I'm sorry. I understand how upsetting the loss must be. And I know that the gallery owner was a friend of yours."

"Yes. John was an old friend."

To me, John sort of sounded like an afterthought. I said, "But I don't see how I can be of any help. I know it seems like a weird coincidence that the thief wound up in our basement, but—"

"It's not a coincidence, it's a sign," Lorenson interrupted.

"It's really not."

"With your insight into human nature and your knowledge of the workings of the criminal underworld, I feel certain you might succeed where the police have failed."

I thought of Jerry and his *your brilliant criminal mind.* I said, "But the police haven't failed. They just haven't found your collection yet. Honestly, I appreciate your confidence in me, but I think I would just be getting in the way of the official investigation."

Irresistible Force meet Immovable Object. For the next five courses Lorenson continued to coax, cajole, challenge, charge and finally command me to take his case. As the dinner portions shrank, so did my patience, but I tried to stay pleasant. By the time we got to the cookie-sized mascarpone cheesecake, I was pretty sure my smile had frozen in place like a death rictus. Lorenson remained jolly and cheerful through the whole ordeal, but the other captives at the table were mostly silent and clearly uncomfortable.

Except for J.X. who kept trying to interrupt, and kept getting talked over by our host. At least Lorenson did not actually command him to silence. That was something to be grateful for.

We declined the treat of an after dinner brandy with Lorenson in his study and left as soon as the meal was officially over.

"Un-fucking-believable," I said as the front door closed behind us. I didn't bother to keep my voice down. I'd already had an evening of that.

"That was…interesting," J.X. agreed as we started down the long, steep hill to where we had left our car.

Lights shone in the windows of the houses all around us as we hiked down from Asgaard. It was amazing to me how many people did not bother to pull their drapes. Interesting though, those brief shadowbox glimpses into other people's lives. All around us people were eating dinner, watching TV, working out…happily oblivious to each other.

"You notice he didn't even offer to pay me? I mean, not that that would have made a difference, but the arrogance of insisting that I take his case simply because *he* wants me too. Can you imagine living with him? I'm amazed nobody in that family has poisoned his Geritol by now."

"He lives there on his own. I was listening to them talk while you were fending off Lorenson. It sounded like they all received a royal summons to show up just like us."

"I don't doubt it. That he lives alone, I mean. I'm guessing his wife threw herself off the roof the first chance she had. Five more minutes and I'd have been looking for a window."

"I've got to say, I'm in awe. I didn't think you'd make it through the cheese plate without using it to clobber him."

"By then it was a test of will," I said darkly. "Is there a Kentucky Fried Chicken anywhere around here?"

* * * * *

We dined at the Colonel's on crispy fried chicken, wedge cut potatoes, cheese macaroni and hot biscuits and honey. The plastic chairs were uncomfortable, the décor less than inspiring, but you couldn't beat the food—or the company.

J.X. looked rather dashing for our surroundings in black jeans and a black turtleneck. Like a John Robie-style cat burglar. Did that make me Grace Kelly? With five o'clock shadow and a truss? J.X. smiled tolerantly at me as I wiped honey from my fingers with the moist towelettes provided with our meal. "Feeling better?"

"Yes," I conceded. "A little."

"Did you catch that bit about Sydney the reporter who used to be a weather girl?"

I sighed. "Yes. And I agree, it's too much of a coincidence. Clearly she's the link between the Lorensons and Ladas. In fact, she admitted to knowing Ladas. She told me she interviewed him about a year ago."

"I guess it's possible she was an unwitting connection."

I shook my head. "She's in it up to her neck," I said wearily. "They're all in it. In fact, I think there's a good chance the old man knows they're all in it. I think he was having a little bit of fun with them tonight."

"Fun?"

"Or maybe not. Maybe he doesn't know. I'm not sure it would occur to him that any of them would have the nerve to defy him."

J.X.'s brown gaze was very direct. "It's not your business, Kit."

"I agree."

"I'll talk to Izzie tomorrow. Tell him what we know. Or at least suspect."

"I'm not arguing," I said. "But I'm not holding out a lot of hope either."

"Hope?" J.X.'s brows drew together.

I took a final noisy drag on the straw of my cola. "That our involvement ends here," I said.

CHAPTER FIFTEEN

"**H**ow's your back?" J.X. asked, climbing into bed when we finally arrived home after our double dinners.

I eyed him thoughtfully. "It's okay."

"Good." He smiled. It wasn't a predatory smile, exactly, but it also wasn't an I-just-want-to-hold-you smile. He leaned over and his mouth came down on mine, his lips warm, the Van Dyke beard soft. I murmured...not protest but not acquiescence either. I was thinking. Which, frankly, is not conducive to kissing. J.X. kissed me harder, the tip of his tongue probed delicately—but determinedly—and I opened to him.

He smiled against my mouth and his tongue flicked inside, touched mine. I can't deny that I felt an instant and overwhelming response. I wanted him. It was that simple. But I also felt a flash of *this is getting out of control*. And that was not at all simple.

J.X.'s hand went to my cock and he handled me with a firm and expert hand.

Readying me.

Because that's what this was. As pleasurable as it was to be brought off by J.X.—and to relax in the knowledge that this was just one of many pleasurable things he would do to me that night—there was also my awareness that he believed himself to be completely in control of this moment. And any other moments we would have.

What was there to object to in that? J.X. was using the right pressure, the right angle, even the right speed from the very second my penis hit his palm. He knew what I liked, *exactly* what I liked, and he was bound and determined to make sure I got what I wanted every single time.

And what he wanted every single time.

Why not? What was wrong with that? Nothing. Not a damn thing. It wasn't like I didn't want him. Not like I wasn't in the mood. I did want it. I was already starting to shiver with the intensity of my reaction to him. There was no greater turn-on for me than thinking of J.X. taking me with that gentle but relentless strength. I wanted it so much. Too much.

Yes, this was the problem: I didn't just want to make love. I wanted to be fucked. I *needed* to be fucked. And not only did I know it. *He* knew it.

I wrenched my mouth away from his and gasped, "Wait."

J.X. drew back, surprised. His eyes were dark with passion and a little unfocused. "What's wrong?"

I put my hand on his, stilled him. "I think we need to take turns."

"Turns?" He sounded like the concept was utterly alien, which simply underscored how out of whack the dynamic between us was getting.

"Yes. Right. We need to...trade off that. If we're always going to do *that.*"

"Always going to do what?"

"Fuck."

He actually glanced around. "What's wrong?"

"No, I mean if *we're* always going to fuck."

Wide eyes, parted lips. No mistaking that look for anything but dismay. "You don't want to?"

I took his face in my hands. "Listen carefully to me, Costello. Yes. I want to. I like sex. I love sex. But I don't always want to be the one being fucked. Okay?"

Something flickered in his eyes. "Okay. Of course. I didn't—"

"We need to take turns. We need to switch off. So you had Monday night. Tonight is my night."

His breath was warm against my face. He didn't say anything. His erection was subsiding—along with mine. Too much talk. I knew it, but I persisted stubbornly.

"That's fair, right?"

I watched him consider and discard a number of replies. But what was there to say? This *was* fair. And he *was* fair-minded, so I knew he couldn't and wouldn't object.

J.X. said finally, "But what if tonight you'd prefer it the other way? Because you do prefer it, Kit."

I shook my head. "No. We've got to take turns. And I don't prefer it. It's too passive."

He repeated very slowly, "It's too…passive. And you think, what? That's not masculine?"

"Of course not. Although, to be honest, it's not society's concept of masculinity."

"Or yours."

"Maybe," I admitted.

He said, "I think maybe you need to be passive in this. You can't control everything all the time. It isn't healthy to try. I think maybe it's a relief for you to let go sometimes."

I shook my head.

J.X. said, "Why is it so hard to admit you enjoy sex a lot more when you're being f—"

I shot him a fierce look and he stopped. I said, "You know, there are other ways to have sex. Nobody has to penetrate anybody."

"That's true."

"We could just…do other things."

He was silent.

"Right?"

"Right."

"But what?"

He sounded troubled as he said, "I don't understand why we're setting up rules and regulations about how we're going to have sex."

"I'm not trying to set up rules and regulations."

"Well, yeah. You are. You're trying to control, to manage how we make love. To make sure nobody colors outside the lines. And that's the last thing you need, Kit."

I opened my mouth and he said, "And it's the last thing I need."

That pulled me up short. "You don't enjoy it the other way around?"

"Kit, I enjoy everything we do together. But there is *nothing* that feels as good as when I'm buried to my balls in that sweet, hot ass of yours. Those little cries you make, the way you push back on my cock like you just can't get enough. It's beautiful, and it's the only time you really let go."

My face felt like it was on fire.

"And I know you're embarrassed when I talk like this, but it's the truth. It's all good, Kit, but..." he put his lips to my ear and his breath was hot against my skin as he whispered, "we both like it best when I'm fucking you so slow...and so hard...and *so* deep."

I groaned. Just like that I was up again and rarin' to go. I *yearned* for him. An old-fashioned word, but an accurate one.

"Don't fight me, Kit," he whispered. It sounded like a plea. And that really was ridiculous because of course I wasn't going to fight him. That was the trouble. It was myself I had to fight.

I shook my head, not trusting my voice. Not refusal. *I'm not fighting,* that was the message. Surrender.

To seduction. Because even as he was taking me, his cock pushing into my wet, slick hole, shoving in as far as he could go, he was wooing me with soft words and sweet kisses and touches that aroused and reassured all at the same time.

"You like this, Kit? You like how it feels with me inside you?"

I swallowed, nodded. Beyond words.

"I like it. I *love* it. It's better with you than anyone else, Kit. That's the truth."

He thrust against me. A few tentative strokes. I let out a helpless sound because it just felt so *good.* And my body had already learned—been trained—to accommodate his thickness, his length. My muscles submitted even while my mind was still worrying at the problem of this dynamic. I was instinctively straining back, wanting more, needing more.

He observed my silent struggle, that naked need. "Yeah, honey," J.X. encouraged softly, almost sympathetically. "I know. I know."

But he was holding still, waiting, withholding until I was writhing, until the words tore out of me, "Jesus, J.X. *Please.* Please..."

He said something—maybe in Spanish—it wasn't the words, it was that dark, emotional tone that reached me. He began to move, hips rocking up hard against my ass, transfixing me with each thrust. I shoved back to meet him, going after what I wanted, what I needed, with a single-minded ruthlessness.

Somewhere in the distance I could hear my own cries and shouts. And it was okay because the wilder and noisier I got, the more J.X. liked it. And that was exciting too. Exciting and freeing.

We found our rhythm. Sped up.

His hands tightened on my hips, he was pounding into me now, and every stroke was sending flares of exquisite feeling through the nexus of nerves and muscles. Pleasure was too small, too frail a word for such enormous, fierce gratification.

"Jesus God," I choked. There it was. The be-all and end-all. I was coming in jets of hot white.

J.X. grunted, thrust harder, strained, groaned, and I felt that spill of liquid heat.

"Kit." He said my name again and again. Just...*Kit.*

We held each other tight, rocking, trying to milk the last drops of sensation. Wring the last flashes of lightening. Riders on the storm.

Thursday was so normal it was weird.

We started the day picking up J.X.'s car at San Francisco International Airport. We had breakfast out and then went shopping for groceries—real groceries—afterwards.

Back at the house, we put the food away and then we got down to the serious business of hanging pictures and artwork.

"I don't think family photos go in the living room," I stated.

"No, I agree." J.X. surprised me. I'd been bracing for a montage of framed photos of Gage and Nina plastered all over the front parlor. "For one thing, you don't want every stranger walking into your house to get a look at the people who matter to you."

Oh. Right. Security measures.

"There are no pictures of you as a little kid?" he asked a while later as we were sorting through framed photos.

"Why would I want a picture of myself as a little kid?" I didn't even like pictures of myself as a grown-up kid.

J.X. seemed disappointed. "I was looking forward to seeing you in your little smoking jacket."

"Ha."

Our taste in art was dissimilar but not incompatible. J.X. liked Jackson Pollock, Lee Krasner and Rothko. I liked Turner's and Sargent's landscapes. And I was forced to confess to an unnatural love of old china plates arranged symmetrically on walls. J.X. took the news bravely. We positioned the traditional paintings with contemporary furnishings and then experimented with a Rothko print in the dining room and Jackson Pollock over the Victorian fireplace. I had to admit it all kind of worked.

There was no sign of Beck Ladas and no word from Jerry Knight. It was all quiet on the western front. And the eastern, northern, southern, water and home fronts.

With groceries in the pantry and pictures on the walls, our house did indeed feel like a home.

J.X. disappeared into his office and a short time later, I heard the faint sound of music. The Black Keys. "Tighten Up." It was actually sort of, well, companionable. Strange too, living with someone who didn't leave the house in order to go to work. I had expected this to be one of the most difficult aspects of living together. Both of us working at home? If David had worked at home, our relationship would have been over within a year.

Nina called. Laura called. J.X.'s agent called. Gage called. I went for a swim. Rachel called while I was outside.

It was a beautiful day. Warm and sunny. Blue skies for as far as the eye could see, and the eye could see quite a ways. All the way to Coit Tower.

"You know, you're going to have to talk to Rachel sooner or later," J.X. told me when he came out to sit at the foot of a lounge chair and watch me swim.

"I know."

"Just tell her…"

"Yep, that's the problem." I folded my arms on the side of the pool, lazily treading water while we talked.

"She works for *you*."

"I know."

"There's nothing wrong with taking time to decide what you really want."

"I agree."

"You're answering me, but you're not really *talking* to me," J.X. observed.

"That's because I don't have anything to say," I replied. I didn't want to be irritated with him. It was a lovely day and I was feeling sort of content—for me—but J.X.'s need to fix everything, to fix *me*, did sort of get on my nerves.

"You've worked your ass off for enough years that if you want to take some time…"

I sighed and pushed away from the side of the pool, slipping into a back-stroke. "I'm listening," I called, but of course I wasn't. I couldn't hear a thing he said over the splash of water.

"I think we should get some hummingbird feeders," I said when I finally swam back to the side.

J.X. stopped talking. "Okay," he said at last.

"And some kind of cushions for those patio chairs. They're very uncomfortable."

"If you want."

"I do."

"Then we'll get some cushions." He rose and went back into the house.

Not happy with me. But if we were going to live together we were going to have to get used to each other. Get used to the ways we were *not* compatible. And figure out our coping strategies.

Rachel and I had been working together a long time. She knew my little idiosyncrasies and I knew hers. And while I appreciated J.X.'s concern, I'd been a bestselling author longer than he'd been writing. I didn't give him career advice. And I didn't want any *from* him.

He came back outside while I was sunning myself in the lounge chair, and—shading my eyes—I saw that he was dressed in author-about-town uniform: black jeans, black shirt, black boots. My boyfriend the MIB. Maybe I'd buy him a blue shirt for his birthday.

"Where are you off to?" I inquired.

"Monthly writers' luncheon. You're more than welcome to join us, by the way."

"Who's going to be there?" If I'd truly been welcome to join them, he'd probably have mentioned it before he was walking out the door. But that was okay. J.X. was assuming I wouldn't want to go, and he was quite right. I listened politely as he rattled off the names of a couple of bestselling thriller writers, and smiled. "Maybe next time."

"If you get nervous, SFPD has a patrol car in the area."

I tilted my head, the better to read his expression. "*Should* I be nervous?"

"No. I wouldn't be going out to lunch if I thought so." He was serious. "Izzie says there's been no sign of Ladas since we spotted him at the Dew Drop Inn. And it's not like they aren't looking for him."

"Right. True. Maybe whoever knocked off Elijah knocked off Beck."

I don't know where the idea came from, but I could see it startled J.X. I waved him off. "Have fun. Oh—are you going to be home for dinner?"

"Of course."

"It's noon now, so—"

"I'll be home for dinner. I thought we'd have roast chicken."

"Okay." He seemed a little sensitive on the topic of dinner and I wasn't sure why.

He leaned down to kiss me and that seemed a little forceful too. Maybe he felt like I was shutting him out? I locked my hand about the back of his neck when he started to rise. He nearly tipped over into the chair as I kissed him more thoroughly. When he finally straightened, his mouth was pink and he was smiling.

"I'll see you later," I told him.

When I'd had enough sun and water, I wandered back into the house and considered the contents of the freezer. I had a very nice selection of frozen pizza to choose from, but I kind of felt like it was time to return to normal eating. I closed the freezer, opened the fridge and considered the glass shelves crowded with all the healthy options J.X. and I had purchased that morning.

Salad? I really hated salad. I wasn't much of a lunch eater. When I was working I didn't want to stop for food. I liked breakfast and I liked dinner. But I liked early dinner and J.X., who did like lunch, preferred late dinners. So I probably needed to figure out something I could eat for lunch. Which brought me back to hating salad.

The phone rang. I let the machine pick it up. There was a rush of noise—like someone was standing by a freeway—and Jerry's irate voice said, "Christopher, I don't appreciate your boyfriend butting in between us. I thought we were friends. If you don't want to talk to me, you should have the courtesy to tell me yourself."

I felt the hair on my head stand up.

"You can't treat people like this. Use me when you need something and then dump me the minute your big famous friends show up."

I started to reach for the phone, but my survival instinct belatedly kicked in.

"It's bullshit. It's fucking bullshit. And you're going to be sorry."

A long, loud dial tone followed before the phone went dead.

"What the…"

I picked up the phone. My impulse was to call J.X. But I stopped myself. For one thing, I couldn't disturb him at lunch with something this ridiculous. Knowing J.X., he was liable to think he needed to return home immediately. While I found Jerry alarming, I wasn't afraid of him. I didn't need J.X. rushing back to hold my hand. In fact, if he had spoken to Jerry without discussing it with me, I was not happy.

At all.

I knew he hadn't been kidding about confronting Jerry, but I hadn't expected this. I hadn't *agreed* to this. What exactly had he said to Jerry? Because if anything, it seemed to me that J.X. had aggravated the situation.

I looked at the window on the answering machine. Two messages. I played the first message. Rachel wanted to know how my Nordic noir proposal was coming.

I made myself a peanut butter sandwich and considered the problem of Jerry—and the problem of J.X.

Contacting Jerry might be the courteous thing to do, but I was pretty sure it would be a mistake. And as for J.X...we were going to have to have a conversation about boundaries.

I got my laptop out and took a look at an article in *The Economist* which Rachel had recommended in one of her many, many emails.

Three factors underpin the success of Nordic crime fiction: language, heroes and setting. Niclas Salomonsson, a literary agent who represents almost all the up and coming Scandinavian crime writers, reckons it is the style of the books, "realistic, simple and precise...and stripped of unnecessary words", that has a lot to do with it. The plain, direct writing, devoid of metaphor, suits the genre well.

Stripped of unnecessary words? Say what? Rachel had gone mad. I was all about the unnecessary words. And probably about the metaphor too.

The Nordic detective is often careworn and rumpled.

Okay. Fair enough. Morose and unheroic sounded familiar. I could probably write convincingly about some life-sized guy with emotional hang-ups and a boring job.

Most important is the setting. The countries that the Nordic writers call home are prosperous and organised, [...] the best Scandinavian fiction mines the seam that connects the insiders—the rich and powerful—and the outsiders, represented by the poor, the exploited and the vulnerable. [...] The cold, dark climate, where doors are bolted and curtains drawn, provides a perfect setting for crime writing.

I gazed out the wall of windows at the sunlit garden. Yeeeah. Not so much.

I sighed.

I couldn't deny that I was enjoying reading Scandinavian crime fiction. I appreciated other people's existential malaise as much as the next middle-class white guy. I thought Nesbø was brilliant. And so did pretty much everyone else. In fact, one of the most interesting aspects of my research was the reiteration from all sources that somehow Nordic noir held more credibility and prestige worldwide than any other crime fiction from any other country.

I was glowering over that assertion when the doorbell rang.

My heart, attempting to flee the scene, instantly wedged its cholesterol-laden self in my throat. I listened anxiously to the chimes ringing musically through the house. Then I remembered that we were still getting shipments and packages and this could very easily be UPS. It was unlikely that Ladas would ring the doorbell. And I could handle Jerry.

Even if I didn't want to.

I went to the foyer, tiptoed to the front door and peered out through the peephole as the doorbell rang for the third time.

A miniature Ingrid Edwards was chewing nervously on her lip as she considered ringing the doorbell yet again. I turned the deadbolt, unlocked the door and opened it.

She jumped as though the last thing she had expected was an answer.

"Hi," I said.

"Mr. Holmes!"

"Who were you expecting?"

"Well…you."

"That makes one of us. Because this is definitely a surprise."

She laughed nervously. "Yes. I guess so. Could I talk to you for a minute? It's important or I wouldn't bother you."

There were so many things I could have said to that, but I had a feeling it would be easier to get it over with. I stepped back and Ingrid came inside. She watched me with uncomfortable intensity as I relocked the door.

"Would you like to sit down?" I asked.

"Oh. Yes. Thank you."

I beckoned to the parlor and she walked into the room and sat down on the nearest chair with her square white handbag perched genteelly on her lap. "Mr. Holmes, why did you refuse to help my grandfather last night?"

Something in the way she phrased it made me feel like the kind of fellow who pushes old ladies in wheelchairs down staircases.

I said defensively, "I'm not a detective. I don't even play a detective on TV. I'm just a writer."

"But you know about solving crimes."

"I know about making up crimes. It's not the same."

"But it is," she said at once. "It's just the flip side."

Flipped being the day's watchword.

"Um…"

"Mr. Holmes, you *have* to help us. You have to help *me*."

"You know, I really don't," I said. "I don't mean to seem unkind or unco-operative or lacking in civic-mindedness, but—"

Ingrid flicked back the flap of her handbag and pulled out what looked like an antique Walther pistol. She pointed it straight at me.

CHAPTER SIXTEEN

"What did you need help with?" I asked.

Tears filled her eyes. The pistol wavered. "I'm a desperate woman," Ingrid told me.

"I can see that," I said. "Maybe you better start at the beginning."

"Don't make fun of me!"

The only thing more frightening than having a pistol pointed at you, is having a pistol pointed at you by someone having an emotional meltdown.

"I'm not making fun of you," I said. "I'm scared out of my wits. Which I handle by chattering incessantly. Is that thing loaded?"

"Yes. And I know how to use it. So don't try anything."

"What the hell would I try? Besides curling up in a fetal position and waiting for you to go away."

"I didn't want to do it like this. I hoped you would be willing to help me without…without coercion."

A horrible thought occurred to me. I glanced at the sunburst clock on the wall. Nearly three. J.X. was going to be home any minute. If he walked in and startled Ingrid, she was liable to lose it and shoot him.

No. No. *No.* I couldn't even contemplate that without a rise of panic. A greater rise of panic. This one tidal wave-sized.

"Tell me what you want," I said. "I'll do whatever I can to help you. I promise. Just…tell me what you think I can do."

"You've met my grandfather." She stopped.

"So far so good," I encouraged. I didn't let myself look at the clock again.

Ingrid said hopelessly, "It's going to be hard to make you understand."

"You're probably right. But try."

"My grandfather is rich, but most of his money is tied up in his coin collection. And as long as I can remember, that collection has been dangled in front of all of us like a-a carrot."

Not a writer, Ingrid. "Go on."

"Grandpa always promised that one day the collection would be divided between my mother and my uncle Nord. My mother didn't care about the collection, but of course it's very valuable, so she certainly wanted her share of it. My Uncle Nord also collects coins."

It was hard not to grip my head with both hands and scream at her. I worked to keep my voice calm. "Right. Okay. Go on."

"But my grandfather likes to, oh I don't know how to describe it. Manipulate people? Control people? Whenever my mother or my uncle did something he didn't like, he would threaten to give the complete collection to the other. Then, after we—Kenneth and Cynthia and I—came along, he began to say that the collection would go to us instead."

I didn't say anything, but what I was thinking was that was a great way to turn loving family members into bitter enemies. And Lorenson had seemed like such a nice old guy at first.

"When we were little, we didn't think so much about it, but as you get older… Well, it would make a huge difference to all of us to have three million dollars each." She clenched her hands. "For me, it means freedom. The chance to live my own life. My parents are…not like me."

"That's usually the way it works."

"No. I'm not explaining this so that you can see what I mean. I'm twenty-four, but my parents still try to control every part of my life. They chose the college I attend and they're the ones who decided I would be a business major. I don't want to be a business major!"

"What do you want to be?"

"I don't know! They insist that I live at home. They try to tell me who I can date, even who I can be friends with. My mother even tries to tell me what I can wear. At my age!"

I said, "See, here's how you fix that. You get a job and you move out and then no one can tell you what to do for a living or who you can be friends with or what to wear."

"You don't understand."

"I understand more than you think. About this part anyway. The trade-off for living under your parents' roof is you accede a certain amount of control to them. I won't argue that your parents sound more controlling than most, but you cure that by becoming independent."

"I can't be independent without money!"

"So, let me skip ahead to the punch line. You and—I'm guessing—your cousins decided to become independent by stealing your grandfather's coin collection?"

"I explained this all wrong. You're looking at it from *their* point of view." The pistol was now pointed at my face.

I swallowed hard. "I'm sorry. Finish your story. Your explanation."

"The coins were going to be ours anyway. Our entire lives that was what Grandpa promised. One day we would have that money."

I guessed, "But your grandfather changed his mind again?"

"Yes. At Christmas he announced that he was planning to donate his collection—the entire collection—to the American Numismatic Society. Just like that! He said he believed that Ken and Cyn and I only cared about the money. We didn't care about the collection at all, and he believed we'd just break it up and sell it off."

"Which was correct, right?"

"Of course!" She looked indignant. "Our entire inheritance is tied up in that collection. He's said again and again there's no money after he dies."

I smothered a groan. "So, again, you and your cousins decided to become independent by stealing your grandfather's coin collection?"

"Cyn wasn't involved. She's just a kid. Ken and I decided…yes."

So did that mean they had decided to cut Cynthia out or that someone would have held onto Cynthia's share in trust? And what did it matter anyway? But against my will, I was curious.

"How the hell did you hook up with Elijah Ladas?"

Tears welled in Ingrid's eyes and spilled down her cheeks.

"You've told me this much, you might as well tell me the rest."

"I can't tell you all of it, but Elijah and I met and fell in love. We were going to go away together with my share of the collection. But then he was murdered. I don't know who killed him and I don't know what happened to the collection."

"That's a problem," I said. "The other problem is that the gallery owner was killed during the robbery. Which makes you all accessories to homicide." I eyed the pistol meaningfully. "Among other things."

"I know." A sob burst out of her. "That was an accident. Nobody was supposed to die. Elijah had done that kind of thing a million times and nobody ever got hurt."

"By nobody getting hurt, I assume you mean physically hurt, because people were certainly being robbed."

"Yes. I know. And that's usually wrong. But this time the money *was* ours. Or as good as. But Elijah brought…someone with him and that person killed John. He didn't mean to. It just happened. None of us wanted that."

"He brought his half-wit brother with him," I said. "Beck."

She gaped at me. "How do you know that?"

"I know everything. And nothing." I spoke automatically. There were some considerable gaps in her story, but the very nature of the gaps was revealing. "Okay. I've heard your story. What is it you think I can do for you?"

Tears filled her eyes again. "I realize it's all going to come out now. The truth about the robbery and everything. But I thought if at least I could help you get the collection back, then maybe the police will go easier on us."

"I think cooperating with the police is your best bet now," I agreed. "I think that's a great idea. But the person to talk to would be a lawyer."

"I can't go to a lawyer. I don't have money for one, and even if I did, everyone would find out. My parents will find out. My grandfather… My grandfather can't know about this until we can give him the collection back. It's the only thing that will make up for what we did."

There was no making up for what they had done. John Cantrell was dead, Elijah Ladas was dead. There was no fixing either of those things. But I kept the thought to myself, saying instead, "Ingrid, listen to me. I write mysteries about an elderly lady botanist and her cat. Half the time the cat solves the crime. Do you understand what I'm trying to say here? I don't *have* any real experience with investigating crimes or the criminal justice system. I want to help, but I'm not the right person to talk to."

"You're all I've got!"

Something snapped inside me and I yelled back, "Then you've got nothing!"

Ingrid waved the pistol wildly. I put my hands up. She burst into tears. "Oh, what's the use! Anyway, it's not even loaded." She threw the pistol to the floor.

The Walther banged down hard, spun around, there was an explosion—and a hole appeared, as if by magic, in the plaster over the baseboard right next to my foot.

Ingrid screamed and threw herself in my arms. I screamed too and clutched her back. The fact that she was taller than me made it interesting.

"I didn't know it was loaded," she cried. "It's my grandpa's gun. I didn't know it had real bullets. I've never fired a gun in my life!"

I stammered, "You nearly sh-sh-*shot* me!"

"I'm so sorry!"

"You're *insane!*"

"I'm sorry, I'm sorry. I don't know what to do. You're my last hope."

I know it's not logical, but I think the fact that she was sobbing in my arms, so clearly frightened out of her wits, softened me. It shouldn't have. She could have killed me. At the least she could have taken my foot off. My skin smarted where the bits of plaster had hit my bare ankle. But I had never seen a damsel in more distress than Ingrid.

Or maybe it was just that, despite everything, I found real life mysteries as irresistibly tantalizing as Mr. Pinkerton found catnip.

"What is it you think I could do?"

Ingrid gave a couple of wet gulps, lifted her face from my now soggy T-shirt and, said, "I thought if you went with me to Elijah's, you might be able to figure out where he hid the coins."

"But the police will have been all over his place. In fact, it's probably sealed off. The police probably consider it a crime scene."

"They did. It was. We've—I've—been watching it. But they've finished with it now. We could go over there. We could get in without any trouble at all. I have a key."

"But if there had been anything to find, the police would already have it."

"The coins aren't there. I know that. Elijah said he had a safe place to keep them."

"He didn't tell you where he hid them?"

"No."

"I thought you were partners."

"We were. But he was worried that the police might be watching any of us or all of us, so he hid the coins in a place he'd used before. He knew more about that kind of thing than we did."

"So he died and none of you have any hint where the coins are hidden?"

"Yes. That's what I keep telling you."

I overlooked that show of snippiness. "And you think I'd be able to figure out where Ladas hid the coins by snooping through his things?"

"If you're as clever as Grandpa says you are, yes. I'm sure you'd spot some clue the police missed."

Ridiculous. Totally ridiculous. And yet.

One thing for sure, it was as much to my advantage to get this matter cleared up as it was to Ingrid's. I was tired of waiting for Beck to show up again.

"I'm sure this is a complete waste of time, but all right," I said. "Let's go have a look."

* * * * *

I made the mistake of letting Ingrid drive.

I hated driving in San Francisco. No wonder everyone relied so heavily on public transportation. I kept getting lost and I loathed all those narrow, ridiculously steep streets. The pedestrians and cyclists all seemed to have a death wish. And it was impossible to find parking. So I thought it would be simpler just to take *her* car. Keep her busy, keep her hands occupied and away from lethal weapons. But it wasn't simpler. It was hair-raising. Never mind my heart being in my mouth, my entire stomach was crammed in there the whole journey.

However, against the odds, we did arrive in one piece at Elijah Ladas' waterfront loft.

A squat brick building took up the corner of an unprepossessing street in a not particularly nice neighborhood. According to Ingrid, the building had been built in the early thirties and converted into a giant loft in the late nineties.

"It just goes to show, crime *doesn't* pay." I clutched my back as I staggered from the MINI Cooper. The air smelled of dead fish and soot and possibly urine.

"It just goes to show how much you don't know about real estate," she retorted. "That's a million-dollar view of the bridge and the bay."

"Yeah, but you still have to live *here*." We gave wide berth to one of Ladas' neighbors, a wino clutching his bottle, huddled in the entranceway of the adjoining condemned warehouse.

Ingrid ignored me and the mutterings of the bum both, heading straight to Ladas' industrial-looking front door, punching a series of numbers into the access pad.

The door unlocked, Ingrid pushed it open and we stepped into an entrance of concrete walls and concrete floors and an old-fashioned cage elevator. Ingrid keyed another code into another access pad and then unlocked the elevator. Ladas had taken his security seriously.

We stepped into the elevator and Ingrid shivered as we began to rise through the gloom.

"What exactly attracted you to Ladas?" I asked curiously.

She lifted her chin defiantly. "We were kindred spirits."

"He was like, thirty years older than you. And a crook."

"He was the most charming man I ever met." She said it like she was throwing it in my face, but I was not—and never had been—under the illusion that I was a charming man. Not unkind and occasionally witty, sure. Charming? No.

I shrugged. "Okay. That's nice for going out to dinner a couple of times, but what did you have in common? Besides the desire to rip off your grandpa?"

She said as though this should settle the matter, "Elijah said we were a perfect match."

"Really?" Well, Ingrid was pretty in a vapidly All-American way and her moral compass was not what one would call tightly wound. She seemed to be a girl in search of a savior, and maybe Ladas had liked thinking of himself as her white knight. From what I'd read of him, he had a tendency to romanticize.

I couldn't help noticing that she wasn't exactly prostrate with grief. Sad, yes. Disappointed, certainly. But she wasn't dying inside. If something happened to J.X.... Well, I didn't want to even let the picture form, lest the gods start taking notes on new things to do that would really ruin my life.

"So after the heat died down, you were going to move in with him?"

"We were going to go to Cuba."

"Cuba?"

"Hemingway lived in Cuba."

"Well, I know. But—"

The elevator reached the top level. The doors opened. Ingrid stepped out and punched more numbers into the keypad. I looked around myself and I had to admit the view really was something. In fact, it was everything.

Personally, I'd have opted for blinds, but if you didn't mind living front and center stage, it was an amazing space. Space being the keyword. Space and light were my immediate impression. There were a few brick walls, some furniture, of course, and some striking McCauley Conner crime fiction illustrations. Possibly originals, given Ladas' day job.

"See?" Ingrid said.

What was I supposed to be seeing? That this really *was* a nice place to live? That there weren't many possibilities for hiding Viking treasure?

"Well..." I wandered around the central rooms, stopping to examine various pieces of furniture or art. I figured he'd probably hired a professional decorator, so we had to take the hints regarding his personal interests and passions with a grain of salt.

The kitchen was all stainless steel and self-consciously utilitarian. "Did he cook?"

"He was a wonderful cook," Ingrid said. "He was a wine connoisseur too."

Of course he was. It was all part of the gentleman thief image.

"Did he do much entertaining?"

"Not a lot. He went out all the time. He loved to party. But he didn't like to have people over."

Okay. That was interesting. Probably not germane, but interesting.

"The police have his laptop," Ingrid volunteered.

"I figured."

"He always burned all his mail. Not that he got a lot. But he burned everything. He said he never kept any papers."

"He can't have burned everything," I objected. "Pink slips, property titles…he didn't burn that stuff."

"He said he burned everything."

"Yeah. Well."

Saying and doing were two different things. As I could vouch for. Somewhere Ladas had a safety deposit box, but we were unlikely to gain access to that. He couldn't have hidden his ill-gotten gains in a bank, but the key to the hiding place might be there.

Or maybe not. I had a feeling Ladas liked games. He liked puzzles. He was a romantic.

Which meant what? I wasn't sure.

I wandered back to the long main room and examined a giant, surprisingly elegant metal shelving unit that contained, among other things, the complete Lazlo Ender series co-written with Richard Cortez. Cortez had been Cuban, come to think of it.

I glanced at Ingrid. She was watching me intently, apparently waiting for an epiphany à la that other Holmes chap.

I pointed to the Lazlo books. "Thumb through those and see if Ladas happened to tuck any papers or notes away between the pages. Or if he wrote any notes in the margins."

Her eyes widened at the brilliance of this idea. At once she began to go through the books, meticulously examining the pages. I didn't think she was going to find anything, but she had made me nervous, watching my every move and waiting for me to say *Ah ha!*

I went back to studying the collection of art, artifacts and books on the shelf.

With the exception of his own work, Ladas' taste seemed to mostly run to non-fiction. There were a couple of books on art and Cuba and the Vikings. Nothing that related to coin collecting or where to hide valuable objects from the cops.

"He did those." Ingrid pointed to the framed pencil sketch I was holding.

"Really?"

"He was very artistic."

So was Hitler. But…Ladas did have a good eye and a sure hand. Useful in his trade, no doubt. These little pencil and ink cartoons were very well done. There was a touch of humor in glimpses of a cat sleeping on a fire escape, an old bag lady with a shopping cart, and a younger version of Beck showing off a tattoo on his bicep.

I studied that tattoo unhappily. I hoped this wasn't going to turn into some weird escapade where the secret to everything lay in Beck's body art. That kind of thing worked great in fiction, but in real life? No. Especially if Beck was lying dead in a ditch somewhere.

"What about Beck?" I asked.

"What about him?"

"Was he going to Cuba too?"

"If he wanted."

"Did he know about Cuba?"

"No." No hesitation there. I glanced at Ingrid. She said defensively, "Elijah was going to tell him once everything was ready. He didn't think Beck would want to go."

Beck would be a liability. But there was that funny little sketch, so I thought Elijah was probably fond of his little brother, liability or not. And Ingrid or not.

"You were hoping Beck wouldn't go, right?"

"He creeps me out." She frowned down at the book she held. "Elijah had a wonderful singing voice." It seemed like a non sequitur, but maybe she was mentally comparing the Ladas brothers. "He really was a special man."

Understatement. I moved on to the framed photos. Unlike J.X., Ladas hadn't worried about visitors seeing who mattered most to him. Probably because, judging by the photos, the person who mattered most to Ladas was Ladas. And, in fairness, he'd been a handsome guy. He looked good-humored too. Like a man who laughed easily—or at least he was laughing in most of the photos.

I moved on down the shelf. There were a couple of small bronzes and a large model of a Viking *drakkar*. One of those expensive models you pay a grand or more for, not something plastic that came in a kit.

I went back to examine the photographs of Ladas. In a couple of them the background looked like sails or rigging or ocean.

"Did Ladas own a boat?" I asked.

"Yes," Ingrid said. "That was the first thing we thought of. We've been over it plank by plank. There's nothing there."

"Hmm."

I had reached the end of the shelving unit. I glanced out the nearest window. The summer sun threw gold dust on the tree tops and a gauzy haze hung over the bay. I spotted a man crossing the street below, walking with swift purpose toward this building. A big, blond man. My heart jumped. Not dead in a ditch after all.

"Shit." I turned to Ingrid. "Beck is on his way up here!"

CHAPTER SEVENTEEN

Ingrid went white and dropped the book she was holding. *"W-w-what?"*

"How do we get out of here?"

"We don't! There's only one way in and out."

We both stared aghast at the elevator.

Beck wasn't the shiniest doubloon in the treasure chest, but even he was probably capable of deducing that if the elevator was up here, so were uninvited guests.

"We have to hide!" Ingrid darted down the room, grabbed open a door and jumped into what appeared to be a coat closet. She closed the door firmly after her.

I spread my hands in supplication and looked ceilingward. I'm not sure if I was talking to the Almighty or Ladas.

From downstairs I heard a door slam.

Maybe Beck didn't know all the security codes. That was possible, right?

The elevator suddenly rumbled into life and began to sink.

Okay. So Beck did know the codes. Or Ingrid hadn't bothered to reset them while we were still in the building. Which would be another clue to Beck that he wasn't alone here.

I ran after Ingrid, yanking open the closet. At least, I tried to yank it open. She was hanging onto the inside handle. It opened a crack and then jerked shut.

"Don't be ridiculous!" I hissed. "Come out of there."

"Go away! Go away!" her smothered voice shot back.

"Ingrid, this is the first place he'll look."

"Go away! Leave me alone! Find your own place!"

Did she think we were playing hide and seek?

Someone whistled sharply from behind me. I spun around. There was no one there. The elevator was still rumbling as it sank to the ground floor.

The whistle came again. I looked about wildly, then realized the whistle was coming from the pocket of my Levi's. My phone.

I fumbled it out and saw I had a text from J.X.

Where r u?

Oh for chrissake. Like it all wasn't bad enough, his final words to me were going to be in textspeak?

From below I heard the rattle and clang of the elevator door opening and closing.

I shoved my phone away and dragged open the closet door again, Ingrid still clinging stubbornly to it.

"Leave me alone!" she whispered frantically. She clawed at me like a cat.

Cat...

"Ingrid, is there a fire escape?" I demanded.

"Go away!" Another effort to scratch my face.

Hastily, I closed her back into the closet and leaned against it, thinking. A building this old, yes. There had to be a fire escape.

Beneath my feet came a grinding of gears and then that telltale rumble of the returning elevator. I left Ingrid in the closet and went looking for the bedroom. I found it behind an arched brick doorway.

The room was unexpectedly small and the bed—mountains of jewel-colored silk pillows and gold satin brocade coverlet—took up most of the floor. There was a pale wheat-colored rug and a small amber chandelier. Another door led to a walk-in closet.

The only window was in a small alcove at the head of the bed.

I jumped onto the bed and went to the window, unlatching the shutters and raising the sash. Sure enough, in the most inconvenient place possible, was the fire escape. Funny how small and flimsy it looked up close. I started to climb out onto the platform. But the thought of Ingrid cowering in that closet, waiting for Beck to do whatever he was liable to do to her, stopped me.

I couldn't do it. Couldn't leave the little lemming to her fate.

I turned around, jumped off the bed and stepped out of the bedroom just in time to see Beck getting off the elevator. He looked straight at me, and his preoccupied expression—and God only knew what preoccupied that slab of raw meat—turned to one of rage.

"You!" he roared.

I don't think until he saw me it had dawned on him that someone else was in the building. Hell, Ingrid and I could both have probably safely hid in that damned closet.

I whirled and ran for the bed and the window beyond. I jumped onto the mattress, bounced to the alcove and scrambled awkwardly out the window. I dropped onto the metal platform, which seemed to wobble alarmingly. I clung to the railing and started down the steps.

It was no use, of course. Beck would take the elevator and reach street-side long before me.

Except he didn't.

The staircase jumped beneath me. I looked up and Beck was coming down after me.

"You think so?" he yelled.

Had we been having a conversation when I wasn't looking?

I ignored him, focusing on not losing my footing as I fled down the next section of fire escape. The narrow rungs reverberated beneath my feet as Beck stomped and banged after me.

It was like some urban version of *Jack and the Beanstalk*.

My phone whistled again.

Not now, honey...

"You're dead," Beck shouted.

I didn't have breath to waste and I wasn't about to look behind me. If he wasn't close enough to grab me, I wasn't going to worry about it. There was nothing I could do anyway. I was moving as fast as I could, concentrating on not slipping, not stepping wrong, not missing a handhold.

I wasn't thinking any further than getting safely to the ground. I didn't have the keys to the car and I couldn't leave without Ingrid anyway.

Hurry. Hurry. Hurry.

Where the hell was the ground? I was on Mt. Everest. I was in fucking outer space.

On and on.

But then suddenly I was out of rungs. The sidewalk was right below me. I jumped to the pavement, ignoring the pain flashing up my shins, and hobbled up the alley, looking for...anywhere. Anywhere there were people.

By *people* I did not mean the homeless guy urinating against the wall of the building. He gave me a hostile look for barging into his bathroom without knocking. I averted my gaze.

Otherwise there was nothing but trash cans and empty cardboard boxes. Or boxes that I hoped were empty.

The opening to the alley was ahead. I ran for it, and darted out onto a street just in time to narrowly avoid getting nailed as a blue Mini sped past. I saw Ingrid, hunched over the steering wheel.

"Stop!" I waved my arms. Yelled to her, "Ingrid! Ingrid, it's me!"

She never glanced my way, never slowed. I doubt if she even saw me. In fact, I doubt she'd have stopped even if she'd hit me.

I watched her bumper sticker—San Francisco State University—grow smaller and smaller. I turned. Saw Beck, still in pursuit, growing larger and larger. I ran.

A restaurant, a coffee house, a bar...anything would do. Eight hundred thousand people in this city and I couldn't find where any of them hung out. I spotted a dry cleaners and crossed the street. I dived inside. The air was warm and chemical scented.

"Where's the back?" I cried.

An Asian girl watering a dead African violet pointed speechlessly to the back, and I ran through the floating racks of plastic film-wrapped garments. I shoved out the emergency entrance, raced down another garbage-strewn alley. There was a trash dumpster next to a concrete wall. With a burst of desperate energy, I climbed—it took three tries—onto the dumpster, climbed over the cinderblock wall, and dropped down into what looked like a construction site.

It had to be well after five by then, and there were only a few workers in hard hats to look on in astonishment as I picked my way across the bulldozer-furrowed yard and went out through the chain-link fence.

I was now completely lost. It seemed the least of my problems. I kept running until the stitch in my side grew too bad. Then I walked—with many glances over my shoulder—and tried to phone J.X.

He picked up at once. "Where are you?" He sounded...hard to say. He sounded like someone who had warned himself not to start yelling the minute I called.

"I'm not sure." I looked around. Liquor stores. Some kind of clinic I didn't want to know about. Single room occupancy hotels. A long way from the Fairmont, that was a fact. "I was on Market Street. Now I'm not sure."

"What the *hell* are y—" J.X. stopped and said very calmly, "Can you look around and give me a landmark?"

"Wait. I think maybe I'm on 6th Street? I'm looking at a closed adult theater called Pussy Katz."

He made a faint sound that might have been dismay or disgust. "Okay. Now listen. As soon as we hang up, put your phone away unless you want to get mugged. Is there a donut shop or some place where you can wait safely?"

I looked around. "There *is* a donut shop, actually. It's called The Donut Hole." I feared that was not artistic license.

"Good. Go have a donut. I'm coming to get you right now."

Three donuts and one very bad cup of coffee later, I dusted the sprinkles off my lips and walked out of The Donut Hole to collapse into J.X.'s Honda S2000.

The car interior smelled comfortingly of apple-cinnamon air freshener and John Varvatos fragrance. We sped away into the evening traffic and into that yawning and abysmal silence I said, "All that you have to say has already crossed my mind."

J.X. replied tersely, but right on cue, "And possibly your answer has already crossed mine."

"I don't doubt it."

"And yet I'm not going to strangle you." He glanced at me. "Are you okay?"

"I'm fine. Or will be. After a drink."

"Are you sure? You look like..." he paused either out of tact or because words failed him.

"I look like a madman chased me through every godforsaken alley in this godforsaken town. Fortunately my tetanus shots are up to date. Although I'm thinking I should have opted for the malaria and yellow fever inoculations too. You can reassure Izzie that Beck is alive and well."

He threw me another look, and this time his expression was shocked. "What the hell, Kit?"

"I know. Believe me, I know."

"I thought...I didn't know what to think. You scared the hell out of me!"

"I'm sorry. Really. You have no notion how sorry I am."

"I almost called the cops. I almost called Izzie."

"Please don't yell at me. Or at least, wait till I've had that drink."

"You leave me an oblique message: *Out with Ingrid.* What am I supposed to make of that?"

I said wearily, "I have no idea. I don't even know what I'm supposed to think. I don't know why I let myself get dragged into it." I proceeded to tell J.X. everything that had occurred that afternoon.

The car swerved twice during my recital. J.X. said very little, but I already knew that was a bad sign. The more quiet he got, the more upset he was.

He said at last, when I finally ran out of words, "If you were going to involve yourself in this, why didn't you just accept Lorenson's offer?"

Good question. "I didn't like Lorenson, that's part of it. He's responsible for this whole mess. Partly. He used his precious collection to try to manipulate and control his family, and I don't blame them for finally getting fed up. But I *didn't* intend to get involved. Period. It just sort of...happened."

"Because you *like* playing amateur sleuth."

"No. I really don't."

He shook his head without answering.

"Don't do the silent head shake at me. Please. That's really annoying. And not fair because it wasn't my intention to get involved in this mess. It's crude and stupid and violent and not an interesting crime at all. It's not anything like what I would write."

He looked at me in disbelief. Did the silent head shake again. Said, "We have to talk to Izzie as soon as possible."

"I know. But if we could just wait until I—"

"No." His voice was harsh. "Kit, do you not understand you just turned yourself into an accessory after the fact? I can't *believe* you would do something so reckless. Criminally reckless."

"*The hell*. I'm not trying to hinder or prevent their apprehension. It helps all of us if I can figure out what Ladas did with the coins. And that's all I'm trying to do. Beck still thinks I'm central to this, and take it from me, nothing that happened today would change his mind."

"*Ingrid confessed planning the robbery to you!*"

"No. She had knowledge of it, sure. But plan it? She couldn't plan her way out of a tea party. *She's* an accessory," I said. "An accessory before the fact."

"Jesus. Christ."

"I'm trying to find a way out of this."

"By getting more deeply involved?"

It's not that I didn't see his point. But I didn't like being yelled at after my already awful afternoon. "You know, I hate to be critical of your friends, but it's been a goddamned week since I found Ladas' body in our basement. And the coins are still missing and Beck is still running around threatening to kill me. At least, I assume that's what the plan is."

J.X. sucked in a sharp breath. "I know you're under a strain, Kit. But that doesn't excuse you from—"

"Oh, spare me. Which reminds me of something else. What the hell did you say to Jerry?"

He didn't answer for a moment. "You heard the phone message," he said finally. I thought he sounded guilty, but he wasn't much prone to guilt, so it was probably chagrin.

"I sure did. I was there when he called. What did you say to him? Because, again, I hate to criticize, but you didn't help matters."

"I told him anything he wanted to say to you could be communicated through me."

I sat up straight. "You told him *what*?"

"That if he had anything to say to you—"

"I heard you. I just can't believe you said something so…so over the top."

"You don't understand the psychology of a stalker."

"I don't even know that Jerry *is* a stalker. He could just be pushy. He could just be socially inept. Now you've pissed him off and he's going to go write a bunch of terrible reviews of my books."

J.X.'s jaw tightened. He said, "He *is* a stalker. I asked Izzie to pull his jacket. His juvenile records are sealed, which right there tells you there's a problem. Even without those records, Knight has a long history of complaints filed against him for harassment and stalking—as well as one conviction."

"He was *convicted* of stalking someone?"

J.X. said grimly, "His creative writing professor."

"He wants to be a *writer*?" I think that might have been the most horrible news yet. On the bright side, he hadn't asked me to look at his work, so there was still something to be grateful for.

"Apparently so. Anyway, he served a year in jail. Mostly because he was suspected of poisoning the woman's dog. It wasn't proved, but it influenced the jury."

I thought of the picnic basket and swallowed. "Fabulous."

"Don't worry. California has the best anti-harassment laws in the country. But the best way to deal with the situation is starve the monster."

"What's that mean?"

"It means Knight feeds off your reaction to him. He knows he makes you uncomfortable and unhappy. There's a bullying component to all stalking. But if he can't reach you, or on the occasions he does reach you, you give him nothing, he'll eventually lose interest and move on."

That sounded fine in theory, but I knew a bit about stalking too, thanks to *A Run in Miss Butterwith's Stalkings*. And inflaming the harasser as J.X. had done with Jerry sometimes escalated the situation.

Not that doing nothing worked either.

Which was why I'd had to conveniently and permanently dispatch the stalker in *A Run in Miss Butterwith's Stalkings*. A real-life solution was unlikely to be so tidy.

* * * * *

"What if you and I took Gage to the zoo this Saturday?" J.X. suggested as we were cleaning up after dinner.

It had been a quiet meal. J.X. and I had both been preoccupied. Him no doubt with my accessory-after-the-fact status, and me with my potential-stalker-victim status. He hadn't mentioned phoning Izzie again, but I knew that he was only biding his time till I was in a more reasonable frame of mind. Or maybe he had phoned Izzie while I was enduring my long and very hot shower. That was possible too. One thing I had learned about J.X.—well, two things, and I'd already known them, but I was being reminded of them daily—he was stubborn and he was used to always thinking he was right.

Two fairly annoying qualities. Which I knew first hand—since I shared them.

"I know," I said. "What if you took Gage to the zoo and I was a really good sport about not getting to spend Saturday with you?"

He sighed. "Kit."

"I'm just thinking of Gage," I said. "He's going to enjoy the two of you going to the zoo a lot more than if I tag along."

"You wouldn't be *tagging* along. It would be you and me taking him. That would be the point."

"I realize that's the theory. And I appreciate what you're saying. More than Gage will. It's just that I've got a lot on my mind right now."

"Wouldn't it help to try to get things back to normal?"

"Maybe. But going to the zoo is not normal for me."

He said, smiling but stubborn, "I really think it would be good for you to get out of the house. Let's change the subject. Let's do something fun. Something relaxing."

Yes, because there was nothing more relaxing than going to a crowded amusement park on a weekend when it would be packed with frazzled adults, screaming children and caged, desperate animals.

It was my turn to sigh heavily. "J.X., I know you're keen on me and Gage bonding, but could you maybe soft-peddle it for a while? I'm not really a kid person. And I kind of need to take this at my own speed."

"I feel like it's important that we start the way we intend to go on."

"So do I," I said. "Which is why I'm asking you not to turn this into a test."

"A *test?*" No vestige of a smile now.

"That's what it feels like."

"It's not a test. It's a chance for you to show a little interest in someone besides yourself."

It stung, but I let it go. "On your timetable."

"If I don't push it, it's not going to happen."

"It's not going to happen this Saturday, that's for damn sure."

"Right," J.X. said. "I should have remembered. You've already planned a busy weekend feeling sorry for yourself."

I saw his eyes flicker the instant the words left his mouth, saw his realization that he had said too much. I saw his regret, but it didn't stop me from firing right back, "Nah, that was last weekend. This weekend I'm busy having second thoughts."

J.X. sucked in a sharp breath. He opened his mouth and I felt a surge of ferocious glee. *Yes, say it. Go for it. Let's get it over with now before I convince myself that it might really work this time. Say it.*

Instead, he exhaled unsteadily, and said, "I'm sorry you're having second thoughts. In that case, maybe it would be a mistake to encourage Gage to get too attached."

I could see he was truly hurt but trying to dial it back, and I wanted to meet him halfway. Part of the trouble was I had learned how to argue from David, and we had developed ugly habits. We didn't fight a lot, but we always fought mean.

I said, "You don't have to worry about that. All the giraffes and cotton candy in the world couldn't soften that kid."

J.X. turned and walked out.

That was a jolt. Neither David nor I ever walked away from a fight. Not while the other had any blood left to pump from his still-beating heart.

I stared after J.X.

I couldn't stand the idea that I had hurt him. I wanted to go after him. Except I didn't think I was in the wrong, and if I went after him that was going to appear like I was relenting. And I wasn't. I had no intention of going to the zoo. Or anywhere else until I was good and ready.

But I hadn't meant to hurt him.

I continued puttering around the kitchen. Not that there was much to putter with. The leftover food had been put away. It didn't look like we'd be having dessert. The dishwasher ran with quiet efficiency. The clock over the sink ticked peacefully.

I walked into the dining room and listened.

I could hear music from behind the closed door of J.X.'s office. The Black Keys again.

Well, hell. I wasn't even sure how this worked. David and I did not apologize to each other. After a fight we just ignored each other until one of us decided to start speaking again.

Sometimes it was a matter of hours. Sometimes a matter of days. I tried to imagine not talking to J.X. for days. My heart sank.

But, as he'd said himself, it was important that we started the way we intended to go on.

Suddenly three thousand square feet seemed way too cramped a space for both of us. I listened to the call of The Black Keys.

It's up to you now

It's up to you now

Yeah, well.

I went out through the side door into the garden. The evening air was mild and sweetly scented. An urban blend of industry and flowers. The sky still held a distant trace of pink and a few stars glittered in the fleecy folds of blue-black.

I walked up the series of little terraces to the pool. The crystal water shone aqua-blue. Something about a pool at night always fascinated me. It seemed magical. Like the entryway to an underwater kingdom. I was always watching for that door, but it never appeared.

I knelt and skimmed the water with my hand. It was warm. Warm enough to swim. I liked night swimming. I liked floating and gazing up at the stars.

Getting out of the pool would be chilly though. June nights weren't usually all that hot.

Something rustled behind me. I turned in alarm. The boxwood hedge shook and then a large gray cat pushed through. Emmaline's cat. Pinky.

He wandered over to me and I ran my hand down his sleek back. He slunk down and then pleasurably arched beneath the caress.

"Wouldn't it be easier to go *over* the hedge?" I asked, picking a couple of small leaves off his coat.

Pinky meowed in reply. He had a very loud meow. He really did sort of remind me of Mr. Pinkerton.

"So it's your job to keep the mice population down? We send our complaints to you?"

Another meow.

Nice to know someone was still talking to me.

I glanced back at the house. I glimpsed J.X. crossing the dining room on his way to the kitchen. Maybe he was looking for me. Maybe he wanted to talk. I was not a big fan of relationship talk—certainly hadn't much practice—but I'd be willing to meet J.X. halfway. More than halfway.

I rose to return to the house. Pinky followed me across the bricks, then suddenly hissed and sprang away.

I looked over in surprise. But I was looking in the wrong direction.

Someone grabbed me from behind and threw me into one of the giant stone urns. I landed on my bad shoulder and the pain was so awful all my breath sucked in instead of whooshing out in a yell for help.

I slid down, landing on my hands and knees. Looking up through tears, I saw Beck, gilded in moonlight, as he towered over me.

CHAPTER EIGHTEEN

"I'm Swiss," I said desperately. "I'm neutral. I don't know what happened to your brother. I got dragged into this. I don't *know* anything."

He picked me up by the back of my shirt, which tore loudly—or maybe that was my spine being ripped out—and hurled me into the urn once more.

I was pretty sure he was going to batter me to death. He was not really looking for an explanation. He was looking for payback. His brother was dead and he wanted someone to take his frustration and loss out on. And I kept popping up on his radar. Looking at it from Beck's point of view, this made sense.

The second time I hit the urn, I did scream. But it came out as a choked sound and I doubted if it carried very far.

I flopped to the ground and started crawling for the house.

I didn't expect to get very far, so it was a dull but welcome surprise when Beck did not instantly scoop me up again and sling me once more into a wall of concrete. Dimly, I heard a thud, a groan, and the earth seemed to jump beneath my hands and knees.

"Christopher? Are you okay?"

I knew that voice. And though it was not a voice I associated with good things, I was abjectly grateful to hear it.

"Jerry?" I stared up through the starring of tears.

Jerry now stood over me. He held a round stone garden sphere about the size of a baseball. I looked past him and saw Beck face down on the ground. There was a dark patch on the back of his silver head. He was groaning.

"Are you all right?" Jerry sounded weirdly calm. Almost cheerful.

"No," I replied.

"Oh hey, that's too bad." Jerry dropped the stone sphere and dragged me to my feet. I swayed dizzily. "Good thing I was here. Seeing that your boyfriend is only interested in sitting around drinking beer by himself tonight."

I looked automatically at the house. No sign of J.X. now.

Beck groaned more forcefully and pushed up on his hands. Jerry unhurriedly let go of me and bent down to pick up the stone sphere again.

I ran.

It was more of a staggering reel, but the motion propelled me forward and I stumbled down the series of terraces, across the brick patio and burst through the breakfast room doors. J.X. was not in the kitchen. He was nowhere to be seen.

"*J.X.!*" I shouted breathlessly. "J.X.!"

I was having trouble getting enough air to speak. Like those old movies where some terrified and endangered person keeps pawing the air and wheezing out the word *help...* but no one notices. That was me. So I don't know how he heard me, but he did. J.X. seemed to erupt out of his office and charge into the kitchen.

"Kit? What's wrong?" His eyes went wide as he got a look at me. "*Jesus.*"

"Beck," I gulped. "Jerry is outside."

Which I'm sure made no sense. But maybe my battered appearance said it all. In two steps, J.X. had his arms around me.

Well, no. That would have been nice. His hands did land on my shoulders, and they were warm and solid and reassuring, but it was only to better inspect the damage. He was swearing quietly, ferociously. He hooked his foot around the leg of one of the kitchen table chairs, dragging it out and pressing me onto it.

"Jerry knocked Beck out," I said faintly.

J.X. shoved my head between my knees. "Don't pass out, Kit."

And he was gone.

What the hell?

I sat up, clutching the table to steady myself. I opened my mouth, but J.X. reappeared—out of his office again—and this time he was carrying a pistol. His face looked hard and dangerous and completely unfamiliar.

He crooked a hand under my arm, lifting me to my feet. "Lock the door after me, Kit. Then call 911."

That cleared my brain like nothing else could have.

"No. Wait. What are you doing? You can't go out there!"

If he heard me, there was no sign of it. He drew me along with him to the breakfast room. "Lock this door behind me. Call 911. Do you understand?"

"Don't go out there!"

"Do. You. Understand?" J.X. rapped out.

"Yes. But—"

But nothing. He stepped outside, turned and gestured furiously to me.

Huh? Oh right.

I locked the door, pressing my face to the glass, watching his lean form disappear into the shadows. The motion detector lights were blazing all around the house. Nothing moved in the darkness beyond. And now I couldn't see J.X. either.

I remembered I was supposed to be phoning for help.

Shivering with pain and shock, I limped back to the phone. I called 911. I poured my disjointed story out to the 911 operator who told me help was on the way and to stay on the line.

She was still telling me to stay on the line when I went out the back door after J.X.

The crickets were very loud as I retraced J.X.'s footsteps. I could hear splashing from the pool area and I stumbled into a run.

I found him in the swimming pool. He was dragging Beck's body to the shallow end. Or trying to. It was slow going because he was keeping the hand holding the pistol above water. There was no sign of Jerry.

Nor was J.X. happy to see me, despite the fact that he urgently needed my help.

"I told you to stay inside with the doors locked," he yelled.

He got a mouthful of pool water for his trouble, so I forbade answering. I splashed down into the shallow end and helped him drag Beck the rest of the way to the steps.

"Is he dead?" I asked.

J.X. didn't answer. Together we hauled Beck, heavy and sodden and dripping, onto the paved deck. I gasped when I saw the front of his face had been smashed in. My stomach did a ladylike somersault and it was all I could do to swallow my revulsion.

J.X. pushed him onto his side. He looked up. "Did you call 911, Kit?"

"They're on their way."

"Tell them they need to send emergency medical services. And stay on the line with them this time."

"Where's Jerry?"

J.X.'s voice was grim. "He was gone by the time I got out here."

"He was here," I said quickly. "I didn't do this."

"I don't give a shit if you did it or not. Just get me some backup."

"He can't have gone far." I looked uneasily at the brightly lit house ringed in white light.

J.X. had commenced life support efforts and did not answer me.

Somehow I managed to get back on my feet. I started down the walkway to the house. Lights were shining in Emmaline's backyard.

"Yoo-hoo!" she called. "Yoo-hoo! Christopher? J.X.?"

"Emmaline, there's a prowler," I called. "Go back inside and lock your doors."

"Are the police on their way?"

"They're supposed to be."

She answered, though I couldn't make out the words. *What was this world coming to?* That sounded about right. It was certainly what I was thinking.

The phone was ringing when I made it back to the house. I picked it with a cautious, "Hello?"

It was the 911 operator. I gave her the latest update.

This time when she told me to stay on the line, I agreed. I was feeling strangely numb. Mentally. Physically, not so much. Mentally...so many things had happened in such a short time, I couldn't seem to make sense of them, couldn't connect the dots. And in any case, the dots seemed less important than my physical woes. There was blood trickling down my face from a cut on my forehead. My shoulder throbbed sickeningly. Had I rebroken my collarbone? My legs were shaking. My hands were shaking. I resisted the temptation to slide down to the floor. Mostly because the phone cord wouldn't reach.

It wasn't really surprising that Ladas had shown up. We should have expected it after my experiences that afternoon. I had been relying too much on those patrol cars and Ladas' own sense of self-preservation. He wasn't smart enough to have a sense of self-preservation.

I closed my eyes, leaned on the counter. I could hear water from my clothes dripping to the floor.

Don't pass out, Kit.

No. I wasn't going to pass out. Anyway, there was something I needed to remember...

What was it?

Right.

Jerry.

A floorboard squeaked behind me. I turned, ready for anything—and yet it still came as a sort of monotonous jolt to see Jerry standing there. *Not this again.*

He was holding a hammer.

No. Holding the meat tenderizer hammer I had joked about with him the first day he'd shown up. He was not carrying the kitchen tool in a threatening manner, but I'd read a lot of Scandinavian crime fiction by then, and I knew only too well what a well-placed hammer could do to you.

"I knew you didn't leave," I said.

"Of course not." He smiled in agreement at the ridiculousness of the idea. "Not without you."

"I have to stay on the phone, Jerry," I said.

"Is someone there with you?" the 911 operator asked.

"Yes, I'm still here," I said.

"Is your assailant in the house with you?"

"Yes."

Jerry said, "What is she saying?"

"She wants me to stay on the line."

"Hang up the phone, Christopher."

"They told me to stay on the line."

He said slowly and clearly, "Hang up the phone."

"How about if I just set it down here?" I carefully set the receiver on the counter and stepped back.

Jerry's face twisted and he smashed the tenderizer hammer down on the phone, which broke apart into several pieces.

Okaaaay. Time to go.

There was really only one way out of the kitchen. The breakfast nook was a dead end. I'd never get the door unlocked in time. So I just shoved right past Jerry, who swung belatedly at me with the hammer—and missed.

I heard it hit the door frame with considerable force though, and that old cliché about adding wings to your feet? I was *jetting* as I darted across the dining room.

I ran into the parlor, hitting the light switch as I passed. The room plunged into darkness. Or at least partial darkness. The light from the dining room cast a faint irradiation over one end. At least there was no real moonlight.

I took a couple of cautious steps. A floorboard squeaked. I froze.

I thought my best chance was to escape through the front door. That meant getting to and across the foyer unseen. But I wasn't sure where Jerry was now.

I listened.

Nothing.

But he was still here. No way had he given up and fled. He was somewhere close by. I could feel his presence like it was a tangible thing. Was he in the dining room? Or had he gone out through the breakfast room to try and cut me off if I tried to get to J.X.?

Arms out, I soundlessly felt my way past chair, shelf, table, lamp, chair—I was getting to know these rooms even in the dark—sofa, table, a solid cardboard box with tissue paper...

The Reading Bear bookends Jerry had given me.

I felt over the cardboard box and whispering tissue paper and lifted one bookend up. It felt solid, reassuringly heavy. As blunt instruments went, not too bad.

A distant sound that had been tapping on my consciousness suddenly made itself known. A siren. My heart lifted as I heard its approaching wail. Help was on the way.

I moved against the wall adjoining the doorway next to the foyer entrance, tucking myself in the corner, waiting.

I fully expected Jerry to enter the parlor from the dining room. My fear was that he would find the switch and turn on the lights. So my heart nearly stopped when he spoke from the other side of the doorway, mere inches away from me.

He knew the house—and me—well enough to try and cut off my escape out the front.

He said in a low voice, "I did it for you. I saved your life."

I stepped silently to the perpendicular wall.

"He would have killed you. I stopped him. But now you're treating me like *I'm* the bad guy." His tone was aggrieved.

I started to reply, rethought, and stayed silent. There wasn't any more reasoning with him than there had been with Beck. Sure, Jerry talked more, but that was the only real difference.

"Christopher?"

I bit my lip. My palms were sweating. The bear bookend felt slippery in my grasp.

"We have to go, Christopher. We have to go *now*." He sounded like J.X. did sometimes when he was struggling to stay patient.

I said nothing.

He laughed. "I can *hear* you, you big silly."

I pressed my lips together, trying to breathe more quietly. Or maybe it was my heart he could hear. It felt like I had a herd of wild horses galloping through my chest. I was shaking with fear and adrenaline and pain. My eyes never moved from the partial outline of his shadow on the polished floor. I could just make out the hammer, which was still by his side as he spoke to me.

Could he see my shadow too? I didn't think so. The foyer light was behind him. Whereas I was standing in deep shadow, tucked into this corner.

Jerry's voice rose, grew shrill. "I don't understand you. We find each other again after all this time, and everything is going great, and then suddenly you start treating me like this. After everything I've done for you, including saving your goddamned life. You're the most ungrateful person I've ever known, Christopher!"

The shadow Jerry suddenly swung the hammer up and lunged around the door frame. The hammer smashed into the wall where I had previously been standing. I heard the crunch of plaster. At the same time I slammed the bookend into where I thought Jerry's head was. *Wham*. I felt hair, skin, ear. Jerry dropped like a bag of wet concrete.

I dropped the bookend from nerveless fingers. Switched on the standing lamp. Jerry was sprawled and unmoving on the hardwood floor he had admired so much. I lifted my gaze.

There was a head-sized hole punched into the wall where Jerry had struck home.

Despite J.X.'s efforts, Beck Ladas was pronounced dead at the scene.

And despite my efforts, Jerry was only knocked out. He was still groggily accusing me of assault and battery when he was loaded into the black-and-white police car and driven away.

That was only the prelude to the very long night's festivities.

First I had to explain my "relationship" with Jerry. Needless to say, our stories didn't match. Once Izzie showed up to cast light on the situation, things improved a little. Or at least everyone stopped looking at me like some kind of gay black widow luring hapless men into my web of deceit and violence.

"It's not impossible that Knight could make trouble for you down the line," J.X. explained quietly during one of the brief breaks in the inquisition. Er, interrogation. "This situation escalated so fast. There was no time to document anything, there's no track record of threatening behaviors. You hadn't even filed a request for a restraining order yet. You let him into the house on two occasions. You accepted gifts from him."

I stared at J.X., aghast. "He was hiding in our backyard! How does he explain that? And there's the message on the answering machine."

"Yes, and I've played the message for Izzie. And Izzie knows I asked to see Knight's record and that, according to me, you felt threatened. Izzie believes you. The cops are on your side. Knight killed Ladas. He dragged him, unconscious or at least stunned, to the swimming pool and dumped him in, leaving him to drown. There's no question that Knight is in deep, deep trouble."

I honestly didn't know what to say. Nor had I missed the *could make trouble for you*—in the singular—comment versus *could make trouble for us*.

Whatever J.X. read in my face caused him to say, "I could be looking for problems where there aren't any. Knight has contradicted his own story a couple of times already, but he does claim you invited him over here tonight, which makes me think he's not unaware that he's got a couple of potential angles for his defense. Don't forget, he's been through this before."

"I don't believe this!"

"Kit, nobody here is doubting your story. And maybe Knight doesn't have a track record with you, but he *does* have a track record. And that record speaks for itself."

"But a good lawyer could make a case in his defense."

J.X. sighed. "Anything is possible. But is it probable? All I'm saying is, be cautious. Don't say anything more than you have to when it comes to your relationship with Jerry."

"There was no relationship!"

"You know what I mean."

Did I? I wasn't so sure. I didn't think I was imagining the new and painful distance between myself and J.X. Was this because of our earlier argument or did he now believe there had been something between me and Jerry?

He *couldn't*.

"J.X.—" I broke off as Izzie returned.

The floggings recommenced.

Okay. Maybe I'm a little prone to exaggeration. But though Izzie had been gruffly sympathetic when we were going over Jerry's attempt to permanently tenderize me, I fell seriously out of favor once we reached the topic of my trip with Ingrid Edwards to Elijah Ladas' loft.

"I was only trying to help," I said for about the millionth time.

"Right. Except when the victim asked for help, you turned him down. When Ladas' accomplice asked for help, you went to her aid." Izzie's brown eyes were narrow and hard.

"I didn't look at it like that. All I was thinking was...I had to get this nightmare over with. I was a nervous wreck waiting for Beck Ladas to show up again."

"So you admit knowing that Ingrid and Beck were in it together?"

"They weren't in it together."

Izzie gave a disbelieving laugh and glanced at J.X. who had, surely against regulations, been allowed to remain in the breakfast room as an observer. He was leaning against the wall, next to the green and pink china plates we had hung that morning. Was it only that morning? His arms were folded and he watched us without visible emotion.

"They weren't," I insisted.

J.X. stared at me without pleasure. Izzie stared at me without pleasure. I could see—without pleasure—why they must have made a great team once upon a time.

I said, "Ingrid was scared to death of Beck. She thought he was a dangerous and unpredictable animal."

"She told you that?"

I shook my head. "She didn't have to. He *was* a dangerous and unpredictable animal. And dumb as a post. What she did say was he creeped her out."

"But you don't think he killed his brother?"

"No."

Izzie slid back in his chair and waved a beckoning hand. "Okay. Go on. Dazzle us. What really happened?"

I said, "I realize you're not serious. But as a matter of fact, I do know what happened."

Izzie stopped smiling. "You're saying *you* solved the case?"

"It's not much of a case," I said. "And I don't know what Ladas did with the coins. But, if you want to put it that way, yes. I know pretty much everything else. I can't prove it. But I'm sure I'm right."

J.X. said, "But then, you're always sure you're right."

That hurt. And it was unfair too, dragging our personal shit into the interrogation room. Okay, the breakfast room, but still. Not nice.

I didn't look at him. I waited for Izzie to make another of those sweeping *after you!* gestures, which he did, right on cue.

I took a sip of water, put my glass down, and said, "Okay. Here's how I think it all came about."

CHAPTER NINETEEN

"**O**nce upon a time—"

Izzie's head fell back and he groaned.

I stopped. "I have to tell this in my own way."

"Go on," he told the ceiling.

"There was a mean old man who used his wealth to control and manipulate his children. And unfortunately they learned these same behaviors when dealing with their own kids. Greed begat greed and manipulation begat—"

J.X. said, "Kit!"

"Anyway, Lorenson took a peculiar and potentially dangerous pleasure in taunting his family about what would happen to his money—most of which is tied up in his coin collection—once he died. He tried to play siblings against each other, and then generations against each other, and when that stopped amusing him, he played his final card. He announced he was donating the entire collection to the American Numismatic Society. With the end result being his grandchildren decided to take matters into their own hands."

Izzie said sarcastically, "And of course you have evidence of all this?"

"Of course I don't. I simply observe and deduce."

J.X. leaned back against the wall like he was welcoming the bullets of the firing squad.

"I used a very similar plot in both *Swan Song for Miss Butterwith* and *Sow Shall Ye Reap, Miss Butterwith*." I frowned. "Or was it *Miss Butterwith Sees Stars*? Anyway. I recognized the setup at once. It's been done a million times, and not just by me."

"Is this going anyw—"

"I doubt what, if anything, would have happened if the Lorenson grand-kids had been left to their own devices, but Kenneth Lorenson has a reporter girlfriend by the name of Sydney Nightingale."

"I know Syd." Izzie was watching me more closely now.

"Then you know that Sydney is smart, capable and gutsy. She's not a sit-around-and-whine-about-things kind of gal. She's the get-out-there-and-make-them-happen type. You kind of have to be in her line of work. And Sydney just happened to know—from conducting an interview a few months earlier—a bored, retired master thief who was just the guy to pull off this kind of job."

Izzie said, "Go on."

"But from the point Sydney put together the deal, things began to go wrong. First off, Ladas was getting a little long in the tooth and he decided to bring his troglodyte brother along on the job. That resulted in the murder of John Cantrell, which I'm sure was a horrible, horrible accident."

"Cantrell's neck was snapped. It was no accident."

"Right, but I mean, murder was not part of the plan. Neither the Lorensons nor Elijah Ladas wanted or expected violence. This was supposed to be a textbook heist. The kind of job Ladas used to pull off in his sleep. But Cantrell was killed, and even though the Ladas brothers successfully made away with their loot, now things were way too hot. The coins couldn't be disposed of through the normal channels. So Ladas hid them."

"But you don't know where."

"No. And neither does anyone else. Ladas didn't tell his partners where he stashed the goods and I think that's because he planned to change the terms of their deal."

"And what was their deal?"

"The most obvious deal would have been a percentage of the total take. That's typically how this stuff works."

J.X. sighed. Heavily.

I ignored him. "I think Ladas would have been willing to work for a percentage because he liked being a thief. He liked the rush. He liked the thrill. I think he missed it. I'm guessing he found retirement boring. And he was a romantic. So I think he probably originally agreed to a percentage.

For old times' sake. But then another thing Sydney couldn't have counted on, happened. Ingrid fell for Ladas. Or Ladas fell for Ingrid. Or they both mutually—"

"Go on," Izzie said.

"And Ladas decided to take Ingrid away from all that."

"All what?"

"All…well, her miserable life. Or at least what she considered a miserable life. Her controlling parents, mostly. Anyway, that's not the point."

"Oh, there is a point?" J.X. put in.

This time I gave him a long look. After a second his gaze fell.

"Here was the situation from Ladas' standpoint. For the first time in his long criminal career, there was a good chance he might actually wind up in prison. Meanwhile there was Ingrid who needed rescuing. So he decided to pull out and start over—in Cuba, where it was unlikely he would ever be extradited. But to do that, he needed a big, big stake. Like ten million dollars worth of a stake."

Izzie said, "So your theory is Ladas was going to double-cross the others and they killed him?"

"Yes. But I don't think it was planned or anything. I think maybe there was an argument and things got out of hand."

"Who killed him?"

"I'm sorry to say—because I like her—I think Sydney killed him."

Izzie's brows rose. He looked at J.X. J.X. said, "Kit, you can't just accuse—"

"I'm not accusing her. This is a private conversation." I looked at Izzie. "Right?"

"That's one word for it."

Two words, if we wanted to be precise. I let it go. "Ingrid is clueless. There's no way she had anything to do with killing Ladas. She had no motive, for one thing. He was her ticket out."

"Beck," Izzie began.

"I'm certain Beck didn't kill his brother. He didn't know what happened to Elijah, which is why he was following me around. His brother ended up here so I became his starting point. From the minute Elijah died, Beck became a-a free floating radical."

J.X. put a hand to his forehead as though he wondered whether he was feverish.

"Then how do you figure Sydney killed Elijah?" Izzie asked.

"Did Ladas sustain any other injuries beyond the knife wound?"

"No."

"No. So there was no fight. And I think if Kenneth or even Beck had been Elijah's killer, it would have all happened differently. I think there would have been a fight. But someone was able to stand right next to Elijah and stab him in the heart with a small blade."

"Huh." Izzie stroked his chin thoughtfully. "That's an interesting angle."

No pun intended. Clearly. "So Elijah wasn't afraid of this person, wasn't afraid to let her get right into his personal space. One thing about hetero-sexual guys, they defend their personal space from other heterosexual guys.

"Secondly, Ladas' death obviously wasn't planned because of the crazy, desperate way his body was disposed of. By the way, that required two people, and the only remaining twosome in that group was Kenneth and Sydney. I think they were terrified of Ladas' body showing up and being identified because Beck was bound to come after one or all of them. So I think Sydney and Kenneth started driving—I think the plan was to dump Ladas just as far from San Francisco as they could. But then they spotted the broken-down moving van and thought they'd found the perfect solution."

"Except, the van was headed for San Francisco."

"Which they couldn't know. Cue the Alanis Morissette."

"But why would Syd kill Elijah? Especially when none of them knew where the coins were hidden?"

"And why would she keep turning up here?" J.X. put in. "She would certainly know the coins weren't here."

"She wasn't looking for the coins. She was trying to keep tabs on the investigation. She figured because of my connection to you and your con-nection to SFPD, we'd probably have the inside track on what was going on. As for why she killed Ladas, I'm not sure. Maybe she just lost it when she realized he was double-crossing them. Maybe he did something to make her feel threatened. He was a big guy and he was no angel, despite the whole gentleman thief act."

They were both silent. Izzie stroked his chin some more. "So that's it?" he said finally. "That's your theory?"

"Yes."

He made a disgusted noise. "All I can say is, if you weren't as good as married to my ex-partner, you'd be on your way to the slammer."

Slammer? There was a golden oldie. Maybe Izzie thought that was what they called it back in my day.

"You don't believe me?"

"What I believe or don't believe is beside the point."

Well, not really. But I kept my mouth shut.

Izzie nodded to J.X. and they both walked out of the breakfast room and went into the garden.

There remained a lot of crime scene personnel wandering up and down the brick walkways. It was still a ways from morning, but the night was starting to fade. The colored solar lights were dimming as the flowers took shape and hue once more. I watched J.X. listening to Izzie. He looked as tired as I felt. He nodded a couple of times, but mostly he was just hearing out all that Izzie had to say. There seemed to be a lot of it.

I resisted the temptation to put my head on the table. My collarbone had not been rebroken, but my shoulder hurt. My face hurt. There was a bruise on my cheekbone and forehead both. My stomach was in knots. I didn't think I was going to be arrested. Izzie's exasperated *as good as married to* seemed to indicate otherwise. But I couldn't help wondering if that hadn't been overstating the current situation between me and J.X. It was clear to me that I had crossed a line there was perhaps no coming back from. Despite all that had happened that night—hell, maybe *because* of it (and who could blame him?)—J.X. was keeping an unmistakable distance.

I'd nearly died twice, but he hadn't even put his arms around me. Oh, he'd been beside me one hundred percent, explaining the situation with Jerry and the situation with Ladas. I had his support and his protection, no question. But there was none of the warmth or affection or tenderness I'd come to rely on.

I could have been any good friend in trouble.

My eyes stung. I wiped at them impatiently.

I shouldn't have said what I had about the kid. J.X.'s family meant every-thing to him. I knew that.

My thoughts broke off as Izzie gave J.X. a commiserating pat on the back. What the hell did *that* mean? My stomach dropped another couple of floors.

They walked back inside, Izzie took his chair at the table, and we began to go through my account of the evening's events again.

The sun was coming up by the time J.X. and I stumbled up to bed.

"Try not to worry," he said as we undressed.

I glanced at him. He met my gaze solemnly and I nodded.

That seemed to be all he had to say. He pulled the bedclothes back, crawled between the sheets and closed his eyes.

I dropped my clothes to the floor and lay down on the bed. The sheets felt cool and caressing, the mattress soft and comfortable. A little groan escaped me.

J.X. opened his eyes. He said nothing. I said nothing. He closed his eyes.

I turned on my back and stared up at the ceiling.

The argument seemed like a million years ago. I wasn't even sure now of everything I'd said. Let alone what he'd said. No, I did remember. He'd said I was self-centered, self-pitying... Probably true. Maybe self-destructive too, if I was going to let this go without a fight.

I could hear his soft, even breaths slowing, deepening.

I found myself studying the painting by Friedlander, the study of autumn wine country. I let myself remember how it had felt when I'd thought J.X. was dead.

My eyes stung just thinking about it. I never wanted to feel that again. Couldn't afford to feel like that again. That kind of emotion could destroy you. If you gave someone that much power and then they changed their mind, decided they didn't want you, didn't feel the same?

That wasn't for me. I wasn't built like that.

And I was kidding myself because it was already too late. Way too late.

I turned my head and said, "J.X.—"

His lips were parted, his lashes never stirred.

Or maybe he was pretending to be asleep.

Either way, the moment had passed.

He let me sleep late.

When I woke, it was to the comforting smells of coffee and bacon. But when I padded downstairs after my shower, the kitchen was deserted. The dishes had been done and put away, but coffee was still warming on the machine and I discovered four pieces of bacon on a covered plate.

J.X. was in his office. The door was closed and music was playing softly.

I'd kind of hoped that the new day might set us right. Offer us a fresh start. But no.

The walls were up, the doors were closed.

So that was that.

Right?

I couldn't do this on my own. And like D.H. Lawrence said, *We've got to live, no matter how many skies have fallen.*

I scrambled eggs and had my breakfast, and then I went out to get the mail.

It was a pretty day. A little hazy, but that would burn off. It was kind of nice to know that Beck wasn't hiding behind the hedges, waiting to jump me. And hopefully Jerry was still busy answering questions downtown. Or uptown. Whatever they called it here in San Francisco.

Maybe I wouldn't be staying long enough to find out.

There were a couple of forwarded letters for J.X., our first utility bill, and a small parcel for me from a bookseller I didn't recognize. I carried the mail inside.

J.X. was in the kitchen pouring a glass of milk. "Hey," he said indifferently.

Okay, I don't know that his greeting was indifferent. It was polite and it was not exactly enthusiastic. But maybe it was just guarded.

"Hey," I replied in the same careful tone. "Mail call." I placed his envelopes on the table and went through the breakfast room to the patio.

Technically, the upper level of the garden was now a crime scene, but I turned my chair so I didn't have to see the yellow-and-black crime scene tape. I put my head back and closed my eyes.

The sun felt good on my face. Despite sleeping late, I had not slept well. I was still very tired. Physically worn out. Emotionally...flattened.

"Yoo-hoo! Yoo-hoo!" Emmaline's voice floated on the warm breeze.

I opened my eyes and sat up.

A small hand was waving to me over the hedge.

I got up and walked over to the hedge. Emmaline looked cheerful enough, though I wouldn't have been surprised to see some dismay after the events of the previous evening. Maybe teaching high school prepared you for anything.

"Christopher! What on earth happened here last night? All those police cars and crime scene people again. And was it my imagination or were police helicopters circling us for a few hours?"

"It's a long story," I said. But since I had no one else to talk to, I launched into it.

"Oh my gosh!" Emmaline exclaimed at intervals. Occasionally, she broke it up with "Oh, my goodness!"

She was not at all like my dear Miss Butterwith, but she was a comfortable sort of person. I could see growing fond of Emmaline. If I stuck around long enough.

When I was finished with my long and rambling tale, she said, "I don't imagine there's been this much excitement in the old neighborhood since Dimitri Foden murdered Julia Clare Hargetter."

"Probably not," I agreed. And then, *"Who?"*

Emmaline's cheeks pinked. "Oh! I took it for granted you knew. About the murder."

"What murder?" I stared and the meaning of her discomfort registered. "There was a murder in our house?"

"Well, yes. I thought you must know. I thought that was probably one of the attractions for a pair of mystery writers."

"No. Not really."

"Well, it was long before any of our time. Julia Clare Hargetter used to live at 321. She was a very famous 19th century painter. Quite eccentric, so the story goes. Anyway, she was murdered by her lover, Dimitri Foden, who disappeared and was never seen again."

She sounded quite chipper about the whole thing.

I said, "Great. I know what that means. I used it in *How Does Your Garden Grow, Miss Butterwith?* Foden's somewhere in our backyard. With my luck, beneath the swimming pool."

Emmaline laughed merrily at the idea. "You mystery writers! What sinister minds you have."

We chatted a little more. Emmaline invited us to dinner Saturday evening, and I told her J.X. would be out with his nephew. So she invited us to dinner on Monday evening. I said I would check with my better half.

We said goodbye and I returned to my place in the sun. I unwrapped the parcel from the bookstore. It was a slim, battered paperback titled *Dead Man's Chest: A Lazlo Ender Mystery*. By Richard Cortez and Elijah Ladas.

I began to read.

An hour later I knocked on J.X.'s office door. He turned down the music and called, "Come in."

I opened the door.

He was seated at his desk, scowling, though the scowl cleared when he saw me. "What's up?" he asked.

I held up the paperback. "I think I know where Ladas hid the coins."

CHAPTER TWENTY

The scowl returned. "Where?" J.X. asked.

I took a deep breath. "Before I get to that, I just want to say that I know you're angry with me. And disappointed. I know I'm not—"

He interrupted harshly, "Did you mean what you said about having second thoughts?"

"Second thoughts, third thoughts, fourth thoughts. Aren't you?"

"Yes."

It hurt. A lot. But in a funny way, hearing it helped. Because I already knew it was true. And if we could talk about it honestly to each other, maybe we could work our way through it.

"But I still want it to work," I said. "I love you and I believe you're the best thing that ever happened to me."

Some of the hardness left his face. J.X. said uncertainly, "Is that true?"

"Yes." Honest. But naked. Too naked. I said hastily, "Well, I mean, next to Miss Butterwith. And Mr. Pinkerton. But you're definitely in the top three."

There was a very faint smile in his eyes. He said, "Right. Of course."

I said, "And I know you love me too and that you really want this relationship to work out—if only to avoid having to move me back to Southern California."

"Do you resent the fact that you're the one who had to move? That you're the one who got uprooted?"

"No." I meant that. "It makes sense because of Gage and Nina. I don't resent them, if that's the real question. And I don't resent that I'm the one who had to make the great migration."

He didn't say anything and I offered a lopsided smile. "So although I know you think I try to control everything and that rules are going to kill any spontaneity between us, I think it's in our best interests if we agree on a couple of things. Like…no matter how mad I get, I'm not ever going to talk about having second thoughts or us splitting up again. Unless I really am packing my bags. I'm not eight years old, and getting mad and threatening to take my ball home is not okay. Unless it really is game over."

J.X. let out a long, unsteady breath and said quietly, "That would help."

"But you have to cut me some slack too." I was startled when my throat closed, cutting off the words. I hadn't realized until that moment how deeply some of his words had cut. "I probably am self-centered and I probably do feel a little too sorry for myself right now. But I'm trying. I wouldn't be here if I wasn't trying. And I'm trying for you. Not because I want to be a better person or for any other reason than I want to make you happy." A swallow caught me at that embarrassing juncture.

"Kit—" J.X. came around the desk.

I waved him away. "Wait. I'm not finished. Here comes the deal breaker."

His brows drew together. "Go on."

"You have a different relationship with your family than I have with mine. And I respect that. And I admire how you're there for Nina and Gage. But I don't know that I can be part of that. Any of that. I'll do what I can. I'll try to meet them halfway. But you have to understand that…it's probably not going to turn out the way you want. I'm not that person. I'm not *The Waltons*."

He said impatiently, "I don't want *The Waltons*. I don't care about that."

"Except you do. You want big family holidays and outings with Gage. You're going to want to have him over for sleepovers and you're going to want to go to his Little League games and then his Demolition Derby shows. And the truth is…I don't even like kids."

"Kit—"

"I don't. They're small and they smell funny. I'll make an effort. Sometimes. But I'm afraid that if they force you to choose between me and them—"

"No." This time he wouldn't be waved off. He wrapped his muscular arms around me and pulled me close. I can't deny that it felt very good, like finding the way back through dark woods when you thought you'd lost the path for good. "Kit, you're wrong about this." He kissed me. "Listen, I fell in love ten years ago and I've never stopped loving you. Nothing and no one is going to—"

I had to protest. "Yeah, you did. Of course you did. You hated my guts when we met up again."

He shook his head. "No. I didn't. Let me finish. Nobody is going to force anyone to choose anything. Or to do anything. I've been going over and over this last argument and I know I escalated it. I already figured out that I'm making it worse by pushing you to participate. So that's over. That's done. Just don't...bail on me. On us. Don't give up before we've given it a real chance to work."

His eyes were dark with pain. I shook my head, wrapped my arms around his shoulders. "I won't. I'm not going to. Hence this. This big emotional scene where I force us both to talk about our feelings."

"I can't bear you thinking this was a mistake."

"I don't. Well, I think it was probably a mistake on your part, but..." He wasn't laughing, so I said, "I meant what I said. You're the best thing that has happened to me...maybe ever. You brought me back to life. That's the truth."

The brown column of his throat moved. "That's...more than I ever thought you'd give me."

"Well, I'll probably only say it the once. So when I'm being a bigger jackass than usual, try to remember that inside this is how I really feel about you." I found his mouth and kissed him deeply, sweetly. His eyelashes flickered against my face. I felt an unexpected wetness and tasted salt. I wasn't sure if the tears were mine or his. They could have been mine.

When we reluctantly broke the kiss, J.X. said, "Did you say you figured out where Ladas hid the coins?"

"That! I almost forgot. Yeah, I think so." I'd dropped the Lazlo book on J.X.'s desk. I picked it up and flashed the lurid cover his way. "When I was reading up on Ladas, finding out whatever I could about him, one thing that stuck in my memory was that he was a member of the San Francisco Yacht Club."

"So? I thought you said Ingrid and the others had already searched his boat."

"They did. And they didn't find anything. Because he didn't hide the coins on the boat. I've been studying the layout on the Web. The yacht club has over fifty dry-storage spaces and I'm betting one of them belongs to Ladas. Somewhere on those premises is a locker or a dock box or some kind of storage unit, and *that's* where he stashed the coins."

"But how would he—"

"The docks and grounds are accessible anytime to members." I handed J.X. the book. "It's right in here. He used it in the book. It's just the kind of private joke he'd have loved. Putting it right out there in front of everybody."

J.X. reached for his cell phone. He hesitated. "Are you sure about this?"

I swallowed. "Yep," I said staunchly.

*   *   *   *   *

I *had* been sure, but I won't pretend it wasn't a huge, huge relief when—several hours later—the yacht club maintenance man sawed off the heavy duty padlock on the unassuming dock box belonging to Elijah Ladas, and Izzie reached inside to heave out a heavy-duty green trash bag.

The sun beat down on our unprotected heads. Gulls circled and swooped overhead. Absently, I was aware J.X. patted me on the shoulder. I couldn't tear my gaze from the sagging bag.

"It's heavy enough," Izzie said. "And it's jingling. He's either got Christmas bells in h—"

The green bag caught on the side of the silver box, tore, and the ring of watching cops and yacht club officials gasped as a rush of glinting, plastic coated squares and a handful of loose coins poured out at our feet. A Viking's treasure.

Izzie, holding the torn bag, gazed across at me. "Not bad," he said.

I nodded coolly just as though I wasn't ready to sag with relief.

Izzie glanced at J.X and then back at me. "I'll still throw you in the slammer if you ever interfere in one of my cases again, but...not bad."

"Not bad at all, Mr. Holmes," J.X. said softly, smiling.

Later J.X. told me that Izzie had confided that when Ingrid and Kenneth were questioned that morning, they had spilled everything. Ingrid had not known about Ladas' murder, and Kenneth was claiming Sydney had killed Ladas in self-defense. Sydney was saying nothing to anyone on the advice of her lawyer.

"What's going to happen to them?" I asked.

"A lot is going to depend on Lorenson."

"That doesn't sound hopeful."

"People can surprise you," J.X. said. He smiled into my eyes, which I took to mean lately I was one of the nicer surprises.

"Speaking of which. Is Jerry still claiming I invited him over to our house so I could bash his brains out?"

"No. He's now claiming that he came over to apologize after losing his temper at all the unfair and undeserved things I said to him. He saw Ladas attack you and rushed to your rescue. He says Ladas got away from him and must have fallen in the pool."

I gaped at J.X. "And what does he say about trying to smash my head in with a meat hammer?"

J.X.'s face was grim. "He says he was trying to get you out of the house because Ladas had escaped from him. He says in your blind panic, you attacked him, and he was only defending himself."

"*What?*" I stared, trying to read J.X.'s expression. "And does anyone believe that cock-and-bull story?"

"No. But that's going to be his defense when it goes to court."

"Oh, that's just fantastic," I said bitterly.

"I don't think a jury will buy it, Kit. Even with a very good defense lawyer, he's going to prison for a while."

I nodded. I wanted to feel reassured. I really, *really* wanted to believe that was the last we'd seen of Jerry.

* * * * *

At an ungodly hour on Saturday morning, Nina Moriarity handed her only child over to her ex-husband and the fiend from hell he currently resided with, and with many doubtful looks—and a few tears—bade us all *Have a nice time.*

I think J.X. had a nice time—and God knows he was never more engaging than when he was getting his way—and I guess Gage was having so much fun even my presence couldn't entirely spoil it.

"Don't stick your tongue out at your Uncle Christopher," J.X. warned, catching one of our exchanges when he returned to deliver a corn dog to the bottomless pit in blue shorts and striped T-shirt.

Gage's little monkey face—so like his real uncle's—screwed up into a grimace as though his corn dog had been dipped in alkali. "*He's* not my uncle."

J.X.'s face darkened. "Gage—"

"He's right," I said.

"Don't you start!"

Gage rewarded me with another display of his tongue while J.X. was busy frowning repressively at me.

I said solemnly, "I feel like it's important that we start the way we intend to go on. Don't you?"

J.X. shook his head at me.

After Gage departed on spindly legs to goggle at some other hapless, trapped creature, J.X. draped a casual arm around my shoulders and said, "Are you hating every minute of it?"

I sighed. "Nah. It's fine. I just wish there was a G&T stand along with all the other refreshments."

He laughed. "I'll fix you a drink when we get home. And then I'm going to give you a nice, long backrub."

"Now you're talking."

He whispered in my ear, "I'm really happy you changed your mind."

"I know."

He gave my shoulders another squeeze. "And I know Gage is tickled."

I managed not to roll my eyes. "Sure he is."

"Uncle Julie! Uncle Julie!" Gage yelled, summoning us at the top of his lungs.

"Uncle Julie," I murmured.

"He'll grow out of it." J.X. sounded pained. "I hope to God."

In fairness, it actually wasn't that bad. As zoos went, the San Francisco Zoo & Gardens were pretty nice. Clean and well-maintained. We arrived for the Grizzly Bear Feeding and stayed all the way until the Giraffe Open House. My favorite thing—per J.X.'s inquiry—was the Penguin Feeding. Gage's favorite thing was, unsurprisingly, the chimpanzees. J.X. did not vouchsafe what his favorite thing was, but every time he caught my eyes, he smiled warmly.

Which made up quite a bit for the fact that every time Gage caught my eyes, he stuck his tongue out. I mean, come on. Couldn't he cross his beady little eyes or stick his hands in his ears and wiggle his sticky fingers for variety?

Finally, I couldn't take it anymore. Not long after we bade farewell to the wide-eyed giraffes on the African Savannah, Gage once again demonstrated how very long his tongue was and how very pointy. I stared at him, then staggered to the nearest bench, put my face in my hands and began to sob. Very loudly.

"What the—*Kit*?" That was J.X., sounding desperately appalled.

I sobbed louder.

People made a wide circle around us, speeding up to pass as quickly as possible.

Through my fingers I peeked at Gage who was pinned to J.X.'s side, looking stricken. He had one hand fastened on J.X.'s belt buckle as though he was about to scale him, seeking safety. The other hand was pressed to his mouth and he was trying hard not to bite his thumb knuckle.

"Kit, he didn't mean it. He's doing it to get your atten—"

I raised my head and stared at them.

They could have been father and son. Those matching dark eyes—as wide as saucers—those gaping mouths—perfect Os of horror.

"Ha!" I said.

Gage's enormous eyes were still bugging out of his head, but as he gazed at me, something sprang to life in his expression. He glanced at his uncle. He glanced at me. He opened his mouth...and giggled.

J.X.'s face changed. "Oh, you *bastard*," he breathed. He began to laugh.

"Gotcha," I said.

AUTHOR NOTES

Keen-eyed readers will note that Christopher's parents have undergone a change in marital status since *All She Wrote*. Yes, it's sad and yes, I did notice. Sometimes these things happen. Everybody said that marriage would never last!

Thanks once again to Keren, Susan, and Janet for getting H&M3 out on time. I don't know what I would do without youse guys.

ALSO BY JOSH LANYON

NOVELS

The ADRIEN ENGLISH Mysteries

Fatal Shadows

A Dangerous Thing

The Hell You Say

Death of a Pirate King

The Dark Tide

Stranger Things Have Happened

The HOLMES & MORIARITY Mysteries

Somebody Killed His Editor

All She Wrote

A SHOT IN THE DARK Series

This Rough Magic

The ALL'S FAIR Series

Fair Game

Fair Play

OTHER NOVELS

The Ghost Wore Yellow Socks

Mexican Heat (with Laura Baumbach)

Strange Fortune

Come Unto These Yellow Sands

Stranger on the Shore

NOVELLAS

The DANGEROUS GROUND Series

Dangerous Ground

Old Poison

Blood Heat

Dead Run

Kick Start

The I SPY Series

I Spy Something Bloody

I Spy Something Wicked

I Spy Something Christmas

The IN A DARK WOOD Series

In a Dark Wood

The Parting Glass

The DARK HORSE Series

The Dark Horse

The White Knight

The DOYLE & SPAIN Series

Snowball in Hell

The HAUNTED HEART Series

Haunted Heart: Winter

The XOXO FILES Series

Mummy Dearest (XOXO FILES Series)

OTHER NOVELLAS

Cards on the Table

The Dark Farewell

The Darkling Thrush

The Dickens with Love

Don't Look Back

A Ghost of a Chance

Lovers and Other Strangers

Out of the Blue

A Vintage Affair

Lone Star (in Men Under the Mistletoe)

Green Glass Beads (in Irregulars)

Blood Red Butterfly

Everything I Know

SHORT STORIES

A Limited Engagement

The French Have a Word for It

In Sunshine or In Shadow

Until We Meet Once More

Icecapade (in His for the Holidays)

Perfect Day

Heart Trouble

In Plain Sight

Merry Christmas, Darling (Holiday Codas)

The PETIT MORTS Stories (*SWEET SPOT* Collection)

Other People's Weddings

Slings and Arrows

Sort of Stranger Than Fiction

Critic's Choice

Just Desserts

COLLECTIONS

The Adrien English Mysteries

Collected Novellas, Vol. 1

Collected Novellas, Vol. 2

Armed & Dangerous

In From the Cold: The I Spy Stories

In Sunshine or In Shadow

Sweet Spot

Male/Male Mystery & Suspense Box Set

NON-FICTION

Man, Oh Man!: Writing Quality M/M Fiction

ABOUT THE AUTHOR

A distinct voice in gay fiction, multi-award-winning author JOSH LANYON has been writing gay mystery, adventure and romance for over a decade. In addition to numerous short stories, novellas, and novels, Josh is the author of the critically acclaimed Adrien English series, including *The Hell You Say*, winner of the 2006 USABookNews awards for GLBT Fiction. Josh is an Eppie Award winner and a three-time Lambda Literary Award finalist.

For more information, go to **www.joshlanyon.com**, or follow Josh on **Twitter**, **Facebook**, and **Goodreads**.